THE FUTURE KING

THE REVENGE OF

MAGIC

THE FUTURE KING

JAMES RILEY

ALADDIN

NEW YORK   LONDON   TORONTO   SYDNEY   NEW DELHI

This book is a work of fiction. Any references to historical events, real people, or real places are used fictitiously. Other names, characters, places, and events are products of the author's imagination, and any resemblance to actual events or places or persons, living or dead, is entirely coincidental.

ALADDIN

An imprint of Simon & Schuster Children's Publishing Division

1230 Avenue of the Americas, New York, New York 10020

First Aladdin paperback edition October 2020

Text © 2020 by James Riley

Cover illustration © 2020 by Vivienne To

Also available in an Aladdin hardcover edition.

All rights reserved, including the right of reproduction in whole or in part in any form.

ALADDIN and related logo are registered trademarks of Simon & Schuster, Inc.

For information about special discounts for bulk purchases, please contact Simon & Schuster Special Sales at 1-866-506-1949 or business@simonandschuster.com.

The Simon & Schuster Speakers Bureau can bring authors to your live event.

For more information or to book an event contact the Simon & Schuster Speakers Bureau at 1-866-248-3049 or visit our website at www.simonspeakers.com.

Cover design by Laura Lyn DiSiena

The text of this book was set in Adobe Garamond Pro.

Manufactured in the United States of America 1221 OFF

2 4 6 8 10 9 7 5 3

The Library of Congress has cataloged the hardcover edition as follows:

Names: Riley, James, 1977- author.

Title: The future king / James Riley.

Description: New York : Aladdin, [2020] | Series: The revenge of magic ; 3 | Audience: Ages 8-12. | Audience: Grades 4-6. | Summary: When time traveling students from a British magic school warn of a coming world war, Fort and his friends at the Oppenheimer magic school try to change the future without making things worse.

Identifiers: LCCN 2019038548 (print) | LCCN 2019038549 (eBook) | ISBN 9781534425750 (hardcover) | ISBN 9781534425774 (eBook)

Subjects: CYAC: Magic—Fiction. | Friendship—Fiction. | Time travel—Fiction.

Classification: LCC PZ7.1.R55 Fu 2020 (print) | LCC PZ7.1.R55 (eBook) | DDC [Fic]—dc23

LC record available at https://lccn.loc.gov/2019038548

LC ebook record available at https://lccn.loc.gov/2019038549

ISBN 9781534425767 (pbk)

To Michelle, Chris, Audrey, Doug,
Sean, and Mallory.
Thanks for letting me in the club.

THE FUTURE KING

- ONE -

S INCE THIS IS YOUR FIRST BRIEFING, I'D just stay quiet and listen," Dr. Ambrose said to Fort as they waited for the elevator in the slowly transforming hall of the new Oppenheimer School. The walls were being repainted from an awful puke green to a less horrible camouflage green, and all the posters talking about some "Red Scare" were being replaced with warnings about magic and not talking to strange creatures.

"I doubt I'll have anything to say anyway," Fort told her, still barely sure what was even happening. Just a few moments ago Dr. Ambrose, the Healing teacher at the school, had collected Fort from his room to head to this mysterious military briefing.

All Fort knew was that according to the short news video Dr. Ambrose had shown him, an enormous black dome now covered the lower half of the United Kingdom. That, and whoever had made the dome wanted Fort—along with his friends Rachel and Jia—handed over to them.

Because of course they did. Just when everything seemed to be getting a little better, this had to happen.

In the last week or so, things had been a bit . . . chaotic for Fort. He'd learned enough Summoning magic to travel between dimensions in the search for the monsters who had taken his father, while also fighting against a dragon, a city of dwarfs, and his own roommate, Gabriel. And that had been the easy stuff.

The truly terrifying creatures Fort had faced were the three Old Ones, creatures as old as time with a hatred of the human race. The Old Ones had tried to offer Gabriel his missing brother back in exchange for the whereabouts of the last dragon on earth. Only it turned out that dragon was actually Damian, a boy from the original class of the Oppenheimer School.

But through all of that, the one thing that had kept Fort going was the idea that he might find his father alive and bring him home. And somehow, someway, he *had*. Fort had located his father, who'd been turned into one of those same monsters that had taken his dad in the first place. Then Fort had restored his humanity and brought him home.

Things still weren't totally fixed. His dad had fallen uncon-scious as soon as he turned back into himself and hadn't woken up since. Plus, Dr. Ambrose had apparently found something weird in his dad's tests. So all Fort wanted to do was go back to his father, hug him tight, and take him home.

The elevator dinged, and the doors opened. "Colonel Charles came back especially for this emergency, after taking his son Gabriel home," Dr. Ambrose told Fort. "And he's none too thrilled with you, I might add, considering what happened."

Fort nodded silently but inwardly wondered how that was different from any other moment at the school. The only time the colonel had seemed to be on Fort's side had been when he assigned Fort to be Gabriel's roommate and basically ordered them to become friends. Gabriel hadn't taken that order very well, but they'd actually had fun anyway.

That was all over now. The last time he'd seen Gabriel, in fact, the other boy had been threatening to drop him into a volcano if Fort didn't take him back to the dimension where his younger brother had chosen to remain with the Old Ones.

Fort sighed, wondering how much worse things could get. "Do you know what the dome people want with us?" he asked Dr. Ambrose. "How would they even know our names?"

"Well, considering you were on international news flying with a dragon yesterday, it might have something to do with that," Dr. Ambrose said with a shrug. "Or maybe they want you because you've faced those Draci monsters twice now."

"Dracsi," Fort corrected, his stomach tightening.

"Right, *that's* what matters now, correcting me about a made-up word," Dr. Ambrose said, and somehow, her annoyance made Fort feel a bit less like things were completely out of control.

Still, the thought of what might be waiting for him in the briefing sent a chill down Fort's spine. Who could have put the dome up? The Old Ones seemed like the most obvious answer, but if they had found a way back, then it wasn't just the UK that was in danger: The entire world would be next.

And if that was the case, Fort wished Dr. Ambrose had left him with his father. He'd *just* gotten to see him again after everything. Who knew when his dad would wake up, if he even would?

"Try not to be too scared," Dr. Ambrose said, patting his shoulder awkwardly. "I'm sure the colonel won't send you three into—"

She stopped in the middle of her sentence right as the elevator did too. But the doors didn't open in front of them, and when Fort glanced up at Dr. Ambrose, he found her mouth open like she was still speaking.

"Dr. Ambrose?" he said, fear beginning to spread through him. "*Dr. Ambrose!* Are you okay?"

And then the doctor and the elevator both disappeared, as the out-of-date paint of the new Oppenheimer School was replaced by a bloodred sky. In the distance was some sort of huge fortress made of shining black stone and surrounded by a landscape devoid of any other signs of life.

Fort stared around him in horror. What had just happened? Where *was* he? Had the people who made the dome just reached out and taken him? But even if they had, where had they brought him?

Maybe this was some kind of dream, or Mind spell? He touched his arm, and it felt solid enough, as did the dusty ground beneath his feet.

"HELLO, FORSYTHE," said a voice from behind him, the power of it vibrating in Fort's chest. His heart began racing even faster, and he slowly turned to find a cloaked creature floating in the middle of the air.

Or at least he assumed it had to be a creature, because

5

it had spoken. Only there was nothing beneath the cloak, which was covered in glowing black symbols. There was no physical body at all, just what looked like a face, or maybe only eyes. As he stared, the cloak seemed to pull Fort in, the world kaleidoscoping around him, as he found himself almost drowning in a thousand different versions of himself. There he was with his father holding him as a baby, and Fort felt every cry he made. Another vision hit him, this time the first day of kindergarten, and he was flooded with too many emotions to deal with, from missing his father to excitement about his new school.

And then he was in D.C., and a giant, scaled hand was driving out of the ground. Terror struck him like a blow, and he couldn't breathe, couldn't speak, could only watch as the hand pushed up out of the Lincoln Memorial—

And then the monster disappeared, replaced by a strangely familiar twenty-year-old man, his body glowing with several different colors of light, as if he knew multiple types of magic. Whoever it was smiled at Fort, and for the first time, Fort felt almost a strange sort of peace. The man started to say something, but then the cloak blew out in the wind, cutting off the vision in midstream.

The emotions of it all disappeared along with the vision, and their absence sent Fort to his knees. What *was* that thing?

"YOU KNOW WHAT I AM, FORSYTHE," the creature said, and for the first time Fort noticed there were hands at the ends of the arms of the cloak. One hand was covered in a spiked black glove; the other was solely bone, like a skeleton.

"You're . . . you're an Old One," Fort said, barely able to look at it.

"I AM," the Old One said. "AND IT'S TIME WE HAD A TALK."

- TWO -

I'VE BEEN TRYING TO FIX THINGS FOR A VERY LONG TIME, FORSYTHE," the Old One said, the force of its voice enough to keep Fort on the ground. "UNTOLD MILLENNIA HAVE PASSED, AND EVERYTHING HAS GONE ACCORDING TO MY PLAN. EVEN YOU HAVE PLAYED YOUR ROLE ADMIRABLY, NOW THAT WE'RE REACHING THE END."

What? What did it mean, play a role? "I'd never help you!" Fort shouted, trying to sound braver than he felt and failing miserably.

An eerie laugh floated out of the empty hood. "YOU NEVER HAD A CHOICE. EVERYTHING HAS BEEN HANDLED, ALL THE DETAILS TAKEN CARE OF. I HAVE SEEN ITS SUCCESS, BRINGING BACK MY WAYWARD FAMILY ONCE AND FOR ALL."

And suddenly Fort felt a *lot* more scared, only this time, not for himself. "Bringing your family back? But that would mean you're—"

"HERE ON EARTH," the Old One said, gesturing with his skeletal hand. "IN THE FUTURE ANYWAY. I AM THE TIMELESS ONE, FORSYTHE, THE ALL-SEEING MASTER OF TIME MAGIC. I HAVE OBSERVED UNIVERSES CREATED AND DESTROYED, WITNESSED THE DAWN OF LIFE, AND WATCHED IT DIE OUT ALONE. EVEN MEMBERS OF MY FAMILY DON'T KNOW WHAT I DO. IT'S BEEN MY CURSE, AND MY RESPONSIBILITY, FOR THEY ARE BUT WAYWARD CHILDREN IN MY CARE."

Fort looked around, wondering if the Old One was telling the truth. Certainly it would have the power to take him to the future, but did the world really end up like this, dead and lifeless? It was almost too horrible to believe.

"OH, THIS REALLY IS YOUR WORLD," the Old One said. "OR IS AS IT WILL BE, ONCE MY FAMILY RETURNS. BUT YOU SEE, THAT'S WHY I'VE BROUGHT YOU HERE TODAY. BECAUSE AS MUCH AS YOU'VE BEEN PERFORMING EXACTLY AS I WANTED

UP UNTIL TODAY, NOW THAT WE'RE APPROACH-
ING THE END, YOU'VE CHOSEN TO DEVIATE FROM
THE PATH I SET FOR YOU. AND WE CAN'T HAVE
THAT, CAN WE?"

"What are you talking about?" Fort shouted, slowly pushing
to his feet. "I would *never* follow any plan of yours, especially if
it brought the other Old Ones back!"

Again, the Timeless One laughed. "YOU NEVER HAD A
CHOICE, CHILD. JUST LIKE YOU DON'T NOW. TO
KEEP YOU FROM INTERFERING WITH MY DELI-
CATE PLAN, I'VE DECIDED TO REMOVE YOU FROM
THE GAME FOR A BIT. A YEAR OR TWO SHOULD
TAKE CARE OF IT."

Fort's eyes widened. A year or two? "What game are you
talking about?"

"THE ONLY ONE WORTH PLAYING," the Old One
said, and reached for Fort, its hands glowing with black light.
"I TRULY AM SORRY ABOUT THIS. YOU AND YOUR
FRIENDS WERE WORKING OUT SO WELL. BUT
SOMETIMES ONE SMALL OVERSIGHT CAN THROW
EVERYTHING OFF, AND I CANNOT ALLOW THAT
TO HAPPEN. BUT DON'T WORRY. I'LL BRING YOU

BACK IN TIME TO WITNESS MY FAMILY'S RETURN. YOU DESERVE TO SEE WHAT YOUR HANDIWORK HAS BROUGHT ABOUT, AFTER ALL."

"No!" Fort shouted, but it was too late. Black light shot out from the creature's hands, directly at him. Fort created a teleportation circle in front of him to block it, but the black light disintegrated the circle and continued straight toward Fort—

Only to stop just before it touched him, and then blow away with the arid wind.

Fort looked up in surprise. So did the Old One.

Standing off to the side was an old man, a human, wearing a brown robe that'd seen better days. His long, white beard was tucked into his belt, and he smiled as he gave Fort a nod. "Don't worry, Forsythe," he said, sounding almost amused. "I've got this."

"*YOU?*" the Old One said, and floated back a few feet. "YOU'RE BREAKING THE RULES. YOU HAVE NO RIGHT TO BE HERE!"

The old man grinned wider. "Oh, no? You're the one who's cheating, my boy. We agreed that there's no changing the past, but here you are, trying to do just that. You'd think you'd have learned that by now, even at your young age."

Fort just stared in confusion, not following at all. Who *was* this man, and how was he intimidating the Old One while *smiling*?

And even stranger, why was he calling this horror in an empty cloak "young"?

"I *WILL* BRING THE OTHERS BACK!" the Old One roared, its hands glowing with black light again. "YOU CAN'T STOP ME, OLD MAN!"

The bearded man rolled his eyes. "So dramatic. Don't get all in a huff: You'll still have your turn. But you're not meant to face these children just yet. And I'm not going to let you cheat, not while I'm around to stop it."

The Old One laughed. "YOU WON'T BE AROUND FOREVER. IF I SUCCEED, YOU WILL NEVER EXIST IN THE FIRST PLACE."

"Probably true," the man conceded, then shrugged. "Sounds like you better get moving, then?"

Without another word, the man snapped his finger, and the Old One disappeared in a burst of black light. Fort just watched in amazement as the man turned to him, now looking much more apologetic.

"What . . . what?" Fort said, struggling to wrap his mind around everything.

"Ah, sorry about all of this," the man said, blushing. "I really should have nipped it in the bud before it got this far. You're not due to fight that one until a little under a year from now."

"A year from now?" Fort said, his eyes widening. "I have to *fight* that thing?"

"Well, you and the others," the old man said. "Granted, you could try taking a different path, but I think you'll find it's hard to change your destiny once it's in motion. And the destiny of you and your friends has been set for thousands of years."

"Thousands of years?" Fort said, completely confused. "But how could that be? I'm only twelve!"

"Fair point!" the man said, and laughed loudly. "But we've known you were coming. We've known *all* of you humans were coming, and what that would mean." He paused. "But I don't know why I'm bothering telling you any of this, as I'll be wiping this all from your timeline. You can't remember any of it, not if you're to choose the path you're meant to."

He raised his hands, and they glowed black just like the Old One's had. "Wait!" Fort said. "I don't know what's happening!"

"Oh, you'll get used to that as you get older," the man said, and the light surrounded Fort. "But don't worry! Next time we meet, I promise I'll try to guide you as best I can." He shrugged. "It won't work, but I'm happy to try!"

"What path?" Fort shouted. "How will you—"

And then the lifeless planet disappeared, and Fort was back in the elevator, with Dr. Ambrose reaching out to pat his shoulder.

"Try not to be too scared," she said. "I'm sure the colonel won't send you three into danger."

Fort flinched away in surprise at her touch, and she pulled her hand back immediately. "Whoa, I didn't realize you were *that* nervous," she said.

"I . . . didn't know either," Fort said. He had the strange sense that something bizarre had just happened, but he had no idea what. He'd been standing here in the elevator with Dr. Ambrose, talking about the dome, and she'd said the colonel wouldn't send them into danger. And then . . .

And then nothing. The elevator was still moving, and Dr. Ambrose was looking at him oddly. So why did he feel so unsettled, then?

"I know none of this is easy, getting it all sprung on you out of nowhere," Dr. Ambrose said as the elevator dinged, and the door opened. "But don't worry about it. Colonel Charles just wants you here to be briefed. You'll be completely safe the whole time."

Fort nodded as she stepped out, clearly expecting him to follow. She had a point: They were in the middle of one of the only schools for magic anywhere in the world. Even the Old Ones couldn't reach them here from their other dimension, not without Summoning magic.

With that, he took a long, calming breath. It was good to remember that if nothing else, the Old Ones weren't coming back, and even if they did, Sierra and Damian were tracking down the books of magic. Granted, Fort didn't trust Damian at all, but with Sierra to watch over him, he'd hopefully have the power to keep the Old Ones away.

And without their threat, how bad could things really be?

- THREE -

ORT'S VERY FIRST MILITARY BRIEFING had already started when he arrived. "Time is short, so I won't keep you long," Colonel Charles said from the front of the Briefing Room, then paused as Dr. Ambrose brought Fort in. Everyone turned to look at Fort, and he felt his face begin to burn as the doctor led him gently toward the back, where Jia and Rachel were seated.

Of all the stares, though, the colonel's was the angriest. The man looked like he hadn't slept in days, which he probably hadn't, not with everything that'd happened with his son Gabriel and the Old Ones. "Good to see everyone's here, *finally*," Colonel Charles said, and Fort winced.

"Sorry," Dr. Ambrose said, as Fort silently took an open seat next to Jia. "Had to make sure my patient was fit for active duty, Colonel."

This earned Dr. Ambrose a similar glare to the one Fort had gotten, but he couldn't help but feel relieved that the doctor was on his side, at least a bit.

"Your devotion to your job is noted, Doctor," Colonel Charles said. "Now if I might continue?"

She waved absently, dropping into a seat along the wall.

"Are you okay?" Jia whispered to Fort. "I'm sorry I couldn't finish healing you. There were so many people that the Old One morphed—"

The memory of D'hea—the Old One of Corporeal magic— turning soldiers two-dimensional or merging them together filled Fort's head, and he shook it off, trying not to think about how letting the Old One into the school had been all his fault. "I'm okay," he whispered back.

"As I was saying, I'll make this quick," Colonel Charles said. "This isn't a surprise, ladies and gentlemen. We knew this day would come. Many of you have been briefed on the situation from your squad leaders already, but for those who haven't, we have another potential D.C. situation on our hands."

A low murmur came over the assembled soldiers as the lights dimmed, and the screens on the wall lit up to show the video Dr. Ambrose had shown Fort earlier, news footage of an enormous black dome now covering half of the United Kingdom. A few of the soldiers actually gasped, while Rachel and Jia just stared in shock. That was understandable; even having seen it before, Fort couldn't help but shudder at how unreal the world had become.

Eight months ago, a monster attack or a dome covering a country would have been unthinkable. Now it was happening every few weeks. And if Fort was terrified by that, he couldn't imagine how the general public must be panicking.

"Another attack was inevitable," Colonel Charles said, stepping in front of the screens. "And since that's the reason you're here, why the TDA even exists, consider yourselves at bat. At 2000 hours yesterday, Unknown Magic Users, or UMUs, created this dome over the countries of England and Wales, the southern half of the isle of Great Britain. The units of the United Kingdom military stationed outside the dome have attempted to breach it without any success. We don't know if the soldiers inside have made similar attempts, as we've had zero communication with them."

"Fort, isn't that where *Cyrus* went?" Jia whispered to him.

Fort nodded, unable to hide his worry. "Sierra's there too," he whispered back, trying not to think about how Sierra hadn't

18

answered any of his mental "calls" since the dome had appeared. Last he'd heard from her, she was going to use her Mind magic to try to "wake up" the Clairvoyance students, Cyrus's old schoolmates who'd somehow come untethered from the real world by using Time magic.

This had to be related. It had to be the—

"Based on the color of the dome, we've ruled out Destruction, Healing, Mind, and Summoning magic," Colonel Charles said, mirroring Fort's thoughts. "Obviously the most likely culprit is Time magic, considering the UK government saw fit to keep that book of magic for itself." His tone made it clear what he thought of *that* decision. "Though we've had a student of Time magic on campus for almost a year, as far as we know, he never exhibited any power of this magnitude and was limited to Clairvoyance spells, by which I mean looking a short period into the future."

A map of the UK replaced the video now, lit up with names as a black dome appeared to cover the bottom half. The colonel pointed at a marked area on the map in Wales. "Our Time student and the school's civilian expert, Dr. Oppenheimer, are presently inside the dome, according to our last available intel. Shortly before it appeared, they had traveled to the UK's school, the Carmarthen Academy, located *here*." He tapped the map. "Based on our available information, which I will share momentarily, we believe this to be the current location of our UMUs, and therefore our objective."

The screens went blank and the lights turned back up as Colonel Charles faced the room once more. "There are around *sixty million* United Kingdom citizens trapped within this dome, people," he said, staring out over the assembled soldiers. Fort's eyes widened as the number hit him. This really was so much bigger than the last two attacks. "And we're their best— and *only*—hope. Your job is to infiltrate the school, find these UMUs, and take them down using any means necessary."

"What?" Fort whispered, and it must have been louder than he thought, as several soldiers turned to look at him. But he couldn't help it. *Any means necessary?* His *friends* were over there! What if something went wrong, and a soldier mistook Sierra or Cyrus for one of these UMUs? They could get hurt!

At least Cyrus might be safer, since some of the TDA soldiers should recognize him from his time at the school. Except none of the soldiers around looked familiar to Fort, which made him even more nervous. After his weeks at the Oppenheimer schools, he'd seen a *lot* of soldiers, mostly guarding the students or the school. But somehow, he'd never run into any of the ones here.

Had they been training somewhere else, away from the students? And if they had, why?

None of this seemed like a good idea, and Fort shifted in his seat anxiously. If he'd known this was coming, he might have just teleported over to the UK school himself before coming to the briefing, to see if he could find Sierra and Cyrus before the TDA invaded. He even knew what the school looked like, since Sierra had shown him a mental image of it the night before, which meant his Teleportation magic could get him there.

Maybe it wasn't too late, even now. He could at least get his friends back, if not see what was going on, and possibly try to stop things before they got out of hand. If he could just sneak out of the briefing somehow—

"As I said before, we haven't had any communication from British forces inside the dome," Colonel Charles said. "But we did receive one message. We traced its origin to the Carmarthen Academy."

The lights dimmed as the screens lit up once again, now showing video footage of six children wearing what looked like black school uniforms, only with black hoodies on top, each hood pulled down to hide their identities. This left them looking awfully creepy in the dim light of the video, with only the bottom half of each of their faces visible.

"Greetings, Oppenheimer School," said one of the boys, stepping forward. His accent sounded similar to Cyrus's, though his voice was very different.

But then a stray, silver-colored hair slipped out from beneath the hood on the boy's face, and Fort's eyes widened.

"It is regretful that circumstances have come to this," the boy said, spreading his arms wide. "But you have left us with no other choice. Your actions have created a future that we cannot abide, and therefore we must take a stand. You—"

"If you give us what we ask for, we'll drop the dome, and everyone will be fine," said a girl, stepping forward to interrupt the first boy. "All we ask is your cooperation to—"

"If you do not do what we say, London will be *destroyed*!" the boy said, before the girl could continue. "Is that what you want?"

"*Whoa*, hold on," the girl said quickly, raising her hands in a calming gesture and looking back and forth between the camera and the boy. "I don't think that's the best way to—"

"And that is only the beginning!" the boy shouted. "London will be the spark that lights the world on fire, if you do not cooperate and fulfill the following demand."

The room was deathly quiet, everyone waiting to hear what they wanted—everyone except for Fort, who already knew, and Colonel Charles, who was glaring at him from beside the video screen.

"You will hand over to us three of your students, *immediately*," the boy said, crossing his arms. "They are as follows: Jia Liang, Rachel Carter, and Forsythe Fitzgerald."

This time, Rachel and Jia gasped, while Fort just tried to sink low enough in his chair to disappear completely as the assembled soldiers turned almost as one to look back at him. Again, even being warned ahead of time by Dr. Ambrose didn't help, not when everyone now knew exactly why he was here and probably blamed him for the dome even existing. And why not? If that was why these kids had created it, to get him, Jia, and Rachel over there, wasn't it his fault?

"Send them to the Carmarthen Academy *alone*, without any weapons or communication devices," the boy continued. "When they arrive we will take down our dome, and London will survive. Disobey us, and the world will suffer for it."

"No, *stop*," the girl in the video said, glaring at the boy. "This isn't what we—"

And then the video jumped, as if it had been edited, and the girl disappeared, leaving the one boy to speak again.

"You cannot deceive us, so do not even try," he said. "We've foreseen *every* possible action you might take, and have prepared for each and every one of them. You've been warned, and we'll await your compliance." He slowly smiled, then raised his hand in a salute. "To the return of the one, true, *future* king!"

The others saluted as well, and then the screen went dark.

Colonel Charles stepped forward again, the hall now so silent Fort could hear his own heartbeat in his ears.

"*Any* means necessary," the colonel repeated. "Do I make myself clear?"

- FOUR -

SIR!" RACHEL SHOUTED, LEAPING TO her feet. "Permission to speak?"

Again, all eyes turned backward, as the soldiers began to whisper among themselves.

"Cadet, I didn't ask for questions," the colonel said, giving her a hard look. "This isn't a training exercise."

Cadet? He'd never called them that before, especially not Rachel, his favorite student.

"But, sir, there's no need to put anyone in danger," Rachel said quickly. "If they can see the future, they'll know you're coming. Turn us over to them, like they asked, and let us handle them. We've got the power to take them down—I *know* we do!"

A few of the soldiers began to laugh quietly but immediately went silent at a look from the colonel. Rachel, meanwhile, set her jaw and kept her eyes on her mentor.

25

"Cadet, you and Liang will not be involved in this operation and only attended this briefing for information's sake. Given that these UMUs are after you, you'll both be confined to quarters, under guard, until the objective is completed," Colonel Charles said.

"But, sir!" Rachel started to object, only for the colonel to interrupt.

"*You have your orders, Cadet.* Am I in the habit of repeating myself?"

Rachel blinked, then shook her head. "No, *sir*," she said, dropping back down to her seat, not looking at either Jia or Fort.

Confined to quarters, under guard? Was the colonel that worried about the Time students getting to them? That wasn't a comforting thought, that someone with bad intentions might be able to reach them here. Fort shivered at the idea of what they might do, before something else occurred to him.

What if the guards weren't there for protection so much as to ensure Rachel and Jia didn't try anything on their own? After all, it wasn't just Fort who'd gone off to the Dracsi dimension. And Colonel Charles didn't seem exactly thrilled with Rachel, either.

All in all, Fort wasn't sure which interpretation was worse and didn't especially want to find out.

"Cadet Fitzgerald," Colonel Charles barked, and Fort quickly turned his attention back to the colonel. "*You* will be facilitating travel to the Carmarthen Academy for our squads. Guards will be assigned to you during the operation, and as soon as the squads have reached their destination, you'll be confined to quarters as well. Do you understand your orders?"

Fort gritted his teeth. "Yes, sir," he said aloud, while inside, his mind whirled with objections.

Rachel wasn't wrong. Sending the soldiers over would just get people hurt, or worse. And some of those people might be his friends! Why *shouldn't* Fort, Jia, and Rachel go? Of everyone at the Oppenheimer School, Jia and Rachel were the best at their respective types of magic, which meant they could handle almost anything between the two of them. And with Fort there to teleport them in and out, they wouldn't be in any danger. After all, what could a bunch of kids who could see the future do against Rachel's fireballs or even Jia's Healing magic?

At the front, Colonel Charles began moving around the room, giving individual assignments to squad leaders. As Fort watched, lost in thought, something smacked into his shoulder, and he turned to find Rachel staring at him from behind Jia's back.

"This is *wrong*," she whispered. "Sending these soldiers into danger is a horrible idea, especially when we can handle this. So be ready, Fort. We're going over there."

"Really?" Jia whispered, turning to look at Rachel. "You're going to disobey an order?"

Rachel's cheeks turned a bit red. "I break the rules *all* the time," she said, crossing her arms.

"The rules, sure. Direct orders, never."

"Orders are just a different kind of rule," Rachel said, but she didn't sound thrilled about it. "Yes, they ensure the proper functioning of the military, and without them there'd be chaos. And when we disobey orders, it puts lives in danger, obviously. So, you know, there's that."

"Is there a 'but' coming anytime soon?" Jia asked, raising an eyebrow.

Rachel gritted her teeth. "*Fine*, I don't disobey orders usually, and for good reason! But we can't mess around with this. I've seen what happens when soldiers get sent to dangerous places. My mom and dad have come back from missions with injuries, once almost . . ." She trailed off, then shook her head. "We're not going to let the soldiers get hurt when we can handle this, and better than they can, because we have magic."

"Not to mention they might accidentally attack Cyrus and Sierra," Fort whispered.

"Okay, so what's the plan then?" Jia asked. "Those are basically six Cyruses over there. They're going to know ahead of time anything we try to do."

"So we improvise," Rachel said. "They'll never see it coming."

That didn't sound exactly right, but Fort let it slide, considering he was on Rachel's side.

"We also have no idea what that dome does, or what else those students can do," Jia said. "Not to mention that this is the whole reason why we've been making weapons for the military, so they can use them in missions like this. Since, you know, they're the adults here, and we're just kids."

"Kids who just rescued Fort's dad from a dimension of ancient evil monsters," Rachel pointed out, nodding at Fort. "Granted, that was a horrible idea, but still, we did it."

Fort sighed. Harsh, but fair.

"And almost let the Old Ones return in the process," Jia said. "Look. You're the one who taught *me* how fun it is to break some rules. But in those cases, *we* were the ones in danger.

Who knows what will happen if we mess up here? Sixty million is a *lot* of people to hurt by accident. And this is the TDA's job. They know how to handle this."

"Yeah, by 'any means necessary,'" Fort whispered, not even liking saying the words out loud. "That's how they'll handle it. You think they'll hold back if Sierra or Cyrus gets in their way? Rachel's right, Jia. We *need* to go."

Jia sighed, as up front, the colonel began to dismiss squads from the room. "This is a *bad* idea. I just want that said." But then she slowly began to smile. "Still, I was going to suggest the same thing from the start."

"What?" Fort said, staring at her in confusion.

"I just wanted to make sure you both knew what we were getting into," Jia said. "Rachel, disobeying an order? That's huge."

Rachel gently nudged her with her shoulder. "I *knew* you were in. So we're going to need to move fast, if we want to beat the TDA there. Fort, can you teleport us to the school right now? Do you need a picture of it?"

"No, I—" Fort started to say, but stopped as he saw Colonel Charles begin to make his way back toward them. As he walked, his look suggested he'd already guessed what they'd been talking about, and he wasn't exactly thrilled about it.

"Did I *ask* for questions, Cadet?" the colonel said as he reached them, turning his angry gaze on Rachel. "Or were you just trying to embarrass me?"

Rachel seemed surprised by this. "Embarrass you? Not at all. I just wanted to—"

"Not at all, *sir*," Colonel Charles said, leaning in so close that Fort could see the red in his eyes from lack of sleep. "Do you have *any* idea what's going on right now, Cadet?"

Rachel looked away. "Sixty million people are in trouble, sir."

"And that's the *least* of my problems," the colonel hissed. "China wants their book of Healing magic back, so they can build up their own defense against the Old Ones. And do you know why? Because they don't think *we* can cut it!"

"That's ridiculous, sir," Rachel said, turning back to him. "The TDA is ready for anything!"

"I agree, but our track record says otherwise," Colonel Charles growled, standing up again. "Even the president thinks we haven't proven we can handle a magical attack— given how badly we've failed over the last two. So he's thinking about shutting us down for good. Not to mention that every news station worldwide has been showing video of a *dragon* flying over half the world's major cities for the last two days!"

Fort winced, looking away. He'd been teleporting D'hea around to keep the Old One away from people while trying to think of a plan, and it hadn't exactly been his greatest idea.

"I've been lenient in the past," the colonel continued, still focused on Rachel. "*Especially* with you, Cadet Carter, given your talents for Destruction magic. But I don't have that luxury anymore, not with everything that's happened. The world's eyes are on us, and we *cannot* fail again. If we do, and they shut us down, who will protect the world, Cadet? Our people would be defenseless, and I for one will *not* allow that to happen! Do you understand?"

Rachel nodded, staying silent.

He glared at her for a moment, then stood back up. "Any one of you who even thinks about disobeying my orders is *gone*, cadets. No more second chances, not for anyone, not anymore. I don't care who they are."

"Sir, I just think we could help—" Rachel started to say, but the colonel whirled on her abruptly.

"Did you not hear a word I said?" he shouted. "You are the last person I want help from right now, Carter! Those UK students asked for you three specifically *for a reason*. That means

I need you as far from this as possible, for your sake *and* ours! Are we clear?"

Rachel nodded, staying silent.

"Are we *clear*?"

"Sir, yes, sir," she said.

"Sir," Jia said, her voice shaking slightly. "About the book of Healing magic: Rachel and I have been working on new spells, just using spell words we already know and trying different combinations. It's possible you could give the Healing book back to China, and that we'd still be able to—"

"Give up Healing magic?" the colonel asked, his eyes widening. "That's literally all we have to fight off the Old Ones, Liang! Our books go *nowhere*, not as long as I'm around. Do you hear me?"

Jia nodded, her eyes wide.

"And *you*, Fitzgerald?" the colonel said, turning to Fort. "No brilliant suggestions from you?"

"I'm just worried about Cyrus, sir," Fort said, not looking up. "I don't want him to get hurt."

"Oh, don't worry—that won't be a concern," the colonel said. "As of tomorrow, you won't remember *any* of this. Last night, while you were still in the medical ward, I put through all the paperwork I need to expel you.. You're heading home with your mind wiped as soon as this operation is complete."

"What?" Fort shouted, leaping to his feet, but the colonel pushed him back into his seat.

"You unleashed an *Old One* into our world, and almost killed my sons! *Both of them!*" Colonel Charles leaned in close once again, his eyes burning with such an intense rage that Fort actually shrank back, not quite sure what the man might do. But the colonel abruptly pulled away and turned toward the front of the room, his fists unclenching as he took a deep breath, apparently trying to calm himself down.

Calm was the last thing Fort was going to feel, though. Colonel Charles thought he'd almost gotten Gabriel and Michael killed? Fort had *saved* Gabriel, after his ex-roommate had tried to join his brother, Michael, at the Old One's side! Without him, the colonel would *really* have lost both his sons. And all of that had been because of Gabriel to begin with. How could the colonel blame Fort for that?

When the colonel turned around, he did look less angry on the surface, and even forced a small, shaky smile. "Fortunately for you, Fitzgerald, I need your magic," he said. "And that means you've got an opportunity here. Do as I say, *exactly* as

I say, and I'll send both you *and* your father back home." His eyes narrowed. "But disobey me even *once*, and I'll personally find reasons to keep your father here for as long as I want, just to be sure he didn't bring back any magical diseases or anything from that other realm."

Fort's mouth dropped open. "What? He's fine. Dr. Ambrose even said—"

"Well, don't worry. You wouldn't remember you'd found him," the colonel said, giving Fort a long look. "Can't have any memories of the school in that brain of yours, now, can we? The last thing you'd know about your father is that a monster took him."

Fort's whole body went as cold as ice, and he couldn't believe what he was hearing. *"No,"* he whispered. "You wouldn't. You couldn't!"

"Maybe not," the colonel said, shrugging his shoulders. "It *would* be very extreme. But if I were you, I wouldn't take that chance, especially considering what you did to Gabriel. So best follow orders, do you understand?" And with that, he stood back up and yanked his uniform down to straighten it. "I said, do you understand me, *Cadet*?"

Fort could barely think, barely breathe. Out of nowhere,

he could suddenly feel the miles of rock above the Briefing Room, as if they were pushing down on him, crushing him with their weight.

For the briefest of moments, Fort considered teleporting the colonel somewhere far away, like the Sahara Desert or the Arctic. Even the moon, maybe.

But wherever he sent him, it wouldn't be far enough. The colonel would find his way back and just think of a worse punishment, if one even existed.

For all Fort's magic, it was the colonel who had the real power. He was in control here at the school and had both the government and military to back him up. Even if Fort did teleport the colonel to the center of the earth, whoever was next in line would just step up and continue whatever the colonel had ordered. There was no way to fight them all.

Which meant he had no choice, as horrible as that was.

Fort stood up and saluted the colonel, his hand shaking as he did. "Sir, yes, sir."

"Good," the colonel said, then turned to Jia and Rachel. "Cadets Liang and Carter, you'll be escorted back to your dorm in a moment. Fitzgerald, you'll be brought down to the Deployment Room at that time. Until then, you'll all be kept under watch." He waved two nearby guards over and turned to them. "If any of these children show even the slightest hint of using magic, taser them and contact me immediately."

"Yes, sir," the guards said, then looked at each other uncomfortably as Colonel Charles strode out of the room, slamming the door behind him so hard it reminded Fort of a jail cell door closing.

- FIVE -

THIS IS *SO* MESSED UP!" RACHEL WHIS-pered as she paced in front of Jia and Fort. "Colonel Charles is making a huge mistake here. We *can't* just go along with it."

Fort didn't say anything, his eyes on the guards standing at attention not too far away, their Tasers in their hands. With the room otherwise empty, it'd still be possible to teleport the three of them out—or send the guards for a quick vacation in Cancún, Mexico.

Why not? he imagined his father saying. *Everyone loves a beach vacation. Just make sure to book them at a nice resort.*

"You're right, but what can we do?" Jia whispered back, throwing Fort a quick look. "If we disobey his orders, Colonel Charles might actually go through with his threat."

"He won't," Rachel said, looking back at them. "He *won't,*

Fort. I don't care how much has happened—he's not that person. He just wants to keep us safe."

"Is that what you call it?" Fort asked. "I'll try to remember that when my mind's wiped and I'm sent home."

"Well, your aunt's house *is* probably a lot safer than this school," Jia said. "It's not like she gets invaded by the Old Ones every few weeks."

"I know what he said sounded terrible," Rachel said, rubbing her temples. "But this is how the military works. They can't have people disobeying orders, or bad things happen."

"We're not *in* the military, Ray," Jia said quietly. "And weren't you just attacking him a second ago?"

"Well I'm conflicted, okay?" she said. "There's a lot to process here! But we can't just sit back and let people get hurt when we could help!"

That's right! Fort heard his father say. *Help your friends, Fort. You know that's what I'd want you to do, if I were there and, you know, awake!*

Fort growled in frustration. Did even his own imagination have to argue with him? "What if he's *not* bluffing, though?" he asked quietly. "What if the colonel really does make me forget about my father? After everything with Gabriel, he looks like

39

he's barely holding it together. You heard what he said about the book of Healing magic and China."

Rachel looked away, sighing. "He's definitely changed, even since you got here, Fort. I wish I could believe he knows what he's doing, but I just don't know anymore. Why would he even think bringing Gabriel to the school was a good idea? He's yelling at *us*, when his own son turned me over to the Old Ones and tried to drop you into a volcano! Maybe check on your parenting skills before judging everyone else, *Colonel*."

"It's not just Gabriel," Jia said quietly. "Fort's right about the Healing book. He's acting like the whole world's against him, and that's scary. But what *can* we do? He's got the books, soldiers, the school . . . plus enough memory wipes to make us *all* forget we were ever here. And we're just kids. Adults are *always* the ones in charge, because they think they know better."

"And they think they have the power," Rachel said, staring down at her hands.

"They *do*," Fort said. "I could get us all out of here right now, my dad included. But what happens next? The soldiers throw us in jail, or chase us down for the rest of our lives if we run. We can't beat them all, not even with all the power you two have."

Neither Jia nor Rachel said anything to that, and Fort dropped his head into his hands, not sure what else to do. Should he tell Dr. Ambrose what the colonel had said? But even if she did want to help, she still wouldn't have the power to go against Colonel Charles. And Dr. Opps wouldn't have been much help either, even if he hadn't been stuck beneath the dome, since the colonel had threatened to kick the headmaster out of his own school already once before.

Lost in his thoughts, Fort almost missed a group of soldiers entering the Briefing Room. "Carter, Liang," one of them said. "We're here to take you back to your dorm."

"Sir, yes, *sir*," Rachel said, saluting while glaring at the soldier, who winced, looking nervous. Fort recognized this guard, meaning he'd been working in the school and knew it wasn't smart to annoy a Destruction student. "Fort," she said, throwing a look at him over her shoulder. "Whatever happens, if you leave . . ."

"We'll make sure your dad is okay," Jia finished.

Rachel nodded. "And we *won't* let you go without saying good-bye."

Fort nodded, unable to think of anything much to say to that, since he knew neither of them would have any more control over that than he would.

But if this was going to be the last time he saw them both, he couldn't handle a good-bye on top of everything else right now. So instead, he just stayed silent, hoping his two friends understood.

"Fitzgerald," another soldier said, and waved him over. "We're taking you to the Deployment Room. You all set?"

"Sure," Fort said quietly, and the soldier gently pushed him toward the door. As they left, Fort threw a look back at Jia and Rachel. Jia gave him a little wave, while Rachel gave him a confident smile. They both wanted to help, he knew, but there was nothing they could do.

His escorts led Fort to the elevator, where they were joined by several soldiers, all outfitted now with weapons created by the Oppenheimer School students over the last few months. A few had Healing staffs, just like the ones Sergeant Tower had trained Fort and other students on, but most carried Lightning rods instead, something that could easily stun a person, or do a whole lot worse.

And Fort was going to teleport soldiers wielding weapons that dangerous to where Cyrus and Sierra were because he had no choice in the matter. The thought of it made his skin itch all over.

They took the elevator down five floors, where they exited and followed a second group of soldiers into a large room that looked almost like an empty warehouse. The corners and ceiling were covered in cobwebs, and there were various items covered in tarps against the walls, but otherwise, the room was empty except for the assembling squads.

His escorts brought him to the front of the room, where a set of creaking wooden stairs led to a raised platform, most likely the spot where he was going to create his teleportation circles for the squads. As he climbed the stairs, the guards waited at the bottom just a short distance away, probably thinking they were close enough to stop him if he tried to escape.

They'd be too late, though, if he used his magic the way Gabriel had. His former roommate had figured out a way to move the teleportation circle instead of making it stationary, which made teleporting a lot quicker if you pulled it up and over yourself. And if Gabriel had made it work without much practice, it couldn't be *that* hard.

For a moment, Fort let himself daydream. He could teleport up to the medical ward, grab his father, and take him somewhere safe, somewhere Colonel Charles couldn't get to either of them. And without Fort, none of the soldiers could get inside the dome, which meant Sierra and Cyrus would at least be safe from Lightning rods.

But where could he take his father? What place was actually safe? His aunt's house would be the first place the TDA looked. And if he did find somewhere to hide them, the government wouldn't stop looking for them, not ever. Not to mention that his father wasn't conscious, and would need medical attention, something that wasn't exactly free, even if they weren't fugitives.

Eh, I'm fine, his father said in his imagination. *Just taking a long nap, really. Don't worry about me!*

Fort rolled his eyes at that, as more soldiers filed in with their weapons. What if he instead teleported to Jia and Rachel, then took *them* over to the dome to find Cyrus and Sierra? Then his friends would be protected, and with Sierra's help, maybe he *could* get his father out safely, by making everyone at the Oppenheimer School forget he'd been found. She might even be able to convince a doctor to treat him with her Mind magic. It'd gotten her and Damian on a plane over to the UK, after all.

Only that would mean leaving his father at the colonel's mercy while he, Jia, and Rachel were rescuing Cyrus and Sierra. And all Colonel Charles would have to do was move his father to a different facility, and Fort would never know how to find him again.

No. There was no choice in the matter. He was heading home either way, but at least if he did what the colonel said, there was a good chance his father would go with him.

"Everyone, to your squads," Colonel Charles shouted as he entered the warehouse with someone at his side. Whoever it was, Fort couldn't make out her face, as it was obscured by the line of soldiers, but she was dressed in civilian clothing.

As the colonel and the woman made their way over, Fort's gaze shifted to several of the troops, who were staring at him. Half looked suspicious, while the rest looked disgusted, like he was some kind of bug to step on.

And just when Fort thought things couldn't get much worse, the colonel and his companion reached the front of the room, and Fort recognized the woman.

"Oh, hello, Fitzgerald," Agent Cole said, smiling at him. "I never got the chance to thank you for your help in apprehending our two missing students at Heathrow Airport. Could never have done it without you."

Fort gritted his teeth to keep from saying anything that'd get him in more trouble. Agent Cole was the federal agent assigned to track down Sierra and Damian and had manipulated Fort into helping her capture them at the London airport a few days ago. The two had only escaped after Damian had turned into a dragon against his will, due to Gabriel giving him up to the Old Ones.

Last Fort had heard, Sierra had implanted an idea in Agent Cole's head that the woman wanted to quit her job and go back to art school. Apparently it had worn off.

"Just remember," Agent Cole whispered, pausing next to Fort as the colonel moved past them. "Your friend Sierra was the one who wanted to 'fix' all of the Time students. So whose fault do you think this is? Try to remember that when our soldiers storm the school, just in case anyone gets hurt. You know, by *accident*."

Fort's fingernails dug into his palms so hard he left imprints, but he didn't say a word.

Colonel Charles turned to stare out over the assembled squads, who all snapped to attention. "We're ready here?" he asked, and got nods from the officers standing in front of the soldiers. "Good."

The colonel turned to Fort and handed him a folder filled with photographs of what looked like the exterior of the school building Sierra had shown him from the inside. "These are the destinations for your teleportation circles. I want portals opened on the wall behind us every five feet in that sequence. Start on the left and work your way right. Do you understand me?"

Fort nodded, staring at the pictures, lost in thought as his mind still offered up ways to save everyone, even though he knew it was impossible.

Colonel Charles leaned in. "I said, *do you understand me? Or do we need to go over the consequences for disobeying me again?*"

"I understand you, *sir*!" Fort shouted, looking up at the man he hated almost as much as the Old Ones at the moment. "Everything is clear, *sir*."

"Good," the colonel said, and straightened up. To the assembled soldiers, he shouted, "We're a go, ladies and gentlemen! Bring me back some UMUs!"

Fort heard an odd noise, and he looked down to find the photo in his hand almost completely crumpled in his fist, he'd been gripping it so hard.

But there was no choice here. For all his magic, the adults in charge would always have more power.

Staring at the photo, he concentrated, then opened a teleportation circle on the wall behind them, creating a portal between the Deployment Room and a spot just in front of the Carmarthen Academy.

Everyone tensed as the green circle opened, revealing a very dark scene, in spite of it being daytime in the UK. The dome must have been blocking out most of the sun's light, leaving everything in shadow and difficult to make out from a distance. It didn't help that a dark, cloudy fog began to seep in through the portal, adding to the creepy feel.

More than anything, it made Fort think of a horror movie, but he had to remind himself that it was just the dome's effect, and horror movies weren't real. It wasn't like the fog and shadows were alive or something.

But then, before any of the soldiers could move, two of the shadows on the other side of the portal pulled out of the darkness and leaped through into the Oppenheimer School.

- SIX -

UMUS!" COLONEL CHARLES SHOUTED as Fort felt his blood go cold in horror. "Move to contain, *now*! And get that portal closed!"

The TDA soldiers immediately leaped to intercept the shadows, even as Fort quickly closed the portal, his hands starting to shake. The first squad moved to surround the intruders, who seemed to fade in and out of view, almost as if they were turning invisible. But as the soldiers encircled them, the shadows disappeared completely, reappearing in a flash just outside the squad, one on either side.

What were these things, and how were they moving so quickly? They couldn't be Old Ones . . . could they?

"Got one!" shouted a soldier in the next squad over as he aimed his Lightning rod, but the nearest black shadow flashed next to him, knocking the rod off course just as he fired. Lightning exploded into the first squad, arcing between the soldiers and knocking most of them to the floor, unconscious.

"Hold your fire until you have a confirmed target!" Colonel Charles shouted, but the shadows disappeared again, and the room went silent as the soldiers all looked for them frantically, their Lightning rods held at the ready.

A moment passed, then another, and no one made a sound. Fort's throat constricted so much he almost choked when he swallowed, he was so terrified of making even the slightest noise.

"There!" someone shouted, and they all turned to see a flash of black across the wall. A lightning bolt struck right behind it, a moment too late.

"Over here!" shouted another soldier from the opposite side of the room, and Fort whirled around just in time to see the shadow disappear, another lightning bolt hitting where it'd been.

Could these things even be human, disappearing and reappearing that fast? It was almost like they were teleporting, or moving too quickly to see. . . .

And then it hit him. The intruders *were* moving too fast to see: They had sped up their own personal time.

This was Time magic. Only it was nothing like the spells Cyrus had used.

And that meant it had to be the Carmarthen Academy students. They'd seen through Colonel Charles's plan, just as they'd promised, and now they were here to punish them all.

Now completely panicking, Fort turned to the colonel. "It's the Time—" he started to shout, but Colonel Charles shoved him back toward the wall, guards moving in front of him protectively.

"Stay down and don't draw attention to yourself!" the colonel hissed at Fort as one of the shadows appeared again, this time in the middle of a squad. The soldiers all moved to aim but stopped as the colonel shouted, "*Do not fire!* Contain it instead: Use your bodies to keep it trapped!"

That might work, actually! Fort peered between the arms of his guards to find the soldiers moving to obey the colonel as the surrounded shadow flashed in and out of existence, each time a slightly different shape, like it was moving in place. The squad closed in to form a fairly solid wall, their shoulders all pushed against each other, their Lightning rods all aimed straight at the shadow.

And then an eerie black light appeared around each soldier,

and they immediately began to wink out one by one, disappearing into thin air.

A collective gasp of shock went up around the room, the loudest coming from Fort, and everything erupted into chaos.

All the soldiers began to shout at once as the shadows appeared all around the room now, baiting the soldiers into firing at each other. Lightning bolts filled the air, creating an almost electric field within the room as more and more TDA soldiers were hit, falling to the floor unconscious.

Even the ones who were careful not to aim at the other soldiers had their shots knocked off course by the shadows, creating more panic. A bolt sizzled past Fort's shoulder, and he dove to the floor, now as scared of the soldiers as he was of the Carmarthen students.

"*Weapons down!*" Agent Cole shouted, then glared at Colonel Charles. "Have you trained these soldiers at all? This is insanity!"

"We *will* take control of this situation!" Colonel Charles shouted, grabbing a Lightning rod from next to an unconscious soldier and striding out into the melee. "Form up on me, soldiers! We will take these UMUs down! Let's—"

And then he broke off as one of the shadows appeared right in front of him.

Fort's eyes widened in shock, but it was too late to do anything. "No!" Colonel Charles shouted, leaping backward and raising his Lightning rod to fire as black light washed over him. As the magic hit him, he immediately froze in place, his mouth hanging open, his Lightning rod just beginning to unleash a bolt of electricity.

But as the shadow cast its spell on the colonel, Fort finally got his first good look at the intruder. Whatever it was, it looked about his height and was wearing all black, just like the kids in the video.

Fort had been right about the attackers and how they'd seen Colonel Charles's plan ahead of time. But he'd been very, *very* wrong about being able to face them with just Jia and Rachel.

Whatever these Time spells were, they were *far* more powerful than anything he and his friends had.

He pushed to his feet, ready to try to teleport one of the Time students away, but something struck him from behind, knocking him back to the floor. For a moment, he was sure one of the Time kids had attacked him, and he tried desperately to fend them off before realizing it was Agent Cole, just as he was about to punch her in the face.

"Stay down!" she shouted as a succession of lightning bolts

passed through where he'd been standing. She looked up and readied her own Lightning rod, looking furious. "I should have brought my own team in. Charles's soldiers weren't ready for this!"

She released Fort and stood up, moving into the squads, yelling at them to lower their weapons. But even as the soldiers obeyed, the shadows grabbed multiple Lightning rods, moving too quickly to catch, and set them off one by one, taking down more of the TDA agents. Another squad disappeared entirely, while a second one slowed to a halt, not freezing like Colonel Charles had, but moving almost imperceptibly slowly.

At this rate, it wouldn't be long before the Time students had taken down the entire TDA. And all so they could take him, Rachel, and Jia for who knew what reason.

"Lock the doors!" Agent Cole shouted as soldiers continued to drop. "We have to contain them within this room. We can't let them out into the rest of the school!"

Two soldiers began to close the doors leading back into the school but disappeared before they could.

"Fitzgerald!" Agent Cole shouted at Fort. "Open a portal to the barracks, and get more—"

A shadow flashed past her before she could finish, and

when it was gone, Agent Cole had disappeared as well.

Fort looked around in horror, seeing only a dozen soldiers left now, spread throughout the room. Agent Cole was right; they needed backup if they were going to keep the Time students trapped in the Deployment Room.

But not soldiers. They'd be useless. No, he needed his friends, and all the other students he could find. Sebastian, the Chads, Rachel's Destruction friends, *everyone*.

As more soldiers ran to block the exit doors, Fort aimed for a spot just in front of them, hoping to protect them by opening a teleportation circle between them and the Carmarthen students.

But as he started the spell, something shadowy flashed before his eyes, and suddenly everything changed in the Deployment Room. Where there had been less than a dozen soldiers left on their feet, now there were none. All of the unconscious soldiers and those frozen like Colonel Charles had disappeared as well.

In fact, the room was entirely empty but for Fort and two black shadows who now stood in front of him.

As he watched in desperate horror, the shadows formed into two children, their hands glowing with black light. Hoods covered their faces, but beneath their open hoodies, Fort could see school uniforms and ties.

These *were* the children from the video, the Time school students.

And they'd come for him.

First one, then the other removed their hoods, revealing a pale-skinned boy and a girl of Indian descent, both with bright silver hair, exactly like Cyrus's.

"*That* was unnecessary," said the boy, wiping some dust off his sleeve. "Adults never listen, do they? They're the worst."

The girl stepped closer with a smile and reached a hand out to Fort, who stared at it in terror. "Hello, Forsythe," she said. "Nice to finally meet you. We're going to need you to come with us."

- SEVEN -

FORT QUICKLY BACKED AWAY FROM both Time students, his hands up and ready to either punch or open a teleportation circle, whichever one was quicker. "What did you do with everyone?" he shouted, his voice cracking. "Where are they?"

"Oh, we just threw them all a quarter hour into the future," the boy said, shrugging. "Calm down. We didn't *hurt* them."

"Well, except for the ones you hit with lightning," the girl said, giving him an annoyed look. "*Speaking* of unnecessary." As she spoke, Fort recognized her voice from the video. The boy, though, didn't seem to be the other student who'd spoken in the message.

"Hey, they were shooting it at us," the boy said. "It's only fair. But they'll all be fine."

"We sent you a few minutes into the future as well," the girl said to Fort. "See? It was completely painless, so there's no need to worry about the soldiers. You probably didn't even know it was happening. And this way you didn't have to wait around while we cleaned things up."

Cleaned things up? That was how she talked about sending all the soldiers into the *future*? Fort suddenly knew how the guards at the Oppenheimer School felt about the Destruction students. These Time kids were on a completely different level, and he had no way of fighting back.

"If we want to avoid some unpleasantness," the boy said, nodding at Fort, "we need to be back at the school before our 'mess' returns, Ellora. Let's get this moving. You know what we have to do."

The girl sighed, then leaned in closer to Fort. "Do boys here like to pretend you know more than the girls too, or is that just a British thing?" She smiled but looked tired. "Now how about you bring your friends here? We don't have *too* much time left, honestly."

"You'd like that, wouldn't you?" Fort shouted, barely able to think from fear. They moved so fast and could freeze people in time, send them into the future! Would he even be able to open a teleportation circle before they stopped him?

The two Time students gave each other a look. "Yes, we *would*," Ellora said to Fort. "Don't worry. We'll explain every-thing back at the Carmarthen Academy. Just bring Rachel and Jia along, and Simon and I will take you there."

"We're not going *anywhere*!" Fort said, now much more thankful that he and the others hadn't disobeyed and just teleported over to the UK themselves. They would have been beaten instantly.

"Ugh, he's been brainwashed by the adults here," Simon said, shaking his head. "You knew this would be how it goes, Ellora. Let's freeze him and quit wasting time."

Fort's eyes widened at the word "freeze," and he stepped backward, ready to bolt. What did that even mean? They were going to freeze him in *time*?

"Whoa, it's okay, Forsythe," Ellora said, glaring at Simon. "We're not going to freeze you!"

"We will if we don't want to get caught!" Simon said.

"We want them to *listen* to us, don't we?" Ellora said, turn-ing to face her fellow Time student. "If we force them to come, they'll just be looking for a chance to run!"

And just like that, Fort realized this was the perfect opportunity to do exactly what she said, to *run*. Now, while they were distracted.

But they'd freeze him if he tried to escape through a portal. No, what he needed was to get some distance first. So instead of opening a teleportation circle near him, he first silently opened a portal below *them*, leading to the cavern beneath the old Oppenheimer School.

"Cooperation is built on tru—*whoop!*" the girl shouted as she and the boy dropped through the circle, and for a second, Fort thought he'd actually caught them by surprise. Maybe they didn't see *everything* coming after all!

But then Ellora and Simon paused in midair, black light surrounding them. And then, as Fort watched in horror, time *reversed* itself: The two Time students floated back up out of the portal, and the teleportation circle closed below them.

"And you knew he'd try *that*," Simon said to Ellora, completely calm as if nothing had just happened. "Can we finally do things my way, or do you still have to waste more time?"

"He just doesn't understand!" she said, turning back to Fort. Her smile now was much more forced. "No one's going to hurt you *or* your friends, Forsythe. We just want to talk. All you have to do is come with us, listen for a few minutes, and that's it: You'll be free to go."

They'd be *what* now? Free to go? That couldn't be right: These kids had put a dome up over half the UK just to get ahold of him and his friends. Who would go to that much trouble just to talk to someone? It had to be a trap.

And if that was the case, there was *no way* he was bringing Rachel and Jia here—

"Let me stop you right there," Simon said, raising a glowing hand. "They're coming too, whether you teleport them here or not, okay? So don't even bother with all the tough talk."

Fort's eyes widened at this. Could the other boy have known what he was thinking? He didn't seem to have Mind magic. But no, it had to be like when Cyrus did the same thing, seeing the conversation before it happened.

"We also don't have time to explain how time visions work," Simon said, rolling his eyes. "You know what? I'm tired of this. Come right now, or I'll freeze everyone in this entire school, and cart you over in a wheelbarrow or something. Sound good?"

Ellora groaned. "Oh, *brilliant*, Simon. Why not just threaten to freeze his heart while we're at it? You need to stop with all the threats!"

"What do you think we're doing here?" Simon said to her. "That was the whole idea, threatening *everyone*!"

"Not *them*!" Ellora said, pointing at Fort. "We need their help!"

"Don't tell him that!" Simon said, rolling his eyes again. "If they know we need them, they'll never do what we say!"

Weirdly, the more they argued, the less intimidating they seemed. Sure, they could move faster than he could see and just mentioned *freezing his heart*, but other than that, they sounded like any other kids his age . . . just with amazing accents.

Maybe there was a way out of this, even without his magic. Granted, it all hinged on Ellora telling the truth, that they really *did* just want to talk, but at this point, it wasn't like Fort had any other options.

"Promise me you'll release everyone!" he shouted over their bickering. "I'll bring Jia and Rachel here *if* you promise you'll drop the dome and let everyone go. Including us."

"Of course!" Ellora said. "Just come with us and talk, and you're free to go."

"*After* you help us," Simon said, and Ellora sighed loudly.

"*If* we come and listen to what you have to say," Fort said quickly, "how do I know you'll actually release us all? How can I be sure that you won't destroy London anyway?"

Simon and Ellora looked at each other again, and Simon snorted. "Destroy London?" he said.

"Forsythe, that's why we're here," Ellora said, rubbing her forehead. "To *save* London. We need the help of you three to do that."

Wait, what? They wanted to *save* London? But that wasn't how it sounded from their video—

"The video? We said those exact words in it!" Simon said, this time annoying Fort more than scaring him. "'If you do not do what we say, London will be destroyed.' How did you not understand that?"

"I *knew* William would confuse them," Ellora said. "He tried to be all tough, too, and look where it got us. He completely made it sound like *we* were going to burn London down if we didn't get what we wanted, not that we needed them to stop it."

"But London's just the beginning," Simon continued. "Just show him what's coming if it gets destroyed, Ellora. We don't have any more time to argue. If we'd done things my way, we'd have gotten away cleanly, but no, you had to waste *all* the time."

Ellora winced. "It won't take long. I'll show him. You go get Jia and Rachel."

"They'll need to see too," Simon said. "I'll do that while I cart them back here. Don't leave him in the future for too long."

What? Leave him in the future? What did *that* mean? But before Fort could ask, Simon continued.

"Oh, and make sure you reverse time to reopen his portal back to the academy, or we won't be going home." He nodded at the nearby wall where Fort had opened his teleportation circle.

Uh, reverse time to *what now*? They could reopen his teleportation circles?!

She rolled her eyes. "Yes, I know. I'm the one who came up with that."

Simon sighed loudly, then disappeared in a flash of shadow, leaving Fort alone with Ellora. Even with just one of the students, Fort didn't feel any better, especially knowing that anywhere he teleported her, she could just reopen the circle and come right back.

"I really did want this to go differently," Ellora said, frowning at him. "This is all William's fault." She shrugged. "But there's only so much time, so . . ."

Her hands began to glow, and before Fort could move, the entire Deployment Room faded out around him, and then returned just as quickly. Only now it was utterly destroyed.

Half the walls had collapsed, with dirt and stone crumbling from various holes. The raised platform where Colonel Charles had stood was almost completely gone, just a foot or two at the side remaining.

All in all, it looked as if a bomb had gone off. And there was no indication that anyone was left, not even a lit emergency-exit sign or something.

And then a raindrop fell in front of Fort's face, and he looked up in confusion.

Then his mouth dropped open in dread.

There was no ceiling on the room. In fact, there were no longer any floors above it either. Now Fort could see straight up to the stormy sky above. Where once had been an underground-facility-turned-school, now there was nothing but open air, with dirt and dust swirling in the wet wind.

The second Oppenheimer School, built in an underground bunker that could withstand a nuclear blast from thirty miles away, was just . . . *gone*.

- EIGHT -

H ELLO?" FORT SHOUTED AS THE RAIN intensified. No one answered, so in spite of his shock, he moved to find cover from the storm.

Only the odd thing was, he wasn't getting wet. Instead, the water droplets were falling right through him, as if he were a ghost, or had cast Ethereal Spirit.

But how was that possible? A Time student shouldn't have been able to use Healing magic, let alone destroy a school. Or was this the future that Simon had mentioned? Had Ellora sent him here to see . . . this?

But he wasn't really here, not fully, not if the rain was passing through him. Was this how the Time-magic users saw the future, like ghosts, unable to touch or change anything?

"Ellora!" he shouted into the empty air, his voice not echoing at all. "Take me back! I've seen whatever it is you wanted me to see!"

But again, there was no reply, and Fort began to panic. What if she left him here, stuck in the future? And what kind of horrible future was this? What could have happened to utterly destroy the Oppenheimer School? It'd been hidden to the point that even the students attending the school hadn't known where it was, so how could it have been found to destroy it in the first place?

And how far ahead in time was he? For all Fort knew, this could be happening a few minutes in the future, while he, his father, and all his friends were still there. In fact, what if the Time students were in on it, and the school was getting attacked while he was stuck in the future? He needed to get back already!

But how? He couldn't use Time magic himself, or really, many other spells. All he had currently were the Teleport spell, Heal Minor Wounds, and one instance of Restore Dimensional Portal, none of which were much use as a ghost in the future.

Not sure what else to try, Fort cast a teleportation circle, but nothing happened. Maybe one had opened wherever/whenever his body was, back in the Deployment Room in the present, but it sure wasn't working here in the future. So what did—

The Deployment Room disappeared around him, replaced by a sandy-white beach, stretching off in both directions farther than Fort could see. The ocean he found himself facing was calm, if strangely low, based on how wet the sand was where he was standing. He glanced behind him, to see how far back the damp sand extended, and gasped.

Thousands of uniformed soldiers stood in formation just a few dozen yards away. Each one was wearing some sort of mask, like the kind you'd wear to scuba dive, connected to two tanks on their backs, but other than that, they seemed to have no weapons or other items of any kind.

Instead, their arms hung at their sides as they stared out toward the ocean.

"I'm sorry, I didn't—I don't—" Fort stammered, having no idea what to say, but none of the soldiers seemed to even notice him. As his shock wore off, he remembered that he wasn't substantial here in the future, so they most likely couldn't see or hear him. Still, it felt odd to be standing in front of them, so he quickly moved off the beach, passing through the two nearest squads of soldiers until he reached the back of the company.

Now safely behind them, Fort turned back to the ocean, wondering what they were waiting for. Part of him didn't want to know, as it definitely wasn't going to be anything good. But Ellora had sent him here for a reason, and she might not bring him back until he'd seen whatever it was he was supposed to.

As he watched, the ocean pulled back even farther, stranding several fish and even a few jellyfish on the sand as it did. A loud roaring noise erupted from out on the water, and the sky began to darken, like a bad storm was coming.

The wind picked up out of nowhere, strong enough to make many of the soldiers almost lose their footing, bracing themselves against the force of it. Fort could only see its effects and hear its whistling as it passed, not feel it, and for that, he was actually grateful.

One of the soldiers shouted out in a language Fort didn't recognize, and he realized for the first time he might not be in the U.S. It'd been hard to tell what nationality the soldiers were, given that they all wore masks.

Out on the ocean, the darkness drew closer, and the soldier shouted again. This time, the others all raised their arms, and their hands began to glow bright blue in the oncoming storm.

Fort's eyes widened as he realized what he was seeing: thousands of magic users, all with Healing magic.

But where had they come from? When had they learned magic? How had they gotten the book of Healing magic from the TDA? Was this China, and Colonel Charles had changed his mind? And since none of the soldiers looked like they were children, how many years in the future *was* this?

But then the roar from the ocean turned Fort's attention back to the growing darkness, and he realized with horror that it wasn't a storm coming toward them. The darkness wasn't from clouds or night falling.

It was *water*.

Extending as far as Fort could see in every direction, a wave was crashing toward them, hundreds of feet high, maybe more. And in the middle of the wave, maybe every ten or twenty feet, was a pair of glowing red lights.

No, not lights. Hands, glowing with Destruction magic.

The wave was an *attack*.

Even as Fort stared in shock and disbelief, the soldiers in front of him began casting their spells, sending Healing magic rocketing into the wave. Each spell that hit one of the Destruction-magic users paralyzed that person, knocking them backward out of the wave with the force of the hit. The water where they'd been began to collapse out of the tsunami, but the other Destruction users spread their magic out, solidifying the wave.

How could this even be real, no matter how far in the future Fort was? It all just seemed so unreal, both because he couldn't feel anything around him, and from how much had to have changed between the present and whenever he was now. All of these adult magic users, fighting a war of some kind? It was too much to wrap his head around!

The one soldier on the beach shouted again, and this time, hundreds of soldiers stepped forward, their bodies glowing blue. Wings sprouted from each one, and they took to the air, soaring up into the fading sunlight. Then, when they were just above the highest point of the wave, they dove straight at it, aiming for the Destruction-magic users.

Some managed to hit their enemy, but others were hit by walls of water or lightning bolts sent from the Destruction casters, dropping the Healers into the ocean below, where they were swept straight into the massive wave.

This attack created more instability in the tsunami with each Destruction user it took out, but even this wasn't enough to stop it. The soldiers near Fort began to get nervous, muttering to each other in their own language.

The one soldier shouted again, and everyone else went quiet. Soldiers in the front began to remove their masks and step forward onto the beach, even as the wave grew dangerously close. The soldiers behind them all turned their magic on the ones who'd stepped forward, their blue Healing light almost too bright to look at.

And then, out of the light, the soldiers at the front began to grow.

Fort involuntarily took a step back in amazement, even as the soldiers cried out in pain as their bodies doubled in size, then doubled again, growing larger and larger. From the sound of their cries, the agony was incredible, and several soldiers near Fort had to look away even as they kept their magic flowing into the others.

And then, just a moment later, the light disappeared, and Fort rubbed his eyes, trying to see what had happened.

Giants now strode the beach, each one easily as tall as a skyscraper. And there were hundreds of them, each one lining up to face the oncoming wave, spreading their arms and readying themselves to deflect as much as they could.

The enormous soldiers shouted as one, the force of their cry sending their regular-sized comrades to their knees from the intensity of it, but again, Fort didn't feel a thing, at least not physically. Mentally, he still couldn't believe any of this was really happening.

And then the giants surged forward, crashing into the surf, and threw their bodies into the oncoming tsunami.

Red Destructive spells flew out at the giants, burning them or sending electricity zapping through their bodies, but the spells were too small to do much. The giants hit the wave, and—

And Fort was back in the Deployment Room, Ellora giving him a horribly sad look.

"I'm so, so sorry we had to show you that," she whispered.

- NINE -

BEFORE FORT COULD RESPOND, HE saw that Jia and Rachel were there as well and looked just as shocked as he felt. Simon stood in front of them both, with a wheeled construction cart abandoned just behind them. Apparently he really had carted them here.

Just behind Simon, Fort's portal to the Carmarthen Academy stood open, which meant Ellora must have actually reversed time on the wall.

"What *was* that?" Jia demanded, her voice sounding like she was on the edge of panic. "What did I just see?"

Simon cleared his throat. "Oh, uh, I actually forget which of you I sent where. Were you the attack on Chicago? That was the disease outbreaks, if I remember right. Smallpox, measles, that kind of thing?"

"No, that was me," Rachel said quietly, her eyes wild. "I . . . I've never seen anything so horrible."

"I saw Destruction-magic users, in Hong Kong," Jia said. "They were floating through the streets, setting fire to everything as they went. People were screaming, running. I saw . . . I saw . . ." She went silent for a moment, holding her arms tightly around herself. "That can't be the future. It *can't*!"

Ellora and Simon looked at each other. "It will be, if we don't stop it," Ellora said. "That's why we need your help."

"How far in the future?" Fort asked, trying to get the image of the tidal wave crashing against the soldiers out of his head. "How long do we have before all of that happens?"

Ellora looked uncomfortable. "That can wait for now—"

"No, they should know," Simon said. "Everything you three just saw? It all takes place right around two years from now. Three, for the reprisal in Hong Kong."

Fort fell back a step, completely in shock. Only two *years*? So soon? But how could that even be possible?

The soldiers on the beach had been grown men and women, and they'd been using magic. Discovery Day was only thirteen years ago, so two years from now, the oldest magic users could only be fifteen or sixteen, tops.

Jia and Rachel looked just as thrown. "How can that be?" Jia asked softly.

Ellora glared at Simon, who just shrugged. "Things are going to change *dramatically* in the next year," Ellora said finally. "If what you just saw was a fire, the spark that lights it goes off by this time tomorrow."

Fort just stared at her. That had to mean . . .

"London getting destroyed is the spark, yes," Simon said, answering Fort's thoughts. "Now you see why we're so desperate to stop it. Other than, you know, it's a city of almost ten million. That's sort of important to us too. Now, are you going to come with us, or would you rather waste more time here with obvious questions?"

"But how can adults use magic?" Fort said. Simon groaned loudly, but Fort didn't care. "It's just not possible."

Ellora gave him a long look before responding, making him feel oddly guilty for some reason. "Come with us back to the Carmarthen Academy. We'll explain everything there."

"What Ellora is avoiding saying is that your Dr. Ambrose is the one who figures out why adults can't use magic and fixes that," Simon said, then jumped as Ellora punched him. "Hey, ouch! What was that for?"

"Enough!" she hissed. "We're not getting into all of that right now!"

"You don't think they of all people should know?" Simon said, looking hurt and rubbing his shoulder.

Dr. Ambrose? She was the one who'd be responsible for giving adults magic? But how? Yes, she had access to most of the books of magic, and a whole school of magic users, the most anywhere in the world, from what Fort knew. But no adults at the school could use magic. What was going to change?

"Wait, hold on," Rachel said, sounding like she was in a daze. "*How* did Dr. Ambrose figure this out? Only people born on Discovery Day or after can use magic. That's not just something a vaccine can fix."

"That's what we all thought," Simon said. "But thanks to Dr. Ambrose's research on—"

And then he paused in mid-sentence, his entire body freezing, glowing with black light.

"I told you, *enough*," Ellora said, her eyes blazing with black light as she glared at her schoolmate. Fort immediately readied a spell to use against her, not that it'd do much good, and out of the corner of his eye, he saw Jia and Rachel do the same thing, but Ellora held up her hands in surrender as she turned

77

back to them. "Sorry about that. It doesn't matter *how* it happens. What matters is that we stop it. And that's why we've come to you."

"You really think you can stop . . . everything we saw?" Rachel asked, her hands shaking so hard she crossed her arms to hide it. "It looked like a war zone."

Ellora winced but, again, seemed to be hiding something. "We *can* stop it, or at least postpone it, if we save London. And to do that, we need you three. Without each of you, our plan fails, simple as that."

Something beeped, and Ellora glanced down at her watch, then made a face. "We've run out of time," she said, unfreezing Simon, who seemed unfazed by his freezing. "We've got about two minutes before all of your TDA soldiers show back up, so I need you to come with us *now*."

Fort glanced between his two friends, who looked as shaken as he felt. Jia especially had a haunted look in her eye—he hadn't seen her this unsettled since the Dracsi caverns. Whatever she'd seen must have really upset her.

If it'd been anything like the tsunami on the beach, he shouldn't be surprised.

But if they went with Ellora and Simon, if *he* went, and

Colonel Charles found out . . . what then? Would the colonel really go through with his threat and make Fort forget he'd ever found his father? The thought of spending the rest of his life thinking his father was lost to the D.C. attack was almost the worst thing he could think of, other than not ever having found his father to begin with.

"*We* could go," Rachel whispered to Fort, apparently reading his mind. "If you stay, you'll have followed orders, so no punishment."

"We need all three of you," Ellora said, shaking her head. "With just one or two, we'll never save London. Without Forsythe, everything you saw will come to pass."

Jia seemed to shudder at this, and Rachel gave him a sad look. "It's your call, New Kid," Rachel said quietly. "I don't know that we can trust these two, but there's no way I'm letting that future happen, no matter what Colonel Charles threatens me with. But things are different for you." She paused. "Maybe we could all tell him we were kidnapped? I mean, considering they already froze Jia and me, they easily could have. And the colonel might believe that if we're gone before he returns."

"What about the security cameras?" Fort asked, remembering Colonel Charles telling him about footage of Fort letting

Sierra and Damian go, back at the original school. "He'd have proof we were lying."

"We froze those when we arrived," Simon said, his annoyance evident in his voice. "Hurry *up*, please!"

"We need a decision," Ellora said, sounding anxious as well. "They'll return in under a minute now." She nodded at Simon, who ran over to the portal and passed through it. Ellora quickly moved to follow, but she paused at the entrance, waiting for them.

"I have to go," Jia said suddenly, and walked to the portal without looking at the other two. "Whether or not Fort comes, I can't . . . I have to stop that future. I *have* to."

Rachel stared after her in confusion for a moment, but turned back to Fort. "I'm with her, even more than usual," she said. "What are *you* going to do?"

For a moment, all Fort could think about was his life before Dr. Opps had arrived: going to school every day, sometimes getting into fights, feeling nothing but numb, an emptiness inside that felt as deep and cold as the ocean. His aunt couldn't afford to take care of him, and he'd had no idea his father was out there somewhere. All he'd had was the feeling that it was his fault his dad had been captured.

And that could be his life again, if he disobeyed Colonel Charles.

But what did that compare to the future they'd seen? If even one person got hurt or died in a battle, could he live with himself? Not to mention a whole city full of people in London was in danger.

When it came down to it, there really wasn't any choice. He had no idea how he could be useful, with just his Teleport and Heal Minor Wounds spells, but if Ellora had seen a need for him, then he *couldn't* stay behind.

"I'm in," he said, barely recognizing his own voice. He quickly ran over to the portal, trying to ignore the consequences for now. Rachel might be right: If they could just get out before the soldiers reappeared, they could say that the Time students had taken them by force.

Maybe Colonel Charles would even believe it.

They all passed through the portal, Rachel slapping him on the back supportively as she went. As they stepped onto the dark, damp grass in front of the Carmarthen Academy, Fort turned around to close the teleportation circle behind him . . .

And a lightning bolt passed right over his shoulder, striking the lawn.

"Close it!" Rachel shouted, but it was already too late. As Fort shut the portal down, he saw the TDA soldiers had already started reappearing. Only it wasn't a soldier who'd fired.

It was Colonel Charles. The colonel now stared at them through the portal, his Lightning rod still glowing from use, looking almost dumbfounded from rage. "Fitzgerald!" he shouted. "I *order* you to—"

But the rest was lost as the portal closed.

- TEN -

FORT STARED THROUGH THE SPOT where the portal had been, frozen in place. In his mind, the colonel's threat ran on a loop, and he almost couldn't believe what had just happened.

"Do you . . . do you think he knew we weren't being kidnapped?" he whispered to no one in particular.

"Pretty sure, yeah," Rachel said to him as she laid a hand on his shoulder, then gently turned him around to face her and the others. "It's going to be okay, Fort. Really. We'll figure this out."

Fort shook his head, barely able to comprehend the words. After everything, losing his father to the Dracsi in D.C., finding him in an alternate dimension, and rescuing him—now, in just a matter of seconds, he'd managed to throw it all away.

Ellora moved to stand next to Rachel, her expression full of pity. "I know this seems bad—and it is. But it's not too late to make it right."

Make it right? It didn't even seem possible. How could anyone change what had just happened?

And then it dawned on him, and for the first time all day, he suddenly felt hope. "You mean we can fix it with Time magic?" he said quickly. "You can go back and make sure Colonel Charles doesn't catch us?"

"No, we can't actually change the past," she said, and his hope died just as quickly as it'd appeared. "But come listen to what William has to say. The way you three will help us save London will . . . change things a bit."

"What do you mean by that?" Rachel asked.

"We don't have time for all these questions," Simon said, sounding annoyed. "If you had just come when we said to, it wouldn't have been a problem." He glared at Ellora. "Or if *she* had let me just freeze you all to begin with!"

Simon's words took a moment to filter through Fort's dark thoughts, but when they did, he turned to the other boy with a mixture of amazement and anger. "Wait a minute," he said quietly. "Back up. Did you know this was going to happen? That the colonel would catch us leaving?"

Ellora stepped between them, raising her hands up again. "Forsythe, we can *fix* it. Really. You just need to—"

"Just think of it as getting a little push in the right direction," Simon said, either not noticing or not caring how close Fort was to teleporting him into the ocean. "If you don't want to make even more problems for yourself, I'd suggest you come with us, *now*."

Simon turned to walk up toward the school but almost fell over as the rock beneath his feet rose up around his ankles, locking him in place. "Explain this to us one more time," Rachel said, her hands glowing with Destruction magic. "You two geniuses *planned* for us to get caught?"

"No!" Ellora said, her own hands glowing with black light as she reversed time on Simon, freeing him from Rachel's spell. "It was a possibility, yes, if we couldn't get you out faster. But we would *never* have planned for it, or done this on purpose. This is why I kept trying to hurry you!"

"But you never said *this* would happen," Fort said, wondering how cold the Arctic would feel at this time of year to the Time students. "You could have warned us!"

"I could have, yes," she said, sounding resigned. "And if I had, you would have taken even longer to decide, and then your headmaster would have returned before we left. The only way to have avoided it completely would have been to freeze you and carry you here, like Simon wanted. But then we'd be treating you no differently than our teachers have been treating *us*, and I wasn't going to do that, not if I could help it."

"See?" Simon said. "I'm not looking so bad now, am I?"

Ellora glared at him. "Not helping!" She turned back to the others. "We threw the soldiers as far forward in time as our power allowed. There were too many to send any further, we just didn't have the strength. But if you help us with the plan, all your problems with the colonel will go away. William's idea is powerful enough to change *all* of our futures, no matter how bad they look now."

"Unless we run out of time because you lot take too long again," Simon said. Rachel sent a tiny lightning bolt in his direction, but he sidestepped it and stuck out his tongue at her. "Nice try, but I saw that—" he said, but froze in mid-sentence as Jia paralyzed him.

As much as Fort wanted to keep shouting at the Time students for not warning them, he knew that it wasn't really them he was angry at. He'd known the consequences of coming, and he'd still chosen to try to stop whatever it was he'd seen in the future.

Colonel Charles was the bad guy here, not the Time students.

Assuming, of course, that they weren't lying about everything.

"Okay, let's go," Fort told Ellora. "But this *better* be the last surprise. Tell us right now if there's anything else we should know about ahead of time."

She looked at Fort sadly. "Later, you'll wish you hadn't asked that, believe me. Come on, let's go see William."

And with that, she turned and walked up the driveway toward the school, leaving Fort to stare after her in disbelief.

"Hey, do you want us to unfreeze your jerky friend?" Rachel asked, pointing at Simon, who was still paralyzed.

Ellora paused, then shook her head. "William will come free him when we're done. For now, it's nice not to hear his voice for a few minutes."

Leaving Simon behind, they followed Ellora up the circular driveway toward the white stone school. Three floors tall, the building was shaped like an L, with the long side running straight perpendicularly in front of them, and the leg of the L extending out parallel to them on their right.

In the dim light of the dome, the white stones gave off an eerie glow. Even after dealing with eternal horrors like the Old

Ones, a small part of Fort actually felt nervous about walking into this old, creepy school. With the way his luck was running, the school was probably haunted by some ancient evil.

"Love voluntarily stepping into horror-movie sets," Rachel whispered to Jia, apparently thinking the same thing. "Just my absolute *favorite* thing to do."

"It's just a school," Jia said, sounding distracted. Not that Fort didn't have enough to think about either, but somehow supernatural terrors had a way of pushing to the head of the line in his mind.

"A school for the dead, maybe," Rachel said, shouldering into Jia. But Jia just shrugged, continuing on even as Rachel stopped in confusion.

"What's wrong?" Fort asked as he caught up to Rachel.

"Gee's acting weird," she said. "You heard her before, she was all excited to break the rules and get over here. But something changed after that Simon kid brought us down to you."

"The future I saw was pretty horrible," Fort said. "She might have seen something even worse."

"That's probably it," Rachel said, then moved on with him, but he noticed her eyes never left Jia as they walked.

A few yards ahead of them, Ellora climbed the stairs, then

pulled on one of two tall wooden doors. It creaked loudly as it opened, and Rachel froze in place again. "Nope!" she said.

"It's really not haunted, Rachel," Ellora said. "Trust me. If any ghosts had been here, our teachers would have scared them away."

That wasn't exactly comforting, but Ellora was waving them through anxiously, so Fort gave Rachel a push up the stairs.

Rachel glared at him, then stomped ahead to where Ellora impatiently held the door. "There *better* not be anything creepy in here," she said as she passed the Time student.

"Other than the boys' egos, we're all set," Ellora said.

Fort walked through the double doors with Ellora just behind him and found himself in a lobby full of wood paneling on all the walls. A dusty fireplace filled the wall across from the door, with two large sets of armor on either side of it. Each set of armor was at least five feet tall and held an enormous sword, pointed at the floor.

"I'm calling it now," Rachel said, pointing at the armor. "Those for sure come alive and attack us. Just a matter of time. Probably when we least expect it."

Fort rolled his eyes, then turned around to say something to Ellora, only for his heart to stop in his chest from fright.

"Whoa!" he shouted, leaping back several feet and pointing at two figures staring at him from one side of the lobby.

"No, don't hurt them!" Ellora shouted as Rachel instantly started a Destruction spell. "They're just soldiers! We had to freeze them, after having our own problems with *our* military. When they realized what we were doing, they came in force to take us captive. But we saw them coming and put up the dome."

"Again, you could have warned us!" Rachel growled in annoyance, then strode over and tapped one of the frozen soldiers' guns. "So that's what the dome does, freezes people under it, everyone but you students?"

"Us, and anyone who comes in after the dome went up," Ellora said. "But to keep this many people frozen takes a *lot* of effort. We've been taking turns, but it's not going to last much longer. But William will tell you more about that. Come on, this way."

She started down the hall past the soldiers, with Jia and Rachel just behind. Fort glanced in the opposite direction momentarily, where he found more frozen soldiers, at least a dozen of them this time.

Wow. The British government *really* didn't like what these

kids were doing, something that he'd noticed Ellora still hadn't given any details on. What did the soldiers know that he and his friends didn't?

"You're going to get eaten by ghosts if you lag behind!" Rachel's voice came floating back from down the hall, and Fort hurried to catch up, passing by an empty reception desk with papers piled neatly on one end.

The hallway they followed had what looked like classrooms on both sides, though they didn't seem to have been used anytime recently. Most had large pieces of cloth draped over the desks to keep things from getting too dusty, and the chalkboards were empty.

The farther they got down the hall, the more soldiers they passed. Most were running in the direction they were headed, but a few were staring back toward the lobby in fear. That didn't help Fort's nerves much, considering from the look of it, at this point they were *running from* the Time students.

"Just up these stairs," Ellora said as they reached the end of the hallway. "Watch yourselves, though: There's a bit of a time warp that somehow got stuck here."

"A *what* now?" Rachel said, her eyebrows shooting up.

Ellora smiled slightly, then started up the steps, only to

disappear, reappearing instantly a step from the top, then toward the middle, and finally back at the bottom of the stairs, where she groaned. "I think it was Simon, trying to save some time at one point before we got . . . lost," she said. "But his spell never worked right, and now it's just annoying, honestly. But you get through eventually."

Got lost? Neither Ellora nor Simon had explained what had happened to the Time students yet. All Fort knew was what Cyrus had told him, about how using the magic had affected their minds somehow. Had they actually gotten lost in the past or future, leaving their bodies behind just like Fort had when he'd seen the tsunami and the future of the Oppenheimer School?

Either way, messing around with the stairs was keeping him from getting answers. Fort glanced up to the top landing, then opened a teleportation circle there and gestured for Rachel and Jia to go through.

"Hey, that's cheating!" Ellora said as she attempted the stairs again, this time getting almost to the top before appearing all at once in both the bottom *and* middle. Both Elloras sighed, then waved at each other.

"We don't have time for this!" Jia shouted at her, and Ellora nodded, her face slowly blooming with embarrassment. A black glow covered her, and she walked up the stairs again without any problem, then passed by them without a word.

Beyond the steps, another short hallway led to a few doors on either side, including one labeled HEADMASTER at the far end, down into the leg of the building's L shape.

"We're going in here," Ellora said, reaching the door. She knocked once, then opened it slowly. "Hello, it's me. I'm here with our new friends."

As the door opened, Fort could make out more paralyzed bodies inside the room: a few soldiers, what looked like a teacher or two, and—

"No," he whispered, frozen in the doorway, unable to move.

Sierra stood on one side of the room, her mouth open in what looked like a scream, her hands frozen in midair like she'd been trying to protect herself.

- ELEVEN -

*S**IERRA!***" FORT SHOUTED, THOUGH HE knew she couldn't hear him. He rushed toward her, narrowly missing her hands flung out in front like she'd been trying to cast a spell but had been stopped by the Time magic.

As he reached her, an odd pressure filled his chest, and he had to look away just to breathe. Not her, not Sierra, too—*he couldn't lose anyone else—*

"She's perfectly fine, my friend," said a voice from deeper in the room, one Fort recognized from the video. "There's no need to worry about her."

Fort turned to find a comfortably decorated office, with a large, brown leather sofa on one side and a desk about three-fourths of the way across the room, just in front of a large fireplace with a crackling fire burning away within it. The

94

boy who'd spoken sat in a large chair at the desk. "I bid you welcome, my fellow wizards," he said. "You have arrived at a most advantageous time, and you have our thanks."

Fort just stared at him, struggling through his shock and anguish to even form a sentence.

"*This* is how you say thanks?" Rachel asked, and Fort realized she was standing next to someone else he recognized, a frozen Dr. Opps. The founder of the Oppenheimer School looked terrified and had his hands out as well, as if to block some sort of attack.

"I regret that such actions were necessary," the boy said, and slowly stood up from the desk. He pulled his hood off his head, revealing long, silvery hair, just like Cyrus's. Except a golden circlet sparkled on top of his head, almost like a simple crown. "But the very fate of the world depends on the actions we take here and now."

"This is William," Ellora said, waving in his direction and not sounding thrilled. "And no, I don't know *why* he's talking like this."

William went still for a second, giving her an irritated look. "I apologize for Ellora," he said. "She has a hard time understanding the importance of the quest you must undertake."

"Oh, I get the importance," Ellora told him. "What I don't understand is why you're speaking like the narrator of a TV fantasy. The video was bad enough, and I told you they'd misinterpret what you were saying!"

William narrowed his eyes but turned his gaze back to Fort and his friends and forced a shaky smile. "Haters must, as always, hate," he said. "I merely feel that a traditional tone might better suit the mood for our heroes here. Perhaps, Ellora, you would be more comfortable checking on our fellow wizards, to see if they need aid?"

She shook her head. "I think I'm good right here, thanks."

William's smile disappeared for a moment but came right back even stronger. "As you wish, of course," he said to her. "But let us move on to the quest you must undertake, my magical friends. Please, sit." He gestured to the leather seats in front of the desk. "We have much to discuss."

"We have *nothing* to discuss until you let Sierra go!" Fort shouted, finally finding his voice.

Ellora sighed, giving him a sympathetic look. "Forsythe, you have to understand—"

"I don't have to understand *anything*," he hissed. "You want our help? Let her go, *now*."

"I'm afraid to free her would require canceling the dome altogether, my young friend," William said, leaning back against the desk, "as she and your headmaster were both frozen by it. And if we do that, we'd be inviting doom."

"I don't think 'inviting doom' is a thing?" Ellora said, then turned back to Fort. "Remember how you felt when you were sent forward in time? You didn't even notice it. This is exactly the same thing: She's completely safe and won't know any time has passed when we release her."

"I don't *care*!" Fort said, feeling the heavy pressure in his chest growing even worse. "She was only trying to help you!"

"And we'll help *her* by saving the world," William said, and again gestured at the chairs. "Now please, sit, my friends, so we can address your part in this upcoming quest."

Fort gritted his teeth but didn't move a muscle, not willing to leave Sierra. Rachel and Jia both crossed their arms by his side, not sitting either. "We have some questions first, actually," Rachel said. "Where's Cyrus? He was here with Dr. Opps. Where are the other students from your video?" She paused. "And seriously, what is with you? I have a regular D and D game, and even I'm embarrassed at *this*." She waved her hand vaguely in his direction.

William snorted. "*Real* dungeons and dragons await you, my courageous Elemental magician. But to answer your other questions, Timothy and Cerise have been tasked with keeping the dome in place." He gestured toward the opposite end of the school. "As for my loyal Simon, you know where he is, assuming Jia paralyzed him as I'd foreseen. As soon as Ellora releases him, then he and Amelia will take over for Tim and Cerise, giving them a chance to rest." He frowned. "The dome shall last for five additional hours, no more. That is all the time we might provide to you for your quest—"

"Where is *Cyrus*?" Fort said, not caring about any of that.

"Cyrus? He's not here," William said, his affected manner of speaking slipping a bit. "I thought he was at your school."

What? But Sierra had confirmed he was here when Fort had spoken to her in the medical ward. "How can you not know he was here? Maybe he's frozen somewhere. Did you look all around the school?"

Ellora snorted. "As if we'd be able to freeze Cyrus. He isn't exactly someone—"

"Someone who we know that well," William finished, giving Ellora a quick look of warning, making Fort even more suspicious. William hadn't wanted her to say something about Cyrus. But what? Why would they need to keep any secrets about his friend? What were they hiding about Cyrus?

Meanwhile, William was still speaking. "But yes, Cyrus may have been caught by the dome's magic, indeed. If such circumstances would be the case, then he's perfectly safe, just like the rest, and will be released as soon as the plan is complete. Now, if we could get back to that plan, and your roles in it—"

"*You* tell us the plan, and *we'll* tell you what our roles in it are," Rachel said, glaring at him suspiciously.

William smiled again, though this time it looked even more forced. "As you wish, my demanding allies. First, let me share a tale of the unfortunate tidings that have been plaguing us here at the academy." He slowly waved his hands, as if setting the scene. "Picture, if you will, seven innocent boys and girls, welcomed to a new school just over two years ago. Quickly, these new students discovered that they all shared the same birthday, the so-called Discovery Day. But what they had yet to learn was that they would be learning Time magic, something that would ultimately—"

"Speed this up, we don't need your entire life story," Rachel said, waving her hand in a circle.

William's eyes narrowed, and he looked about as irritated with Rachel as he had with Ellora. "*Of course.* I suppose we have no time for storytelling. To sum up, when we first used Time magic to view the future, we found it . . . difficult to return to the present. You've all now seen what's to come, the world war that—"

"A *world war*?" Jia said. "We didn't know it was that bad! All we saw was the U.S. and China . . ." She trailed off, shaking a bit. Fort noticed her fists were clenched at her sides.

"It's worse than you think," Ellora said. "But William would get to it faster if he'd talk normally."

"Ellora, seriously, you're *ruining* the mood!" William shouted. "Do you think I started a fire in here because it's cold? It's all to create the right atmosphere!"

Ellora rolled her eyes. "Oh, I didn't realize this was about you and the fireplace. I thought it was about *Damian*!"

Damian? Fort had almost forgotten about the dragon boy completely upon seeing Sierra frozen in time. He should have been here too, frozen next to her. Where was he, then?

"What's Damian got to do with this?" Rachel asked. "I

thought he got freed from the Old Ones' control."

William broke off glaring at Ellora to turn to Rachel. "You still don't know? Damian's going to destroy London if you don't stop him. I mean, how did you not get that? I told you this quest would involve dungeons *and* dragons!"

- TWELVE -

WHAT? DAMIAN WAS THE ONE who'd destroy London? But that didn't make any sense. As much of a jerk as he was—and he was a *huge* jerk—Fort couldn't see the boy ever actually attacking someone, let alone destroying a city.

Unless he was possessed by another Old One.

"Damian?" Jia said, his name shocking her out of whatever was going through her head. "There's no way. He'd never hurt anyone."

"We've seen it, Jia," Ellora said quietly. "And you've seen what it leads to yourself."

"But why take our word for it, when you can see for yourselves?" William asked, his voice lowering again as he gestured dramatically, his hands glowing with black light.

"William, *wait*—" Ellora shouted, but the room had already

disappeared around them, replaced by a sort of shimmering, dreamlike vision of a long room with red velvet wallpaper and tapestries hanging every few feet.

And everything was on fire.

Fort immediately raised his arms to protect himself, but just like with the tsunami, he couldn't actually feel the heat from the flames or smell the smoke filling the air. But as real as the water attack had looked, this vision now seemed much less concrete, like watching something through the heat haze coming off asphalt in the summer.

A roar shook the room, and even though he wasn't able to be hurt, Fort still unconsciously took a step backward in fear as a dragon faded into view out of the shimmering fog just yards away, roaring and shooting flames from its mouth. Held tightly in one massive foot was what looked like a large, leather-bound book, but it was hard to make out as the haziness seemed to be emanating from the book itself.

And then the haze obscured the dragon again as the roof above began to crack from the heat, crumbling into the room below.

"This is the *palace*," said a dazed voice next to him, and Fort almost leaped out of his shoes as he whirled to find Rachel and Jia, both transparent as ghosts, standing right beside him. Apparently more than one person could see the future together. And not only that, but they could talk, too? "Buckingham Palace. It's where the British royals live."

"Was that Damian?" Jia asked, staring at the spot where the dragon had disappeared. Another roar echoed down the hall, and Fort realized it hadn't left. They just couldn't see it. But why?

"It sure looked like him," Rachel said. "We saw his dragon form when the Old Ones took him over in the Dracsi dimension, and he looked exactly like this dragon. Right, Fort?"

Fort nodded but jumped again as the dragon swirled back into view, sending another plume of flames into the walls as the roof above them began to collapse in on itself. "You're all traitors!" the dragon roared in Damian's voice, breathing even more fire into the walls. "I'll burn you all to the ground before I let you take this book!"

He disappeared again, but worse now, huge timbers had begun falling from the roof, cracking through the marble floor below.

"We have to get out of here! It's not safe!" Fort yelled, forgetting in the heat of the moment that this was the future.

"Fort, we're not really *here*!" Rachel told him, then leaned over to push her hand right through his body. "See?"

"But other people are," Jia said quietly, pointing at several people on the opposite end of the hall, cringing away from the fire.

Without even realizing it was futile, Fort tried to open a teleportation circle for the people before the fire could reach them or the roof fully cave in. But just like the last time, no portal appeared, which of course he should have known, since he wasn't actually here.

Except green light did appear in the room—

And then the room, the green light, and the fire all disappeared, replaced by rooftops over a city, sprawling out in every direction.

For a moment, the new height sent a wave of dizziness through Fort, and he desperately grabbed for the railing on the fence surrounding them, only for his hands to pass right through it, just like Rachel's had through him a moment ago. Still, he managed to catch himself before falling through the fence, at least, and straightened up to find large glass triangles rising up around them.

But where was he? He peered over the fence as close as

he dared, knowing he wouldn't be able to grab it if he fell—though hopefully he wouldn't be able to fall, since he wasn't even here—and noticed a familiar sight: Not too far was a bridge with two castle-like towers spanning a river.

He'd seen that bridge before. This was London.

"Look!" someone shouted from behind him, and Fort whirled around again to find Rachel, with Jia beside her, pointing out over the city from nearby. He ran over to them, but froze in place as he saw what Rachel was shouting about.

Orange light from a thousand different sources was flooding into the domeless sky, like streams of magic. And as they stared, more and more appeared, all emptying out into a sort of humanoid form that stood as tall as a skyscraper.

"What kind of magic is that?" Fort asked softly, not sure he wanted to know.

When neither of them answered, Fort turned to find Jia looking as confused as he felt, which made sense. But Rachel, always confident and fearless, looked *terrified*.

"It's . . . it's Spirit magic," she said finally, holding her arms tightly to her chest. "That's . . . that's what the Old One Q'baos used on the dwarves. And on *me*." She shuddered. "It changes who you are, down to your core. Into whatever the caster wants. That's why the dwarves worshipped Q'baos. It's that powerful."

They were too far to see clearly, but even from a distance, Fort could tell that the orange light was forming around something large, with huge wings. A dragon, it had to be. The center of the light even shimmered the same way Damian had, back in Buckingham Palace.

Wait. Hadn't Cyrus mentioned something like this, when looking into the future? He'd said that the books of magic fogged things up, making them really hard to pin down. Something about how they were too powerful, too chaotic for seeing their future clearly.

Was that what this was? Had that really been a book of magic being held in Damian's foot? Was that what was causing the shimmering in the vision?

And if so, was it Spirit magic?

As the orange light continued to stream in, it formed a sort of massive creature, which began to reach down to swipe at nearby buildings. Apparently it was solid, because wherever it touched, the buildings collapsed to the ground.

Buildings with people in them, maybe.

Again, Fort cast Teleport, trying to open a portal over to the monster, not knowing if he could help, but not being willing to just sit and watch. But just like the last two times, no teleportation circle opened, and—

"There's someone on those rooftops," Jia said, pointing now as Rachel looked away. Fort followed Jia's finger, squinting enough to make out a few figures on the roofs near the monster, just as she'd said.

As he watched, one set off a green light, and the three disappeared into what looked exactly like a teleportation circle.

Fort gasped. "Was that . . . me?"

"Who else even knows that spell?" Rachel asked. "Just Damian, and Gabriel . . ."

But there was no chance to answer her as the skyline of London faded momentarily, then reappeared.

Only this time, where the orange monster had once stood, now there was nothing but destruction.

Whole blocks of buildings were razed to the ground, leaving behind devastation and chaos. Soldiers walked in formation through the remaining streets as ambulances' sirens rang out through the air, so many they all seemed to come together as one.

Below them, even in the blocks where buildings still stood,

people lay on the ground unmoving, like they'd been knocked unconscious. Here and there, thin tendrils of orange light flittered back to the ground like discarded ribbons, where they seemed to explode with a light too intense to look at. Fort covered his eyes, but when the light faded, he discovered that there was now a dazed, confused-looking human lying where the light had landed.

Was the orange light . . . people? How could Spirit magic do that, though?

Another siren went by, and something flashed in Fort's mind, the National Mall and police sirens racing toward the Reflecting Pool as a giant monster clawed its way up from the depths below. He flinched at the memory of the Dracsi attack, only to find something similar unfolding below him, this time real, not just in his nightmares.

A wave of dizziness hit him again, but not from the height, and he wanted to cover his eyes, to look away, anything, but he knew he couldn't.

It was all happening again. And this time, he knew who'd caused it.

"Take us back!" he shouted into the air, making Jia jump next to him, though Rachel didn't seem to notice. "We've seen what you wanted us to see, William. Bring us back, *now*!"

But the sirens continued to shriek through the air, and shouts from people below echoed up to them, even high above the rest of the city. Fort finally did look away, shutting his eyes, not willing to watch any longer. "We'll stop this, okay?" he shouted again. "We will. Just bring us back and tell us what we need to do! We don't need to see this anymore!"

"Okay," said William's voice, and Fort's eyes opened to find he was back in the Carmarthen Academy's headmaster's office, with William and Ellora in the same spots they'd been in, as if no time had passed. Next to him, Jia and Rachel both jolted as if coming out of a dream as well, which Fort wished had been the case.

But even with the shimmering, even with the fog, that had been far too real.

"Now, my fellow wizards," William said, his smile more genuine this time, "you have seen the enemy, and the awful future he seeks to bring about."

"I don't get it," Rachel said. "I thought you couldn't see the future when a book of magic was involved, but we saw plenty."

"Only William's been able to see that much," Ellora said. "That's why he had to show you. If the rest of us look, it's all fogged up. Probably had to do with him getting trapped in the near future, so he had more time to—"

"False," William said, shaking his head. "I was destined to see it, and to be the messenger of our future peril!" Ellora rolled her eyes as he continued. "Now, brave souls, tell me you'll follow my lead in our endeavor. Our plan is truly the world's last hope."

Fort took a deep breath, then looked at his two friends. Jia seemed distracted, like she was lost in the future still, while Rachel had her arms wrapped tightly around her chest, like she was freezing cold.

"We will," Fort said. "Tell us the plan."

William gave him a tight-lipped smile. "No."

- THIRTEEN -

N O?" FORT SAID, NOW EVEN MORE confused. "You *don't* want our help? Then what—"

"If I share the full plan with you, Damian will pluck it from your mind like a flower from a garden," William said. "In order to keep it safe, none of us know the full plan. It is the only way."

Rachel sighed loudly, but at least her annoyance seemed to be bringing her out of the funk she'd been in. "First, you really need to talk normally, or I'm going to explode. Second, if you can't tell us the *full* plan, we still need to know how to stop Damian."

"And why Damian is acting like this," Jia said quietly. "He must be possessed. He'd never do this."

"Oh, he's not possessed," William said. "But I can't fully

112

explain his actions, not without taking a peril-filled journey into *his* mind—"

"What did I say about the language?" Rachel said, taking a step closer to him.

William sighed, rolling his eyes. "Great art is never appreciated in its time. I can use simpler words if that helps you. Is that better?"

"*Yes,*" Fort, Jia, Rachel, and Ellora all said at once.

"Philistines," William said, then held up his hands in surrender at a look from Rachel. "Okay, okay, I'm sorry. This all started yesterday, when Sierra brought us back to the present. From where, you ask?" His face lit up a bit. "Ah, that's a story worth telling—"

"*Another* time," Ellora said.

"*Fine,*" William said. "Sierra brought us back from *somewhere*. And that's when things get interesting. Because before we came back, I'd foreseen what was to come. Originally, we'd have returned, and Damian would use his Mind magic to try to find out where the book of Time magic was. Only, we didn't know, because the teachers had taken it. But instead, he found something much more interesting."

Ellora waved her hand for him to hurry it up, and he shook

his head in disgust. "Damian found that one of us knew where the book of Spirit magic was, *okay*? Long story *way* too short."

Fort winced at the mention of Spirit magic and saw Rachel shudder out of the corner of his eye. So they'd been right about the type of magic they'd seen back in the vision of London's destruction. He really wished they hadn't been.

"So then Damian goes and gets the book," William continued. "Probably planning on using it on our teachers, to find the book of Time magic too. Only what he doesn't know is that Spirit magic can affect the weak of mind, tempt you with its power. And Damian, who'd just found out that everything he ever knew about himself was a lie, had quite a bit of anger boiling around inside him." Here he paused, giving Fort a long look. "Though you three probably know just as much about that as I do, eh?"

Fort turned bright red in response. But that wasn't even fair. *Gabriel* had been the one who'd betrayed Damian to the Old Ones, not Fort. And that had been how Damian had found out about his dragon heritage.

Yes, Gabriel would never have been in that position if Fort hadn't gone looking for his father, lying to his friends about it, but . . .

He sighed. Maybe it was time to stop making excuses.

"I don't get how Damian finding out he's a dragon makes him destroy everything," Rachel said. "What exactly did the magic do to him?"

William leaned in close, an excited glow in his eye. "You think of magic as a power, a tool you can use like electricity or gravity."

"Gravity's not exactly a tool . . . ," Ellora said, but William ignored her.

"Magic doesn't care about your physics or laws of nature," William said, getting closer to Fort, Rachel, and Jia to the point they all stepped backward. "Magic has a mind of its own, one not too happy with humanity, from what I've felt."

Felt? Fort frowned. How had he "felt" that? What was he even talking about, magic having a mind of its own? That couldn't be possible. Magic couldn't have its own opinions on things and just not like human beings.

. . . Could it?

"He's making this up," Ellora said. "None of the rest of us felt anything like this."

"None of the rest of you were sent where I was," William said, his face going pale. "And from what I've seen, magic has

115

it in for us. It *wants* us to fail, to fall before its masters. And it'll help them in any way it can. Especially Spirit magic. No other type has as strong a will as Spirit, and when someone as conflicted about things as Damian messes around with it— BOOM." He shouted this last bit, making them all jump.

Could that be true? Damian hadn't exactly seemed calm and together when burning down Buckingham Palace. And stealing all the people in London to form a giant Spirit monster didn't help either. But how could magic itself have such an impact on someone's mind?

"I don't know about the rest, but Damian definitely thinks everyone's out to get him, even his former friends," Ellora said, nodding at Jia. "You must have seen yourselves there in the future, trying to stop him."

And failing, from the look of it. Fort frowned. *That* didn't bode well.

"There's no reasoning with him," Ellora continued. "Whatever Spirit magic is, he uses it to absorb the power of every citizen of London and destroy the city. After seeing the TDA powerless to stop Damian, all the other countries decide they need to protect themselves any way they can. And that means they want their books of magic back, *now*."

"To which your government says 'no thank you,'" William continued. "And in the department of unfortunate timing, this is when the discovery is made about how to give magic to adults. Word gets out, books of magic are stolen, and the world goes to war, resulting in scenes like the ones you all saw."

For a moment, everyone was quiet, each lost in their own memories. Visions of the tsunami and of Damian destroying London flooded into Fort's head, no matter how hard he tried to push them out. Was this going to be how the world ended, in a war because Damian couldn't control his magic?

No. It'd be a war because Fort couldn't let his father go. Everything else had come from that, and there was no one else to blame but himself.

But if he hadn't gone to the Dracsi dimension, he'd never have known if his father was still alive. His dad would have been left there, living out his life as a monster. That couldn't be the better choice, no matter what came of it!

But maybe there was a better way to do it. One where he worked with his friends instead of lying to them. Where, together, they found out what Gabriel was up to before he almost gave the Old Ones the whole world.

"You know, of course, about the war," William finally said,

breaking the silence. "You've seen parts of it. And I know Simon was going to share how adult soldiers could use magic—"

"He told them it was Dr. Ambrose who made the discovery, that's it," Ellora said, giving Fort a quick look.

"Really," William said, turning his gaze on Fort as well. "So not the whole story?"

"They know all they need to know, for now," Ellora said quickly, staring at William. "I told you what would happen if we tell them *too early*."

"Oh, right!" he said, winking entirely unsubtly at her. "To everything its proper time, of course."

What was going on? Ellora and William were definitely hiding something from them, from *Fort* especially, but what was it? Something to do with Dr. Ambrose? "I think we need to hear the rest *right now*—" he said.

"Not yet," Ellora told him, looking away. "Sorry. We can get into that later. Tell them about the dome, William."

He nodded. "Because I had foreseen all of this happening, I came up with the idea for the dome and put it up the moment we returned. Almost fainted from the effort, but there was no way to tell everyone what was going on without alerting Damian to what I was doing, so I didn't have a choice. Once they heard it all, the others pitched in and took the weight off my shoulders."

"We don't care about what you went through," Rachel said. "What was the reason for the dome?"

"It was meant to freeze everyone, including Damian, so that we could figure out what to do," William told her, then paused, looking uncomfortable. "But somehow, he was able to resist the magic. I'm not really sure how. He escaped, and we don't know where he is now."

"Maybe he's with Cyrus," Fort said, more bitterly than he'd intended. "Maybe they're all hanging out together."

"You better hope Cyrus isn't helping him," William said, narrowing his eyes. "We'll all be in for it if they're working together. But no, he probably just managed to sneak a Mind spell or something into my head and made me leave him out of the dome's effect."

"So basically it's useless," Rachel said. "And you're just freezing half the country for nothing?"

"Not exactly," Ellora said. "You saw the soldiers below. They were coming for us the moment they figured out Sierra could bring us back. Our teachers weren't going to let that happen."

She shuddered, and Fort again wondered where exactly

they'd all been this whole time and why they couldn't come back. Had the school's teachers kept them away somehow, like some kind of detention or something? But how? Their teachers wouldn't have been able to use magic any more than the Oppenheimer School's teachers could.

"The dome's good for something else, too," William said. "Getting to the book of Spirit magic without any outside interference."

What? "Are you joking?" Fort said.

"He better be," Rachel said. "Or we're going home *right now*."

"Oh, I'm not joking," William said. "Why do you think we needed you three here? The only way to stop Damian from destroying London is to get the book of Spirit magic before he does. And to do that, I'm told you three each will play a part."

"And who told you that?" Fort asked.

"I did," Ellora said, looking him in the eye. "Because I'm the only one who knows where it is."

- FOURTEEN -

YOU KNOW WHERE THE BOOK OF Spirit magic is?" Fort said to her, both his eyebrows shooting up. "How? Where is it?"

"Hey, no!" William said, throwing up his hands. "I told you already: She can't say. If Damian's out there, he could be listening in to our conversation as we speak, reading our minds. Ellora's the only one who knows, and it has to stay that way until you three get the book before him!"

Ellora coughed, then reached into her hoodie and pulled out a familiar-looking silver necklace. "Dr. Oppenheimer had a medallion that protected him from Mind magic, so I took it, to keep the secret safe."

Fort turned to look at the terrified, frozen Dr. Opps, cringing. There was so much wrong with *all* of this, so many secrets that the Time kids weren't sharing. How could he trust them, when they kept so much to themselves?

"Anyway, it's time for you to go," William said, looking at his watch. "We can't keep the dome up for much longer, and once it falls, we'll have far more than just Damian to worry about. Ellora, take them to a neutral spot first, and then—"

"We're not going *anywhere*!" Rachel shouted. "I'm not bringing that horrible magic into the world, no matter what. You yourself said that it takes you over, changes who you are."

"I said it does that to people with weak minds, or who are conflicted, like Damian," William said. "Someone prepared for it might be able to use it for good."

Rachel's eyes widened. "Oh, doubly no way then. You think I'm bringing that thing back here for *you* to play around with, Mr. Bean? No chance on *earth*."

"Rachel," Fort said, and she immediately whirled on him with a wild look in her eye. "Hey, I'm on your side here! I totally agree with everything you said. But we still have to keep Damian from getting it. You saw what happened."

"Yeah, well, if she's the only one who knows where it is," she said, pointing at Ellora, "then we'll wipe her mind or something, and Damian will never find it!"

"He'll take the medallion from her before we got anywhere close to finding a way to take the knowledge from her mind," William said. "We've looked at this a thousand different ways, and finding the book before him is the only way. If you want to save London from being destroyed and stop the coming war, then this is how you do it."

In response, Rachel lifted her glowing hands toward him. "I said, *not going to happen*, Captain Britain!"

William's eyes turned black with Time magic, and Fort wondered if he'd have time to throw up a portal between the two to keep things from getting out of hand. But before he could, Jia stepped between William and Rachel, glowing with Healing magic. She put her hands on Rachel's, and gradually her blue light extinguished Rachel's red, leaving Rachel looking exhausted and empty.

"I know we have to stop him," Rachel said, her voice quiet and strained. "I *know* that. But—"

"The whole world goes to war, Ray," Jia told her. "We can't let that happen, no matter what."

"I know," Rachel said, her voice quiet, almost strained. "But does it have to be like this?"

She wasn't wrong. The things Fort had seen done with Spirit

123

magic gave him nightmares. The Old One Q'baos used the spells to keep the entire population of dwarfs under her thrall, making them all worship her. And he'd even briefly had it used on him by Q'baos, when he'd been in the shape of a dragon to fool the Old Ones.

But he'd been prepared for that. Rachel had been taken over without any warning and been made to follow the Old Ones. He couldn't imagine what that had done to her.

"We'll follow their lead," he told her and Jia. "And we'll get the book." Rachel started to object, but he moved on quickly. "But when we do, we destroy it, then and there, so *no one* can use it. Deal?"

Rachel stared at him for a moment. "Last time you made this deal, you were lying."

"Ask them if I'm lying," Fort said, nodding at Ellora and William.

The two Time kids looked at each other. "The books of magic kind of fog things up," Ellora told them. "So it's hard to see. But even so, we can talk about that later—"

"We destroy it, end of story," Fort said to Ellora. "Otherwise, you're on your own. Those are our terms. You brought us here to listen, and we did, and now we're willing to help, but only in a way that won't make things worse."

Unlike everything else he'd ever done.

"But that's—" William started, but Ellora stopped him.

"Good enough for now," she said, giving him a look. "I agree. But we do need to get started. So if there's nothing else, William . . . ?"

"Just one more thing," William said, clapping his hands together and standing up. He closed his eyes for a moment and took a deep breath, then opened them again, the excitement now back. "Brave adventurers. You have embraced your destiny and accepted your quest to battle for the future of the world. I commend you." He saluted them all in turn, then smiled broadly. "Now, to make it complete. You number four, as in four companions. And I shall call you *the fellowship of the—*"

"Nope!" Rachel shouted. "Time Girl, tell Fort where to teleport us before I open Mount Doom up underneath this guy?"

"Forsythe," Ellora said quietly. "Can you take us somewhere out of sight, so we can get started?"

He nodded hurriedly, not wanting Rachel to really create a volcano in Wales. "I think I know a place."

Fort opened a portal, but as he did, the room disappeared around him. Instead of a headmaster's office with wood paneling, now he was surrounded by actual trees in a deep, dense forest. A small cottage looked like it'd been built when the trees were young, and now had branches growing through the roof in places.

But the cottage and the forest weren't the biggest surprise. No, that went to the silver-haired boy standing in front of him.

"Hey, Fort," Cyrus said, looking a bit nervous. "Got a minute?"

- FIFTEEN -

CYRUS?" FORT SHOUTED, BARELY ABLE to believe this was real. He stepped forward and hugged his friend . . . except his friend wasn't there, and Fort stumbled right through him.

"Oh, sorry about that," Cyrus said, stepping out of his way. "You're not really here, and I should have said something. The me in your present time sent you forward to speak to the me a few hours in the future, so I could give you a message. You know how it goes."

Fort straightened up, staring at the other boy. "No, I really don't, at all. What are you doing here? When are we?"

Even as he responded to Cyrus, Fort realized that was ridiculous. The other boy couldn't actually see or hear him, because only his consciousness was here. He wasn't exactly sure how Cyrus had known he went for a hug—maybe he just assumed—but there was no way he could actually hold a conversation with Cyrus.

"Oh, we're only a few hours from your time," Cyrus told him. "Maybe . . . two? And as for what I'm doing here, I just wanted to help you and the others. See this place?" He turned around and gestured at the cottage behind him. "When you get the book of Spirit magic, before you destroy it, bring it back here. I'll be waiting, and we'll be safe here."

Wait, what? "You can actually hear me?" Fort said carefully.

Cyrus nodded. "Every word."

"But how? I didn't think I was really here!" And then something occurred to him. "Wait, can people in time visions *always* see you? Because we saw Damian burning London down in the future, and if he saw us—"

"Oh, no, it's just me," Cyrus said, smiling widely. "Nothing to worry about there. I just had more time with the book of Time magic than the others, before they were lost."

"Yeah, they mentioned being lost, but wouldn't tell us where they went," Fort said. "Do you know?"

"Of course," Cyrus said. "But you'll find out soon enough anyway. For now, just focus on this cottage, so you can teleport back here when you have the book." He stepped out of the way and vaguely waved at the cottage, like he was presenting a prize on a game show.

"I'll remember what it looks like," Fort said, getting a little irritated with yet another Time student not telling him anything. "But I have so many more questions. Were you here when the dome went up? What is this place? Why didn't you help Sierra? She's frozen back at the Carmarthen Academy, Cyrus. Not to mention that I'm expelled, and Colonel Charles might make me forget I rescued my father because I broke all his rules to come save you both. And now I find you hanging out in the woods?"

"Oh, don't worry about Colonel Charles," Cyrus said. "He's not going to make you forget about your dad, not after what you end up having to do to him."

Do to him? "Do to *who*?" Fort said. "Did you mean Colonel Charles or my father? And what do I do to . . . whoever?"

Before Cyrus could respond, a loud crash came from inside the cottage, and Cyrus sighed. "Eh?" shouted a voice from inside. "Do we have visitors, boy?"

"No, it's nothing!" Cyrus yelled back, making Fort even more confused. "Just talking to myself out here!"

"Bad habit to get into," the voice shouted, and more than

anything it sounded like an old man inside the cottage. "Better quit it now while you can. I've been doing it for centuries."

Centuries? "Who *is* that?" Fort whispered.

"No one," Cyrus hissed back. "It doesn't matter. I'm trying to shut him off, but I can't get it to work. Hopefully he'll be gone by the time you get here."

Shut him off? What did *that* mean? Talking to Cyrus was always a bit confusing, but this was a whole new level. "Cyrus—"

"I have to send you back now," Cyrus said, as something else crashed in the cottage, making him cringe. "Well, the me in the past will have to do it, but you get the point. He's here too, in your time, dealing with *him* just like I am." He nodded back at the cottage.

"Is that Forsythe?" shouted the voice from inside, and Fort's eyes widened. "Why didn't you say so? Bring him in already!"

"It's not time yet!" Cyrus shouted back. "And *you're* not even supposed to be here!" He turned back to Fort, looking a bit desperate. "Come back when you have the book, okay? It's vital that you don't destroy it until then. Tell the others, and try not to get Damian too angry!"

"Too angry?" Fort said, barely able to keep up with the conversation, let alone the old man yelling from the cottage. "He's about to destroy London!"

"And he'll destroy you, too, if you get him angry!" Cyrus said. "So stay calm, and whatever you do, don't let the others get into a fight with him, okay? Just trust me!"

Before Fort could respond, though he wasn't even sure where to begin with *that*, the forest, cottage, Cyrus, and strange old man's voice all faded away, replaced by the office once again.

A wave of dizziness hit him, and he stumbled slightly, only for Rachel to catch him. "You okay?" she asked, giving him a worried look. "Casting a teleportation spell hasn't ever taken it out of you like that before."

Fort looked up at her in surprise, finding everyone in the exact same spots they'd been when he'd opened the portal. In spite of talking to Cyrus for the last few minutes, his consciousness hadn't been gone for any time at all. How was that even possible?

"I'm okay, just thrown for a second," Fort said, giving Rachel a quick smile. He glanced over at Ellora and William, the former standing next to the portal, and the latter leaning on the desk. Both seemed to be giving him a curious look, so he straightened up. "Totally fine now, don't worry."

He could have told them all about Cyrus's warning, and how they had to go to the cottage after they found the book of Spirit magic. But somehow he didn't think that Cyrus wanted the other Time students to know about it. If he was hiding in the cottage now, then he had to have a good reason for it.

Besides, the Time students were keeping so much from him that it felt kind of good to have a secret from them.

"So you're ready, then?" Ellora asked.

"As I'll ever be," Fort said, and waved for her to go through the portal.

"Where did you pick for us to hide out?" Rachel asked as she walked toward the teleportation circle next to him.

"Somewhere totally out of the way, where no one will think to look," he told her. "Trust me—we're going to be completely hidden there."

- SIXTEEN -

*T*HIS IS YOUR IDEA OF 'COMPLETELY hidden'?" Rachel asked, pointing at the tour group frozen in time next to an enormous bell as an unmoving tour guide gestured toward it.

"It's Big Ben!" Fort shouted, as surprised as anyone. "I didn't think there'd be anyone up in the bell tower. Who knew you could even take a tour?"

"Well, I did," Ellora said. "And probably everyone else who's ever lived here, visited, or considered it for a moment." She gave him a small smile.

"I can take us somewhere else," he said, his mood getting worse. After whatever that had been with Cyrus, with all the confusion and offhand remarks about things he was going to do to Colonel Charles or his father, not to mention whoever that old man had been, all on top of everything with Damian and the Time kids, the very last thing in the world Fort cared about at the moment was where they went over the plan. "Is Stonehenge better?"

Rachel just stared at him. "You literally only know tourist spots, don't you."

He glared at her. "No, of course not! I know . . . the airport here too. Because the Old One flew me over it."

Rachel groaned, turning away, but Ellora just shook her head. "This is fine, Forsythe," she said. "They can't hear us or anything. Though I'm glad you know how to get to Stonehenge, since that's where the book of Spirit magic is."

"*Stonehenge?*" Rachel said, suddenly much more excited than annoyed at Fort. "Really? Why?"

"It doesn't matter, Ray," Jia said, staring at the frozen tourists for some reason. "We just need to get it and stop this war."

Rachel threw a concerned glance at Fort over this, and he felt the same way. Even with everything going on, Jia seemed to be upset by something, beyond *everything* that was happening. But if she wasn't going to share, now wasn't exactly the time to ask about it, at least not with Ellora around. After all, they barely knew the Time girl.

"Unfortunately, that's not exactly true," Ellora said to Jia.

"You *will* have to know a bit more, if just to prepare your-selves for what we might find." She cleared her throat, and Fort noticed that her cheeks were turning red. "It's also a bit, ah, ridiculous, all things considered."

Jia turned around to face the others as Fort and Rachel both leaned in. "Ridiculous *how* exactly?" Rachel asked. "Consider-ing some of what we've been through so far, I'm thinking that might be a higher bar than you know."

"Not like this," Ellora said, picking at a fingernail anxiously. "There's a lot of British history that sounds unbelievable, espe-cially concerning its kings and queens. Did you know that Wil-liam the Conqueror, who the current royal family is descended from, was actually French? He came from Normandy."

"What does this have to do with anything?" Jia asked.

Ellora shrugged. "I just always thought that was odd, con-sidering how many times France and Britain have gone to war. But I suppose all the European royal families are related at this point."

Jia seemed like she might turn away again, so Fort jumped in. "That is pretty funny," he said. "But why would the book be at Stonehenge? What's there, other than some stones standing in weird places?"

Rachel rolled her eyes at this. "It's like five thousand years old, New Kid. And the stones line up with the sun rising and setting twice a year, so maybe give the builders a little more credit."

"Plus, it's been associated with magic for all of its history," Ellora said, blushing more now. What was she so embarrassed about? "So it would only make sense for the book of Spirit magic to be there."

"Fine, so we go," Jia said. "I don't even get why we couldn't just teleport straight there from the school."

Ellora looked over her head for a moment, like she was scanning the sky. "You'll know in a few minutes. But there's more I have to tell you. I don't really know how to bring it up, but . . ."

"It's okay," Fort told her, mostly so Jia didn't start yelling. "Just take your time."

Jia glared at him for that.

Ellora, though, took a deep breath. "So, before Sierra helped bring us back to the present, each of us was stuck in a different time, without a clear idea how to get home. Our bodies were here, but our minds were in other times. You all know what that feels like now. William was the closest to the present, and Simon just a year or two out from him, but the rest of us were all further away. Me most of all, I think."

"You must have been in the past, if you know where the book of Spirit magic is," Fort said. "How far back were you?"

She shrugged. "It's hard to say. There weren't many calendars. But if I had to guess, it was around the year 500 AD or so, give or take a century."

One thousand five hundred years in the past? What had Ellora seen, that long ago? How different was life back then? And was there magic still? She might even know what had happened to it—

"Wait a second," Rachel said, her face lighting up. "You were around here in *500 AD*?"

"For much of it, yes," Ellora said, looking almost relieved. "So you know what was happening then?"

"I mean, no one knows for sure, but yeah, that's right around the time of . . ." Rachel trailed off, her eyes widening.

Ellora nodded, and Rachel gasped loudly.

Jia shook her head, looking as confused as Fort felt. "How about you back up a bit and explain? Not all of us are up on British history."

But Rachel didn't seem to hear her. "So? Did you see him? Was he real? How much of it was *true*?"

Ellora winced. "Not all of it. A lot of the stories were made up by French writers, after all. Strange how many times France has affected the British, isn't it?"

"I don't care," Rachel interrupted. "Tell me you *saw* him. Did he have the sword? Was there a huge castle for all the knights?"

"Seriously, who are you talking about?" Fort asked, but again, the other two just kept going like he and Jia weren't there.

"He had the sword, yes," Ellora said. "I'm so glad you don't think I'm mad, bringing him up like this. I thought you all, especially as Americans, wouldn't believe me. *I* wouldn't have believed it, and my grandparents came here almost sixty years ago. But I've never understood the British and their love for him."

"*I* do!" Rachel shouted. "Are you kidding? All the quests, the legends? *The sword?* I always wanted it to be true. I can't believe it actually is! What else did you find?"

"His mantle," Ellora said, looking away, like talking about it bothered her. "That was basically an invisibility cloak. Also a dagger and spear, I think. But that's not—"

"Hello, some of us aren't following here," Jia said, sounding as annoyed with them as Fort was feeling.

"Who cares about all of those things!" Rachel asked, ignoring Jia as her excitement grew. "What about the *sword*?"

"*What* sword?" Jia said. "Can you—"

"Buried with him, as far as I could tell," Ellora said.

"*What are you talking about?*" Jia shouted, grabbing Rachel and turning her around.

"Oh, sorry!" Rachel said, giving her a guilty look. "I thought it was obvious. We're only talking about, like, the most famous sword in history."

"It was actually called Caliburn," Ellora said, still not looking at them. Instead, she stared off over the nearby railings into the city. "I got sent after an Irish sword at one point with a similar name, because they weren't sure if the two were related."

Sent after a sword? What did that mean? Hadn't she said she was stuck in the past somehow, lost there? Who would be sending her places?

"Caliburn," Jia said, giving Rachel a strange look. "Am I supposed to have heard of that?"

"You might know it by its more common name," Rachel said, not able to contain her grin. "Some called it the sword in the stone, but that was only until a young boy pulled it from—"

"*King Arthur?*" Fort shouted, his mouth dropping open in wonder.

Jia groaned loudly. "*Who?*"

- SEVENTEEN -

KING *ARTHUR*! GEE!" RACHEL SHOUTED. "You never heard all the stories about Camelot when you were a kid?"

"I heard something about an American president and Camelot," Jia said, frowning. "But no, my parents read me stories about Chinese heroes, like Lady Mu Guiying."

"Who?" Rachel said.

This time, Jia gasped. "The famous general from the Song dynasty, still commanding troops into her eighties? How have you not heard of her?"

Rachel just stared in awe. "I don't know, but I *want* to!"

"Wait a second," Jia said, looking up at the ceiling of Big Ben. "Arthur's the one with the round shield?"

"That's Captain America," Rachel told her. "Also a great

hero, but less real." She paused and looked at Ellora. "Unless you know something?"

"Just about King Arthur, sorry," Ellora said. "But only one Arthur had the round table."

"Only one?" Fort and Rachel said at the same time.

"There were actually several," Ellora said. "From what I saw, it was more of a title than anything: Artorigios, meaning 'great warrior' or 'bear king.'"

"Bear king!" Rachel said, and swayed a bit like she was going to faint. "This is everything I ever wanted."

"But why does it *matter*?" Jia shouted. "Why do we need to know? Why can't you just tell us where the book is so we can go get it and fix everything?"

"Because the book of Spirit magic is buried with the last King Arthur, Arthur Pendragon, in his tomb," Ellora said quietly.

This brought Rachel up short. "Why would he have the book?" she asked, her excitement fading quickly. "It's evil. King Arthur would have known that. His whole thing was justice and honor. Spirit magic is the opposite of those things."

"He, ah, didn't feel that way," Ellora said, wincing. "In fact, he used it himself to create Camelot."

"What?" Rachel and Fort both shouted.

"He didn't take control of his people," Ellora added quickly. "Instead, he took out their bad impulses. When he was done, no one wanted to hurt anyone else, or steal from their neighbor. It was a paradise."

Fort began to rub his forehead, far too much coming at him at once. King Arthur, the man who led the Knights of the Round Table, not only wasn't made up, *or* the only King Arthur . . . but had used Spirit magic on his own subjects?

But from what Ellora said, was it really that bad? If he hadn't taken them over, and instead just basically made sure everyone followed the law by not wanting to break it . . . wouldn't that make for a better world?

Or would it be taking their freedom still, just in a much sneakier way?

"Wait, you can use Spirit magic like that?" Jia asked. "I didn't know."

"You didn't know because it *can't* be true," Rachel said, then turned to Ellora. "I don't care what you think you saw, I don't believe he'd do something like that."

"You thought he was made up a few minutes ago!" Jia said.

"Yes, and the made-up version would *never* use Spirit magic!"

142

Rachel shouted back. "So why is the real one breaking my heart like this?"

Jia rolled her eyes, but Ellora held up her hands for calm. "I'm not saying he's right or wrong, Rachel, but there's a reason we've all heard about Camelot. It really was like heaven on earth. No one hurt anyone else; no one broke the law. No one even *wanted* to. Would that really be so bad?"

"*Yes!*" Rachel shouted, and she and Jia began to argue about it.

But Fort wasn't so sure, and from the expression on her face, Jia wasn't either. If Spirit magic made it so no one committed violence, how was that different from a law saying the same thing? Wouldn't it be better, because the violence would never happen with Spirit magic, but it obviously still did even when there were laws against it?

But Rachel wasn't wrong, either. Using Spirit magic like that on someone would change them, even if it was for good reasons. And what right did anyone have to do that to someone else?

Unless it was to help more people? Ugh, this was *way* too big a question for Fort to figure out at the moment.

"Um, we're going to need to be going soon," Ellora said, her eyes on the sky outside the clock tower again. What was she watching for? "Forsythe, I'm going to give you a photo of the exact spot we need to teleport to." She reached into her pocket and pulled out a folded paper.

He took it from her, wondering why this was necessary. It wasn't like Stonehenge was *that* big, was it? He started to unfold the paper.

"Not yet," she said, putting a hand over it. "Wait until right before we go, okay?"

"Uh, okay," he said, as confused as ever. "Shouldn't we go now?"

"One more moment," she said, scanning the sky. She nodded. "Ah, okay, I see him now."

"See him?" Fort asked, as Rachel and Jia looked over. "See *who*?"

Ellora pointed, and Fort followed her finger to what looked like a dark dot against the black dome, only visible because it covered the weird glow of the Time magic. What was that?

"Is it some kind of airplane?" Rachel asked, and then gasped. "Oh, right. *Him.*"

Fort frowned, squinting off into the distance. As the dot grew closer, he began to make out something moving up and down every few seconds, like huge wings flapping. But no bird could be that large. No, the only thing he'd seen that size that could fly was—

"Damian," he said, his eyes widening. "We have to go!"

"There's no point," Ellora said. "He's going to reach us before we can escape."

"What?" Fort shouted. "I thought the whole point was to get the book before he does! Why are we waiting around for him to capture us?"

"I didn't say capture," Ellora said, then turned to face the direction where the frozen tourists were. "I said he'd reach us first."

As she finished, a green, glowing circle opened in the middle of the clock tower, right where she was looking, and a dragon maybe half the size of the Old One who'd flown Fort around the world landed with a roof-shaking thump on the floor.

And then the dragon shrank down, its wings disappearing into its back as its enormous front legs pulled up into arms, leaving them facing an annoyed-looking boy in a long, black coat that looked just like his scales had.

"Sorry to burst in on you like this," Damian said. "But we need to have a little chat."

- EIGHTEEN -

OH, THIS WAS BAD. THIS WAS VERY, *very* bad.

Rachel immediately moved to stand in front of the group, while Fort prepared a teleportation circle, not exactly sure what he'd be doing with it. But considering what they'd seen Damian do in their future vision, they might need to get off the clock tower *fast*.

"Damian," Jia said, her own hands glowing with Healing magic. "The Time students have shown us the future, what's to come if you use the book of Spirit magic. William can show you, too; it's horrible. Please—"

"Oh, I saw it," Damian said, shaking his head. "Used my Mind magic on him once they put the dome up, to see what was going on." He smiled. "Don't worry, it won't happen." He turned to Fort. "You're that boy Sierra talks about, the one who almost tried to stop us leaving the school. What's your name again?"

Fort clenched his teeth. Was he so unimportant that Damian couldn't even be bothered to remember who he was? "It's Fort."

"That's right," Damian said. "You're her good friend, aren't you? Do you think she'd be trying to help me get the books of magic if she thought I'd do what William showed you?"

Fort felt a wave of anger pass through him. Damian was trying to use his friendship with Sierra against him? "She hasn't seen what we saw," he said quietly. "If she had, she'd be against all this too."

"You never did trust me, did you?" Damian said. "She always wished you would." As Fort fought to hold himself back, Damian turned to Rachel. "As for you, I don't think we've met."

"My parents named me Dragonslayer," she said. "But you can just call me D.S."

Damian rolled his eyes, then turned to Ellora. "And hey, the girl from the Carmarthen Academy. I don't think I ever got your name either, before you and your friends all attacked Sierra and me."

"There wasn't much time for introductions, I guess," Ellora said. "Considering we were trying to save the world."

He sighed loudly. "You've got no idea what you're talking about. Do you know what your friend's future vision looked like to *me*?"

"You burning down Buckingham Palace, then destroying London?" Rachel asked.

He glared at her. "It looked like I'm under someone's spell, *actually*. Probably Spirit magic. Which makes it even more important that I get it first, before anyone else."

"Oh, someone used magic on you?" Rachel said. "Then it's *totally* okay that you destroy London! Why didn't you tell us before?"

"Damian, all you have to do is disappear for a few days, just to be sure it doesn't happen," Jia said. "Once the danger passes, we'll figure out what's going on, and make sure no one uses the Spirit magic."

He made a face. "Unfortunately, that doesn't work for me, because someone showed the Old Ones where I am." He gave Fort a quick look, and now it was Fort's turn to blush. "If the dome above us weren't masking any magic inside of it, they'd have already found me again, considering I had to teleport to catch up to you. For all I know, they *do* find me, and it's the Old Ones who take over my head like what you saw. So no, I can't just sit it out. I have to find the book of Spirit magic, if just to defend myself. And once I have that and the book of Time magic, I can actually fight them off, and for real save the world, unlike whatever you all think you're doing."

Rachel growled low in her throat. "Are all dragons this big of a jerk, or are you just special?"

Damian smiled. "Oh, I'm probably special. That's what Dr. Opps has been telling me my whole life, at least."

"Damian, let us get the book," Fort said. "Then we can have it just in case the Old Ones do come for you, but also make sure that nothing happens to London. We can work together here; it doesn't have to be like this."

"Like what?" Damian asked. "You all are the ones being insulting, telling me I need to be stopped and calling me a jerk.

"Because you won't listen to us," Jia said. "Fort's right. Let us take the book, and—"

"Oh, because this kid is so good at keeping things safe?" Damian said, pointing at Fort. "No way. It's way too dangerous to leave in your hands. Your *human* hands."

Rachel snorted. "Wow. You've been a dragon for what, two days now, and you're looking down on us?"

Damian's eyes narrowed. "No, I've been doing that my

whole life, actually. I just never knew why the rest of you were so slow and cared about such unimportant stuff. Now that I know where I come from, though, it explains everything. Especially how you humans couldn't keep up with me magically, either."

Rachel laughed. "Oh yeah, Lizard Butt? *Bring it.*"

And then the floor beneath Damian's feet reached up and grabbed his legs, pinning him in place.

Oh *no*. Attacking him was *not* a good idea. They were going to have to get out of here, *now*. As much of a jerk as he was, it wasn't like Damian was wrong about being talented at magic. Dragons were even created from magic itself by the Old One of Healing magic, so it made sense.

Fort readied a portal to Stonehenge but realized if he cast it now, Damian would probably be able to see where they'd gone. Stonehenge was too well-known a spot to escape to for him not to recognize it right away. But maybe Fort could send them to a spot nearby, something that Damian wouldn't know?

Except he needed to have seen a spot like that, and all Fort had ever seen of Stonehenge was the actual site itself, in pictures.

Damian looked down at the flooring holding him in place

and sighed. "Really? I didn't come here to fight any of you, mostly because I'd have to be way too careful not to permanently injure you. Why would you want to do this?"

"Sounds like someone's full of talk," Rachel said with a smile, then threw Fort a quick, terrified look. "Get us *out* of here, now!" she whispered too softly for Damian to hear.

Wait, she'd been stalling? So she did actually get how out of their league Damian was. Fort nodded and quickly opened a teleportation circle directly beneath them, to the London airport instead of Stonehenge, just so he didn't give them away.

All four of them dropped through, landing on the runway. But before they could move, a second portal opened beneath them, and they landed back on the floor of Big Ben, right in front of Damian.

"Did you enjoy your trip?" Damian said, then casually brushed the flooring off his legs like he might a bug.

"Damian, you're right—we don't want to fight you," Jia said, and Fort nodded vigorously in agreement. "But we can't tell you where the book of Spirit magic is!"

"Oh, I took that from your heads the moment I got here," Damian said. "Stonehenge, huh? In King Arthur's tomb? If I hadn't seen it in your minds, I'd have called you all liars."

Fort gasped. He *knew*? That changed everything then. They couldn't run, because Damian could just go to Stonehenge and take the book. And if they tried to get it first, he'd be able to stop them with no trouble at all.

That meant they'd have to stop him here, now. But how? There was no way they could beat him, not with magic. Maybe one of Ellora's Time spells might freeze him or send him forward a few minutes, but for all Fort knew, Damian would be able to brush those off as well. The boy was just *way* too powerful.

"King Arthur is not only real, but he's someone who wouldn't back down, even if the odds were totally against him," Rachel said, throwing a look at Fort and Jia. She wasn't exactly being subtle about her message, but Fort still didn't know what to do. He could try teleporting the boy away, but Damian could just bring himself right back. He knew a lot more Summoning magic than Fort did, after all.

Damian, though, made a disgusted face at Rachel's comment. "I always thought those stories were so dumb."

"*What?*" Rachel shouted. She stared at him in anger, probably half real, half to just distract Damian from Jia, who was standing behind Rachel, her hands glowing blue. "You take that blasphemy back!"

"A bunch of good-guy knights going off on quests? So boring," Damian said. "And totally wrong, too. They weren't good people at *all*. Did you hear the story about how Merlin told Arthur he was going to lose his throne to a boy born on May Day, so Arthur rounded up all the boys born that day and sent them out on a boat? He tried to drown them all, just to save himself. Only the boys all survived, and probably *wanted* to take him down after that. Talk about your self-fulfilling prophecies."

"That's not *true*," Rachel said, her voice low and threatening.

"It actually was," Ellora whispered, but at a look from Rachel, she winced and went quiet.

"Never trust a hero," Damian told her. "They're all hiding something." He shrugged. "Anyway, this has been fun and all, but I really have to go find the book of Spirit magic, and then use that to get the book of Time magic."

"You're not going anywhere!" Rachel shouted, and launched a series of fireballs at him. As they drew closer, Damian blew out at the fireballs, snuffing them like candles.

"You could have all just *helped* me, you know," he said, sounding irritated about it. "But I get it. None of my classmates ever trusted me, right, Jia?" He smiled mockingly at her. "So this is nothing new. At least now you can pretend it's because I'm a dragon."

"It's because you're a jerk!" Rachel shouted, and shot lightning at him.

This time, he made circles with one hand, and the bolt of lightning curled into a ball in the air above him. "You're just wasting your time—"

Out of nowhere, a blue light covered him, and he released the lightning bolt in surprise, letting it sizzle out over the city of London beyond the clock tower. His movements slowed as he yawned widely and started to wobble. He quickly raised a hand, sending the blue light exploding in every direction. Instantly, he seemed wide awake again.

"Really, Jia?" he said. "A Sleep spell? That's just embarrassing, and this is getting annoying. So I'm going to go before I lose my temper and accidentally hurt one of you." He raised a hand, and it began to glow red with Destruction magic. "That said, if you follow me to Stonehenge, then I can't be held responsible for what happens. I'm not letting you or *anyone* stop me from my mission."

"And what's that?" Fort asked, trying to stall him any way he could. Maybe Ellora could try to freeze him, or Jia could paralyze him instead of putting him to sleep? "What *is* your mission exactly? Because it seems like the more magic you learn, the easier a time the Old Ones will have finding you."

"Good," Damian said. "Considering they turned all the other dragons into those monsters, I *want* them to find me. By the time they do, I should have all six books of magic and will have the power to *destroy* them. Now, I'm sorry, but I really can't waste any more time with you humans. Hopefully, we won't see each other again, but if we do, feel free to thank me for saving the world from the Old Ones."

With that, he saluted them, then disappeared in a blink of green light.

- NINETEEN -

N O!" JIA SHOUTED, LOOKING ABSO-
lutely distraught. "Fort, take us there *now*. We
have to stop him!"

"I have no idea how we'll do that, but she's right," Rachel
said, giving Fort a worried look. "We have to try."

He sighed. Rachel was right. What choice did they have,
even if they couldn't beat Damian? They couldn't just let
him get the book, not with the future they'd seen.

"Everyone get ready," Fort said, and pictured Stonehenge in
his mind. Maybe they could distract him somehow, get the
book first, and destroy it—

"Wait, Forsythe!" Ellora shouted, grabbing his shoulder and
pulling him around to face her. "Don't open that portal yet.
We're *not* going to Stonehenge."

"What?" Fort said, completely confused now. "But Damian's there, and he'll get the book!"

"We can't just sit here; we have to stop him!" Jia shouted. "I thought that was the whole reason you brought us here!"

"It was, but here's the thing: The book isn't actually *at* Stonehenge," Ellora said, blushing again. "I, um, might have told you all that so he'd get the wrong information from you. Arthur Pendragon's tomb is actually somewhere else completely."

They all stared at her in shock. "You . . . lied?" Rachel said, then slowly smiled. "Wow, Time Girl. Normally I hate that, but right now, I'm pretty impressed."

"Well, it's a bit easier when you can see things coming," Ellora said. "And I knew Damian would find us with his Mind magic. So at least I bought us some time. Not much, but a little."

"Okay, that's great, but where is it?" Jia asked, shifting from foot to foot anxiously.

Ellora turned to Fort. "Remember the photo I gave you? Take us *there*."

The photo? Right, the one she'd folded up. He pulled it from his pocket and unfolded it, frowning.

This definitely wasn't Stonehenge. Instead, the photo showed a large hill with tiers on it, like a wedding cake almost, and a tower at the top.

"I have no idea where this is," he said to her, and she rolled her eyes.

"Just take us there," Ellora said. "The less we call it by its name, the harder a time Damian will have finding it."

That was fair. Fort concentrated on the photo and opened a portal to the top of the hill, right next to the tower, and they all stepped through. He quickly closed it behind them, then turned to look around.

Just like in the picture, the grassy hill had strange tiers on it, covered in grass as if the hill had been formed that way. But that couldn't be possible; it had to have been cut by humans. Other than the light being much darker below the dome, the only other big difference between the hill in the picture and here in the present was how many construction machines were surrounding it, everything from bulldozers to excavators.

Someone was planning on digging into the hill. But from what Fort could see, nothing had actually been done yet. All the construction people below were staring at the hill in confusion, frozen in that state by the dome.

"Hey, I know where we are!" Rachel said, looking around. "This is Glastonbury Tor! I *knew* this was where King Arthur was buried! It all made sense, what with that abbey nearby finding a gravestone—"

Ellora sighed loudly. "What did I say about not calling it by its name? Damian will be looking for us soon, and he'll find us faster if he can read the name in your mind!"

Rachel made a face. "Okay, right. Let's call it . . . Strawberry Fields. Damian for sure has never listened to the Beatles."

Fort just stared at her, having no idea what was going on. So the hill was called Glastonbury Tor? "What abbey? And what's a tor?"

"Don't use the name!" Ellora shouted.

"A tor is just an old way of saying a hill," Rachel said, then noticed the workers below. "What's going on down there? Are they digging for the book?"

Ellora shook her head. "Not exactly. They're with the government. Fortunately, since they're frozen in time, we don't have to worry about that now." She stared at them for another moment, then shuddered and pointed at the tower. "Let's get under cover for now and talk about what's next."

The others all started walking toward the ruined tower, and

Fort moved to follow, having had far too few of his questions answered. But as he did, the scene around him disappeared, and this time, he found himself standing over a large wooden table in the middle of what looked like an enormous but cozy cabin, lit by a fireplace with a bubbling black pot hanging over it. The walls were all made of wooden logs, each one unshaped by human hands, yet where there should have been cracks or holes, there were none.

Even stranger, sitting at the table was Cyrus, holding his hand out as a teacup floated in midair toward him from a steaming kettle near the fire.

This couldn't be the same cottage Cyrus had shown him before. It looked easily five to six times bigger in just this room than the entire exterior had been.

"Cyrus?" Fort said in surprise. "You brought me back?"

But Cyrus didn't look up. Instead, he seemed to be concentrating on a large book that looked like an instruction manual of some kind. "I don't get it," he said out loud. "There's not even any electricity going to him. How can he still be here?"

"Cyrus?" Fort said again, reaching out to tap the boy on the shoulder, only for his finger to pass right through him. Of course it did, this was just a future vision. "What's going on here—"

Before he could finish his sentence, a strange force yanked him bodily away from the table, straight into a nearby door. Fort raised his hands to protect himself, but again, he passed through it without a scratch and found himself in a dimly lit study, filled with bookshelves that held some of the strangest things Fort had ever seen.

Books were everywhere, of course, but so were bottles of bubbling liquids labeled in a language Fort didn't recognize, some sitting next to the skull of an animal that couldn't be natural in any way, not with that many bony spikes sticking out of it. A small box sparked every so often with a jolt of electricity, while a mirror on the wall startled Fort as an older version of himself looked back. The mirror Fort had a brown beard and looked tired but waved at the real Fort in an almost friendly way, and Fort couldn't help but wave back.

A large desk took up most of the room, and seated there was an old man in a tattered brown robe, his long, white beard thrown back over his shoulder, and his hair wispy on top of his head. As Fort turned to him, the man spun around in his seat and smiled at Fort widely.

"It's about time," he said. "Nice to see you again, boy." He frowned. "Wait, you wouldn't remember that. Forget I said anything. Uh, nice to meet you, I meant!"

"Um, what?" Fort said, completely confused. "Sorry, who are you?"

"You haven't figured it out?" the old man said with a wink.

"Who are you talking to?" Cyrus shouted from the other room. "You better not have brought anyone here, old man!"

The old man rolled his eyes. "Mind your own business, you ignorant lump!" He turned back to Fort. "That boy has so much to learn. So much potential he's going to waste. But that doesn't matter. I brought you here so we could speak privately, without all the judgment." He nodded at the door, meaning Cyrus.

"But . . . why?" Fort said. "Who are you? I don't understand any of this."

The old man shrugged. "Who I am isn't important, and you'll find out soon enough anyway. For now, I brought you here to try to guide you, Forsythe, as well as Rachel and Jia, as I promised. It won't work, but I did give my word."

Fort felt a chill go through his insubstantial body. Jia and Rachel? How did the man know about them? Cyrus could have told him, yes, but considering how Cyrus seemed to feel about the man, that didn't seem too likely.

"But . . . how—"

"My advice is this," the old man said, leaning in with a much more serious expression, his voice now low and eerie. "*Beware the queen of Avalon.* Every Arthur I ever knew fell victim to her, and I don't wish it to happen again. Rachel must not take the sword. Jia must not bargain with the queen." With this, the old man rose from his chair and towered over Fort. "And under no circumstances should you accept *any* deal to save your father!"

- TWENTY -

WHAT? HIS FATHER WAS IN *DANGER*? Fort felt dizziness begin to wash over him, and he reached out to the nearby wall to catch himself, only for his hand to pass through it.

Fortunately, he was able to regain his footing before falling over and turned back to the old man in shock.

"What do you mean? What's wrong with my father?" Fort asked quietly, the most important of the thousands of questions now cycling through his head. He had no idea what Avalon was or why he couldn't trust its queen, let alone what sword Rachel shouldn't take and what bargain Jia shouldn't make. But all of that paled before his father. "Is he not okay? Why would I make a deal—"

"What's going on in there?" Cyrus said, the handle of the door moving back and forth slightly. "Why is this door locked? That shouldn't even be possible. Let me in!"

"You'll discover those answers and more on your quest," the old man told Fort. "Above all, you must find your true future, and accept the consequences of your past, or you will lose *everything*."

Lose everything? What was the man *talking* about? Why couldn't he just say things in plain English? "What's my true future? And what consequences of the past?"

"Fort?" Cyrus shouted. "Is that you? Why can I barely hear you? Are you hiding him from me, old man?"

He began to bang on the door but stopped abruptly as the entire door began to glow with black light. As Fort watched, the nails all turned to red dust and dissolved away, leaving the wooden boards to fall to the floor.

Cyrus stood in the doorway, glowing with a stronger black light than Fort had seen on any of the other Time kids, his face a mask of anger. "Fort, you need to go, *now*!" he shouted, and waved a hand.

The cottage began to dissolve, then reappeared out of nowhere. "Not just yet," the old man said, not even moving.

"You really want to do this?" Cyrus said, his eyebrows rising. "I *told* you not to interfere. What did you tell him?"

"Only what I promised I would," the old man said, crossing

165

his arms. "And don't presume to lecture *me*, boy, until you're a few thousand years older."

Whatever *that* meant—Fort couldn't think about it now. "Cyrus, what is going to happen to my father?" he shouted. "Why did this guy tell me not to make a deal to save him?"

"*That's* what you had to tell Fort?" Cyrus said, sighing loudly. "You probably just ensured it'd happen now by making him ask questions he shouldn't. You'll put into motion everything you wanted to avoid! Talk about your self-fulfilling prophecies."

"I have faith in the boy," the old man said, nodding at Fort. "And knowing the full truth might be painful but is always better over time."

"None of them will live long enough to see a better time if you keep messing with things!" Cyrus said. "Why are you fighting me on this? You know how things are supposed to go!"

"I know how *you* think they should, but it remains to be seen if I agree," the old man said, settling back into his seat with a smile.

"Cyrus, *what is going to happen to my father?*" Fort shouted, not caring about plans or the past or anything beyond that.

"See?" Cyrus said to the old man, then turned to Fort. "Fort, what else did he tell you? Other than that your father is in danger?"

Fort gritted his teeth. What did he mean, *other* than that? "He warned me about a queen in someplace called Avalon, that Rachel shouldn't take her sword, and Jia shouldn't make a deal with her."

Cyrus groaned, then dropped his head into his hands. "Ignore *all* of that," he said. "He's misleading you, sending you down the wrong path." He picked his head back up to glare at the old man, who was watching him, still smiling. "Why are you torturing me like this? Do you have any idea how long I've been working on all of it?"

"Not as long as I have," the old man said, and stuck out his tongue.

Cyrus just stared at him in silence.

"I can't ignore what he said if my father is in trouble!" Fort shouted. "Cyrus, you *need* to tell me what's going on here, or . . ." He trailed off, having no idea how he could force either of these two to answer his questions. They had the power to bring him forward in time or send him back whenever they wanted, after all.

"Ask Ellora—she'll tell you," the old man said. "I wouldn't trust a word *this* boy says."

"Don't worry about it all, Fort," Cyrus said, his hands beginning to glow with black light. "I'm so sorry he brought you here, but I'll figure out a way to fix what he's done before I send you back. It shouldn't take long, and you won't remember it anyway. Just hold on for one minute—"

"Oh, we don't have time for that," the old man said, and before Cyrus could object, Fort was back at Glastonbury Tor just a few feet behind his friends walking toward the tower.

"No!" he shouted, making the others all jump and whirl around.

"Whoa, what's wrong?" Rachel said, looking for the source of a threat. "Is Damian coming back?"

"No, it was . . . ," Fort said, then trailed off, having no idea what to tell her.

"It was . . . ?" Rachel asked, while Jia just looked impatient. "A headache? You just yelling out 'no!' for fun? *What?*"

Fort sighed. He'd have to tell them *something*. But what? Cyrus had seemed pretty convinced that Fort shouldn't have heard anything the old man had told him. He wasn't wrong there, since learning that his father might be in danger would *definitely* make Fort look for a way to save him. Maybe the same thing would happen with Jia and Rachel, too, about their warnings.

But what if Cyrus was wrong, and they needed to beware this queen of Avalon lady, whoever *that* was? Cyrus hadn't said the warnings were actually wrong, had he?

Either way, Fort *had* to find out what was going to happen to his father, no matter what Cyrus thought about it. And that meant talking to the one person who knew.

"Cyrus reached out to me, using his magic," Fort said finally. "He brought me just a few hours into the future and showed me a place we should go after we get the book of Spirit magic."

Ellora's eyes widened. "*Cyrus* reached out to you? Where is he?"

"I don't know, probably in this same place now," Fort said, shaking his head. "It was all really confusing. But someone said that something might be happening to my father, that he might be in danger. And that I needed to ask *you* about it, Ellora."

At this, the blood drained from Ellora's face, leaving her pale in the dim light of the dome. "But it's not yet time," she said quietly. "I don't know what will happen if I tell you now. It has to wait until you're committed—I've seen it. I can't tell you what causes the war until—"

Jia jumped at Ellora's last words. "What do you mean? I thought Damian destroying London sets off the war."

"That, and adults learning magic," Rachel said, giving Ellora a suspicious look. "Which you wouldn't tell us more about, other than that it's Dr. Ambrose who figures out how to do it."

"Because if I told you more, you might . . . take it the wrong way at the moment," Ellora said, looking miserable. "We should go, *now*, if we're going to get to the book before Damian—"

"I'm not going *anywhere* until you tell me what's going to happen to my father," Fort said, both needing to know and deathly afraid of actually finding out. But he couldn't go on if something was going to happen back at the Oppenheimer School, and he'd be too late to save his dad. Was Colonel Charles going to send him away? If that was the case, what could a queen of a strange place do to save him?

More importantly, if she *could* do something, shouldn't he consider it?

"Tell us how adults learn magic, too," Jia said. "If there's something else we'll have to do to stop the war, then we need to know about it *now*."

Ellora nodded, looking dejected. "I do know something about your father, Fort. And I can tell you all how adults gain the power over magic. But *none* of you are going to like it. And this really isn't the time. If we waited, you'd come to accept what needs to be done with Spirit magic. But now . . . I just can't be sure."

"All we're *going* to do with Spirit magic is destroy it," Rachel said.

Ellora gave her a pleading look. "Please, you don't know what we could accomplish with it—"

"Tell us what's going to happen with my father!" Fort shouted.

"And the war!" Jia added.

Ellora turned away but nodded. "Just remember, you asked to see this now. I wanted to wait until you were ready." She raised a hand glowing with black light, and for the second time, Glastonbury Tor disappeared around Fort.

But this time, instead of a cozy dining table, he found himself in a familiar spot: the medical bay at the Oppenheimer

School. And there was his father, lying in a hospital bed, just like he'd left him.

Only now there were a number of Healing students surrounding him, with Dr. Ambrose standing close by, watching carefully.

"I'm so sorry," Ellora said quietly. "But it's here that everything goes wrong."

- TWENTY-ONE -

WHAT DID SHE MEAN, EVERY-thing was going to go wrong? Fort pushed through the assembled students, passing right through them insubstantially, to reach his father. Thank-fully, nothing looked like it'd changed since the last time Fort had seen him.

But maybe something was about to?

One by one, the students on each side of the bed raised glow-ing blue hands over his father, then sent the Healing magic into him. As they did, Dr. Ambrose seemed to be taking notes, her eyes on the machine readouts, but as far as Fort could tell, nothing was happening.

As each spell was cast, the student would then return to where the book of Healing magic sat on a nearby table and read it over.

"She's having them try different spells on him to wake him up," Jia said. "Looks like stronger magic than they've mastered. So maybe it's both practice and an experiment to see if they can wake him up?"

"Are they going to hurt him?" Fort asked Ellora, his eyes on each of the Healing students. He didn't know any of them that well, but if it came down to stopping them to save his father, he wouldn't hesitate to teleport them a few miles away.

Except he couldn't, not watching from the past. Here, he was completely powerless.

"No," Ellora said, her eyes on the floor.

"When is this?" Rachel asked.

"A few months from now," Ellora said, and Fort's throat tightened. If his father was still here at the school, then that meant Colonel Charles had sent Fort home without his father. Did he even know his dad was here, rescued from the Dracsi? Or did this future Fort now have no idea his father was even alive?

He reached out to touch his dad, but his hand passed right through him.

"None of these seem to be working," Moira, one of the Healing students, said to Dr. Ambrose. "Do you want me to try a different spell?"

"No, I . . . *wait*," the doctor said, leaning in closer to one of the machines. "What's this? It's almost like—"

Out of nowhere, Fort's father bolted up in bed, surprising everyone in the room, including Fort himself. They all leaped backward as Fort's father began to shout out words Fort had never heard before, words that disappeared the instant Fort heard them. As the words continued, blue light began to glow from his father's body, just like whenever a Healing-magic user cast a spell.

But that wasn't *possible*. His father couldn't be using magic!

"What did you do?" Dr. Ambrose shouted at the students, but they all looked as surprised as she was. "Is one of you doing this?"

"No!" they shouted as the glow grew brighter, filling the room, before it exploded out from his father, blinding both the students and Fort's group.

And with that, his dad fell back to the bed, unconscious once more.

"I recognized that spell," Jia said, sounding shocked as Dr. Ambrose called for help, and several medical personnel came running in, all talking at once. "It was the same one Moira just cast. How could he do that? He can't have access to the magic!"

"And even *I* can't hear someone else's spell and repeat it," Rachel shouted from elsewhere in the room over the nurses and Dr. Ambrose. "What is going on here, Ellora?"

"It's exactly what you think it is," Ellora said, not facing any of them. "I shouldn't have shown you this, especially you, Fort. It wasn't fair, and it's something we can fix."

"What happened to him?" Fort asked, not able to pull his eyes off his father as the nurses tried to wake him again without any luck. "What did he just do?"

"We don't know for sure," Ellora said. "By which I mean, no one knows. But after Dr. Ambrose sees this, she comes up with a theory and shares it with Agent Cole and Colonel Charles. She thinks that when the Old One restored your father to human from his Dracsi form, he remade him into a human being just the way the Old One remembered them. And the last time he would have seen a human being was from before magic disappeared."

Jia gasped. "Dr. Ambrose had some kind of odd neurological readings from him when we brought him back," she said. "And they matched Sierra's readings. Does that mean—?"

Ellora nodded. "She thinks that whatever changed in your dad's head, Fort, was what allows *us* to use magic, but not adults. And by putting it back the way it should have been, the Old One not only gave your dad access to magic, but at an even more advanced stage than we have. Like if we're exercising a muscle, he was just given a bodybuilder's version."

"No," Jia whispered. "If she knows that much, she could have Healing students try to duplicate it in other adults. And that would lead to . . ." She trailed off, staring in horror at Fort, who hadn't caught up yet.

"Lead to what?" he shouted, not liking her expression at all. "What is going to happen to him?"

"He's fine," Ellora said. "But she uses that knowledge to experiment on TDA soldiers, under orders from Colonel Charles. And her experiments work. She figures out how to give adult soldiers the same access to magic your dad has, a more powerful version of what we have now. And that, combined with Damian's attack on London, leads to *war*."

Her words hit Fort like a hammer to his gut, and he shook his head in disbelief. If his father's condition led to a war, then it was ultimately because Fort went looking for him and brought him back. So all this was *his* fault?

"This doesn't have to be a problem!" Rachel shouted, as the medical professionals gradually gave up, leaving Dr. Ambrose and the Healing students staring at Fort's father in wonder. "What we're seeing hasn't happened yet. All we have to do is stop it. How hard can that be? We just have to fix Fort's dad—"

"He's *already* fixed," Ellora said, looking nauseous. "He's how humans are supposed to be, and how we are, having grown up with magic. She explained it all to the colonel, but I didn't understand most of it. Something about nerve bundles in your brain, and how not using them early on would have led to them being used for something else, I guess? But since magic existed when we were born, *we* could use them, even without knowing it." She shook her head. "It's all beyond me, but I can take you there if you need to hear it from the doctor."

But hearing more about it was the last thing Fort wanted. He felt the room begin to spin as he realized everything he'd set into motion. Just by rescuing his father, not only had Gabriel revealed Damian to the Old Ones and almost given them power over him, but now it turned out that his own father was the source of adults gaining magic.

And he'd seen firsthand what that led to: a tsunami used as a war weapon. Not to mention that Rachel and Jia had witnessed massive outbreaks of diseases in American cities from Healing soldiers and Hong Kong being set on fire.

An entire world at war, and all because of Fort.

Cyrus had tried to warn him, back before Fort had gone to the Dracsi world. He'd said Fort would lose someone, which apparently meant Gabriel, who now hated Fort and had been expelled over his actions. But Cyrus had also said it'd lead to a dark future, and this had to be it.

And it was all his fault.

It took him a moment to realize the others were still talking, and he tried to steady himself by paying attention again.

"So then Healers could replace that nerve," Jia said, and Fort noticed her hands were shaking, oddly. "It wouldn't even be complicated. No wonder the world goes to war . . . all other countries would need is one Healer to . . . to do it, and . . ." She began to tremble, and Rachel reached out to her, but she shook her head. "No! We need to stop this, *now*! Ellora, how can we make sure it doesn't happen?"

Fort clenched his fists, knowing there was only one way Ellora could intend to fix things. "Isn't it obvious?" he said quietly. "She wants to go back in time and stop me from rescuing him." And there was no way he was ever going to let *that* happen.

The others were silent for a moment before Rachel spoke up. "You're not the one who builds an army from this," she told him. "You might have made it possible, but you didn't make the choice to go to war, Fort. This *isn't* your fault, and we're not going to stop you from rescuing your dad."

"But what if there's no other way?" Jia blurted out. "We can't just let the world go to war without trying to stop it!"

They're right, Fort, he could hear his father saying, but even in his imagination, the voice seemed more distant, like it was disappearing. *This isn't your fault. But that doesn't mean you can't fix it. And you know what my vote would be here.*

Of course he knew. His father would want to save everyone, because that was who he was. Who he *is.*

But he couldn't lose his father again, not just when he'd gotten his dad back! It was too awful to even think about—

"Well, that's not even an option, so don't worry about it," Ellora said, shocking Fort out of his thoughts. "It's not possible, not with the Time magic we know. The past is set. But the future, that's something we can still change, like Rachel said a few minutes ago."

What? Fort looked around the room in surprise as he suddenly began to feel hope again. "So I could just go back to the school, take my father way, and hide him?" he said. "And that'd stop the war?"

Ellora hugged her arms around herself tightly, not looking at him. "Unfortunately, no," she said. "It's way too late for that now. There's nowhere you could take him that they wouldn't track you down, and they wouldn't stop hunting you. Your Colonel Charles will make it his mission to do just that if you kidnap your father."

Fort deflated immediately, feeling dizzy again. Of course it couldn't be that easy. He'd made the choice to rescue his father, and now he had to deal with the consequences.

"So what options does that leave us?" Rachel asked, giving Fort a worried look. "There has to be some way to stop this!"

"There *is*," Ellora said, sounding almost like she was pleading with them. "If we get the book of Spirit magic, we can use it *ourselves*. We could take away our leaders' desire to go to war, all their paranoia and hate. We could stop it before it happens, no matter who has access to magic!"

Wait a second; she was right! They *could* use Spirit magic to fix things! That must be what Ellora had been talking about all along, but she couldn't tell them, not without sharing everything about Fort's father. With Spirit magic, they could keep the whole world from going to war, just like King Arthur had used it to keep Camelot peaceful. It wouldn't be easy, but it was possible!

"No!" Rachel shouted, making Fort jump. "There *has* to be another way. We can't just take away people's free will like that. There must be something else we can do to stop the war!"

"The only other option we've found is . . . terrible," Ellora said. "And it's why we didn't tell you how it happened. Forsythe, I wanted to spare you from finding all of this out. You never needed to know, not if we used Spirit magic."

"What's the other way?" Fort asked, dreading her answer.

"The only other way to stop the war," Ellora said, taking a deep breath as the medical ward faded out around them, replaced by Glastonbury Tor again, "is to remove your father from time, *completely*."

- TWENTY-TWO -

REMOVE HIS FATHER . . . FROM *TIME*? Fort fell to his knees in shock, barely even breathing.

"Fort!" Rachel shouted, diving to his side to make sure he didn't fall. "She's exaggerating. That's never going to happen."

"If we don't use Spirit magic, that's the only other choice we have," Ellora said. "Healing magic won't work—it's too complicated to remove part of his brain without damaging it forever, and there'd be questions as to why it was done. Believe me, we've looked into every possibility, and it's either send him away forever, or use Spirit magic."

Even with Rachel supporting him, Fort felt the ground beneath him begin to sway, like the world was spinning away from him. He'd have to lose his father . . . forever?

"We're not killing anyone!" Rachel shouted at Ellora. "How can you even say that's an option?"

"I don't want it to be!" she shouted back. "And it wouldn't kill him . . . he'd just be frozen, not knowing any time had passed. Only he'd never be brought back, at least not while any of us are still around." She shook her head. "This is why I wanted to wait to tell you. The later I told you, the more you'd have gotten used to the idea of Spirit magic, and the more open you would have been to it."

"I'll *never* be used to it," Rachel told her, then turned to Fort. "We're not going to do anything to your dad," she said to him, and gently helped him to his feet. "We'll find another way."

"There already is another way," Jia said, giving Rachel a sad look. "I don't like it any more than you do, Ray, but we can't let this war happen!"

Rachel just stared at her for a moment. "What did you see, Gee? In the future? I mean, I saw things no one should ever have to witness, but it seems like yours was even worse."

The question seemed to surprise Jia, and her face contorted through several emotions before she finally settled on resignation. "I saw . . . *me*," she said, almost too quietly to hear. "My future self was there, in Hong Kong, waiting there . . . waiting for me. On top of a roof, where I could see everything happening. It wasn't like she knew I was there for sure, but I think she—*I*—remembered what I'd seen, and made sure to be there at the same time, when I arrived."

"You were in Hong Kong?" Rachel said quietly as Fort separated himself from her, letting her move to comfort Jia. "Like living there?"

Jia shook her head, rubbing her eyes before finally looking up at Rachel. "I was a soldier," she said, her voice quavering a bit. "Fighting against the Americans for China. My future self, she just started talking, not even knowing for sure I was there. She told me that when the war breaks out, my parents and I have to return to China, and the Chinese government drafts me into service to teach their soldiers everything I know. She said she tried to keep things peaceful, to encourage everyone to talk, but it just got so bad . . . and when the fighting started, we . . . *she* lost our . . ."

She began to sob then, unable to talk, and Rachel quickly hugged her, holding her tightly as Jia cried on her shoulder.

Parents. That was what she was going to say, it had to be. Suddenly Fort felt terrible for how lost in his own head he'd been. All this time, Jia had been dealing with a future maybe even worse than his and not saying anything.

"We *won't* let it happen," Rachel whispered, just loudly enough for Fort to hear. "If it takes using Spirit magic to stop it, then we will. I promise."

Jia pulled away and looked at her in surprise. "But . . . you hate Spirit magic. And you're totally right about it. You'd be willing to . . . ?"

"Oh, you're not going anywhere, not as long as I have something to say about it," Rachel said to her with a smile, though even the smile seemed shaky to Fort. "We can destroy the book *after* one of us uses it to save the world. Deal?"

Jia sniffed loudly and nodded. "One hundred percent deal."

Ellora cleared her throat. "I know you don't want to hear this, but there's so much we could do with that book. Just like Camelot, we could make heaven on earth, do away with crime—"

"We destroy it after we use it to stop the war," Fort said, nodding at Rachel. "If that's the only way to keep it from happening without . . . sending my father way, then we do it. But that's *it*."

Rachel nodded back. "And only one of us should use it, just in case. I can do it, if you want."

An image of Rachel falling victim to the magic the same way Damian was going to, and destroying London, or maybe New York or Chicago this time, filled Fort's mind, and he shook his head. "It should be me."

"You?" Rachel said with surprise. "No offense, New Kid, but you're not as powerful as me or Jia. Don't you think one of us should use it?"

"That's exactly why it should be me," he said, standing up straighter. "Think about it. If either of you fell under its control somehow, who could stop you? You'd be too powerful. But if *I* use it in a way I shouldn't . . ."

"Then we can still take you down," Rachel said, nodding, then made a disgusted face. "It's a terrible plan, and I hate it."

"I know," Fort said. "I do too. But I don't know what other choice we have."

"You're right," Jia said, running her sleeve over her eyes. "I'm in."

"Me too," Rachel said, then dug her finger into his chest. "But at the first sign that you're out of control, I won't hold back."

He nodded as well, far too relieved about his father to care. Besides, if he did get taken over by the magic, he couldn't think of anyone he'd rather have there to stop him than Rachel and Jia.

Not to mention that if anyone was going to get hurt in all of this, it should be the one who had caused all of it.

"Okay, so we've decided," Rachel said, turning to Ellora. "What now, Future Girl? How do we get into the tor and find King Arthur's tomb, anyway? Is there a door or something?"

Ellora shook her head, still seeming a bit distracted by her own thoughts. "Oh, no, sorry. We're going to have to go in the hard way."

The hard way? "You mean use the machinery at the bottom of the hill?" Fort asked.

"We'd never have the time," Ellora said. "Damian will figure out we lied to him soon enough and track you all down by Mind magic. We have only ten, fifteen minutes until he arrives."

Fort, Jia, and Rachel looked at each other in horror. "Why didn't you say so earlier?" Rachel shouted.

"Because it would have started even more arguments!" Ellora shouted. "You think any of this is easy? I'm over here just trying to choose the best of all the bad choices."

"Okay, okay," Fort said, holding up his hands. "No one's blaming you."

"I am," Rachel said, glaring at her.

"But we do need to know how to get in," Fort continued. "What's the hard way?"

Ellora winced, then pointed straight down. "We dig."

"We *what* now?" Fort said. "Like with our hands?"

Rachel sighed loudly. "She means me. *I* dig, with my magic."

Ellora nodded. "It'd be best to start from the tower over there. We can close it off, at least, and give ourselves a bit more time before Damian locates us."

"Digging, awesome," Rachel said, tromping past the others in the direction of the tower. "You know what? I'm *really* beginning to hate this quest."

- TWENTY-THREE -

THE TOWER AT THE TOP OF GLASTON-
bury Tor turned out to be a roofless ruin made of
stone, part of what had once been St. Michael's
Church, according to a helpful sign. Even if Fort hadn't been
told that, the religious icons carved into the stones would
have been enough of a clue that it'd been used for worship of
some kind.

Rachel fell to the ground as she entered and tapped the floor,
her hands glowing red. "Okay, it does feel like there used to be
a tunnel here leading down. It's all filled in now, but it'll still
help support my digging, so that's good. It'll make the Destruction spell less exhausting, at least."

"You know, back in the Pendragon's time, they used to call
that Elemental magic," Ellora pointed out, making Rachel roll
her eyes.

"We were just talking about that a few days ago," Jia said, sounding a bit more like her old self now that she'd opened up about what she'd seen in the future. "Ray actually thinks Destruction magic *should* be called Elemental magic, because that's what it is. It controls the base elements, like fire, water, air, earth . . ." She trailed off as Rachel raised an eyebrow at her. "But that can probably wait."

"The tunnel I feel down there seems to branch off in places," Rachel said, looking at Ellora. "Which way are we going?"

Ellora's eyes turned black again, and she pointed to the floor. "Down, as far as we can. The Pendragon was buried with the book of Spirit magic, and his tomb should be on the lowest level. At least, that's where I see us going." She frowned. "But I can't see the tomb itself. There must be some sort of magical protection down there. I also . . . huh."

"Huh?" Rachel said. "Huh what?"

"I also don't see us coming out," Ellora said quietly.

Before Rachel could say what she *clearly* wanted to say, Fort jumped in. "That just means we find a different exit," he said. "Rachel, we need to get moving if we're going to find King Arthur's tomb before Damian gets here. We should start. You know, to find the tomb of King Arthur. Remember King Arthur?"

191

"Subtle, New Kid," she said, but even so, she couldn't hide the excitement in her eyes. "I do want to see how cool his tomb is, I'll give you that." With that, she began digging into the ground with her magic.

First, she pulled up the stone floor and floated it over to the tower's four entrances, splitting the stone to fill them in. Dirt came next, and she solidified it using her power, then filled in the rest of the holes in the tower, gradually closing them in. She even covered the open gap in the roof, fusing the sides of the tower over the top.

Now hidden from outside view, Rachel set to work with a vengeance, digging straight down with her magic. Within moments, the tunnel was large enough for them to enter, so they all jumped in, with Rachel increasing her speed again. Now the dirt fairly flew past them, filling in behind them and creating a bubble of space for them to stand in beneath the ground.

"Hey, whoa, we need to breathe!" Fort shouted as what little light there was began to fade.

"Don't be such a baby," Rachel told him. "Just hold your breath."

"She's joking, Fort," Jia told him. "She can make more air with her magic."

"Don't tell him *all* my secrets," Rachel said, grinning at her as the dirt closed over the top of them, shutting off their tunnel completely.

Immediately everything went dark, but Jia lit her hands with Healing magic, and the blue glow illuminated the tunnel with enough light to see by. Rachel didn't pause, moving the dirt from below to above them as they slowly followed her tunnel deeper into the ground.

Minutes passed, and Fort could see the strain on Rachel as she paused for a break, wiping sweat off her face. "Can we help?" he asked.

"Do you have a shovel?" she asked back.

Jia used her Healing magic on Rachel, and it seemed to give her *some* energy back.

"Maybe distract me," she said as the dirt flow sped up again. "It helps if I'm not thinking about how hard this is, and how I'm the only one here doing anything."

Fort nodded and tried to think of what to talk about. After everything that'd been happening in the last few hours, he still had a thousand questions for Ellora, but most would lead to places that none of them would really want to dig deeper into, no pun intended.

But there was one thing he still didn't understand. "You said you all were lost, when you used Time magic for the first time," Fort said to Ellora. "How is that possible? What happened to you?"

She didn't answer for so long that Fort began to wonder if she'd heard him. Finally, just before he repeated himself, she spoke. "It wasn't our first time using the magic, but it was close. We'd mastered a few other spells already, which you've seen: spells for speeding up time, freezing people in it, that kind of thing. But seeing the future, that was the big one. We were all so excited . . ." She stared off into space, only to get pushed forward by the dirt accumulating behind her.

"Oops, sorry," Rachel said, but didn't seem that upset.

"When we first visited the future," Ellora continued, "we weren't really sure where we were going. Magic doesn't use time or dates, so it was more like . . . we jumped into the ocean of the future, hoping to find something fun. But when we arrived, most of us in different spots, none of us knew when we actually were. It wasn't like there were calendars waiting for us, showing us how far we'd come.

"Once we were there, we had no idea how to get back," Ellora continued, still not looking at any of the rest of them.

"We knew we wanted to travel into the past, but even that didn't help, because we had no idea how far we wanted to go. So what happened was we got ourselves even more lost. It was like we'd jumped into that ocean blindfolded and had no idea which direction the surface was, or how far we'd have to swim to reach it."

Fort just watched her as she spoke, not even wanting to imagine what that must have felt like. Getting lost in the woods or on a street in a city you'd never been to before was one thing, but they wouldn't have been able to ask directions or touch anything—assuming someone like Cyrus hadn't been waiting for them.

"That sounds awful," Jia said, healing Rachel again.

"Definitely not fun," Rachel grunted, sweating much harder now. "Kinda like this isn't."

"At first, the teachers tried to help us from a distance," Ellora said, like she hadn't even heard Rachel. "Since our physical bodies hadn't left the school, we could still hear them, even as we heard everything around us in whatever time we were in. It was incredibly confusing, but I guess magic doesn't have to make sense. So they tried to suggest things we could look for, places or landmarks that would help orient us in time, so we could find our way back."

"Did it help?" Fort asked quietly.

Ellora nodded, glancing over at him. "It did . . . until they decided they didn't *want* us back."

His eyes widened, and this time the dirt hit *him* in the back as he realized he'd stopped following Rachel's tunnel downward. "What do you mean, didn't want you back?"

"To help guide us, they'd been asking us all questions about the future," Ellora said softly. "None of us knew the others were in the same situation until later, but we compared notes when we got back. The more the teachers heard about the future, the more they began trying to guide us to places and times they had more questions about. They'd describe places or events to help us lock in on them, like landmarks when you're lost. That included the war, among other things."

"So they decided they wanted to know the future more than bring you home?" Jia asked, making a disgusted face.

"Not just the future," Ellora said. "Some of us, like me, they sent to the past, had us overshoot the present. From what little I picked up, it sounded like you Americans were digging up magical treasures around the world. So they told me it was my *duty* to protect the UK by finding our own. They directed me using stories, legends, anything that might guide me to see what was real and what wasn't."

Above them, something loud rocked the ground, and they all went silent for a moment.

"I hope that's not . . . from my tunnel," Rachel said, sounding out of breath. Still, she restarted her dig, and they continued on.

"Were they trying to get ready for the war?" Jia asked, and Fort could hear the edge in her voice when she mentioned it.

"I don't think it was even about that, honestly," Ellora said. "They just didn't want your country to have something they didn't, so they used us to find their own."

"Their own what?" Rachel asked.

Another loud rumbling from above made them all look up. As they did, Jia's Healing light went out for just a moment, leaving them blind.

"Weapons," Ellora said from somewhere in the dark. "*Magical* weapons."

- TWENTY-FOUR -

JIA QUICKLY RESTORED HER LIGHT, and as the blue glow returned, Fort and the others—including Rachel—all turned to look at Ellora.

"Weapons?" he asked. "What are you talking about? What kind of weapons could you find in the past?"

"Before the Dark Ages," Ellora said, "Britain was a crossroads of great magic. I mean, that's what all the stories said, but I've seen it; it's all true. Not just humans, either. Lots of those pointy-ear people—what do you call them?"

"Elves?" Rachel shouted, momentarily alive with excitement before her exhaustion hit her again.

"Right, them," Ellora said. "They made the weapons everyone wanted, I guess. But the stuff I saw, it was so powerful. Maybe stronger than what we have today, even nuclear bombs."

Fort's eyes widened. Magical weapons made by *elves* that

were more powerful than a nuclear missile? And the British government had the Time students out looking for these? *That* was all pretty terrifying . . . or the plot of a fantasy novel. Maybe Rachel would write about it someday.

"But you were looking in the past," Jia said as Rachel restarted her digging. "How did that help the government in the present?"

"Mostly I was supposed to see what was real and what was just a story," Ellora said, shaking her head. "But if something *was* real, I'd try to track it to its last known spot, and they'd go looking for it in the present in that same place." She nodded at the tor beyond their tunnel. "That's why they were going to excavate here next. Fortunately, Sierra brought us back before they could get started, or who knows what they'd have found if they started digging."

The ground around them shook harder this time, sending bits of dirt and stone tumbling down around them. Rachel stopped digging to stare at the ceiling with the rest of them. "I think maybe the government's here," she said, sounding like she could use a long nap.

Except it wasn't the government. From the looks on their faces, Fort figured they all knew exactly who it was.

"If *someone* is up there following us, is this tunnel going to hold?" Fort asked, his heart beginning to beat faster.

"The tunnel's secure, Mr. Engineer," Rachel said, turning back to her digging. "But if it's *him*, then a bunch of dirt isn't going to slow him down much."

Fort started to respond but instead shouted in pain, along with Jia and Rachel, as yellow light flooded over his head, and he heard a voice inside his mind.

I FOUND YOU, YOU LIARS! Damian shouted in their heads. YOU THINK YOU CAN TRICK ME LIKE THAT? I'M RIGHT BEHIND YOU, AND IF YOU DON'T TELL ME EVERYTHING YOU KNOW ABOUT WHERE THE BOOK IS BY THE TIME I CATCH UP, I'LL JUST HAVE TO FORCE IT OUT OF YOU!

"Are you *okay*?" Ellora shouted, reaching out to Fort, but he couldn't answer, he was in too much pain. It felt like the Old One, Ketas, in his mind again, and that was one thing Fort would have given everything to never feel again.

But just as he was about to collapse from the pain, the voice went silent and left, leaving so quickly that Fort almost collapsed anyway, like a puppet whose strings had been cut. "I think it's him, yup," he said, wincing as he rubbed his temples.

200

"I don't understand," Jia said, looking just as much in pain as Fort felt. "Why didn't he just take over our minds?"

"Um, what?" Rachel said, leaning heavily against the wall as she took in deep breaths. "Am I missing something? You *wanted* him to control us?"

"Not at all, but I don't know why he wouldn't," Jia said. "He's got the power."

"He doesn't know what's coming below," Ellora told her. "And he can't read my mind, not while I have Dr. Oppenheimer's amulet on. So I'd guess he's going to let us get closer to the book, then just take it."

They all looked at each other nervously. "Rachel," Fort said quietly. "Do you think you can take him?"

"Not even if I was at full strength," she said. "Maybe Jia and I together might have a chance, but not as tired as I am now."

"You've got me, as well," Ellora said. "He doesn't know Time magic yet and hasn't had to face one of us. You've all seen what we can do."

Right! Fort had almost forgotten how powerful Ellora and Simon had been, back in the Deployment Room. Suddenly he didn't feel *quite* so doomed. "Okay, so we get to the book as fast as we can, with you and Jia ready to stop Damian if he catches up," Fort said to Ellora. "Rachel, can you get us down to the tomb?"

"I was serious when I said you could get a shovel and help!" she shouted, but moved back to digging. "At least Damian's going to be tired too from making his own tunnel."

As she said this, the rumbling above them increased, and they began to hear sounds accompanying it. It almost sounded like . . . claws scraping against stone.

"I don't think he's using magic," Fort said, cringing in fear. "We have to go *faster*."

Jia moved to use her Healing magic on Rachel again, while Ellora gave Fort an anxious look. That didn't bode well, since he was sort of counting on her Time magic to make the difference . . . not to mention that she could see if they made it or not.

"Do we get to the book first?" he whispered to her, hoping the others wouldn't hear over the sounds of the digging.

"I don't know," Ellora said, looking away. "You saw it yourself—the books make it hard to get a clear vision."

He turned her to face him. "But you do know something, don't you. What aren't you saying?"

She looked at him, her eyes filled with worry. "He's going to catch us at the tomb. And from what I can see, we're not going to stand a chance against him."

Fort's eyes widened; then he stumbled forward as the back of the tunnel reached him, pushing him along. "You're saying we *lose*?" he said as quietly as he could.

"No, I'm saying he's going to defeat us easily," she whispered. "But that doesn't mean we can't still get the book. I can see a portal of some kind, all green and glowy. Maybe you teleport him away?"

"If I did, he'd come right back," Fort said as the sounds of the clawing grew louder. "He's got a lot more Summoning spells than I do."

"Then we *might* be in trouble," Ellora said, swallowing hard.

"Ellora, we better be going in the right direction," Rachel said from the front of their tunnel, sounding exhausted. "I'm going to be really annoyed if we missed our turn somewhere along here."

Jia continuously sent Healing magic into her, but it seemed to have less effect the more she did it, and Fort started to worry that Rachel might just collapse completely. As soon as she did, they'd have to face Damian here in the tunnel, with one less magic user to stop him.

Even worse, from the sound of it, Damian's digging was a lot faster than Rachel's, as the scratching above them got louder and louder the farther they went. Also, Rachel's digging seemed to be slowing, as even Jia began to tire from the healing.

But they couldn't just run, not now! If Fort teleported them away to escape Damian, they'd be leaving the book of Spirit magic to the dragon, and there'd be no stopping the world war to come. And Fort couldn't let that happen, especially if it was his fault to begin with, bringing his father back to earth with the discovery of the millennia in his head.

But what he *could* do was send his friends out of harm's way if it got too bad. Damian wouldn't follow them; he just wanted the book, no matter how angry he was. So if it came down to it, Fort would teleport Jia, Rachel, and Ellora to safety and just find some way to get to the book before Damian.

If that was even possible.

Another few minutes passed before Rachel seemed to shudder, then fell onto the floor, struggling to breathe. Fort quickly joined Jia next to her, using his Heal Minor Wounds spell on Rachel just in case it helped. "I'm feeling like . . . ," Rachel said, taking in deep breaths, "whoever built this tomb . . . went too far down!"

"You can't sense anything below us?" Fort asked, glancing above them anxiously.

"I can't sense . . . *anything* right now," she said. "We could be . . . on top of it . . . and I wouldn't know."

She just seemed so done, like she'd used every bit of energy left in her. But without her to dig, there was no way Fort could get the book away from Damian. And that meant he'd have to do something he knew he'd regret.

"You know, I didn't honestly think Damian was a better magician than you," Fort said quietly. "But I guess there's no denying it now."

She looked up at him in surprise, then narrowed her eyes. "That's low, Fitzgerald."

"Oh, is it time for excuses?" Fort asked, trying to hide how nervous he was, though more from Damian's arrival or poking the bear that was Rachel, he wasn't exactly sure. "When he gets here, I'll just tell him this doesn't count 'cause you felt all sleepies, okay?"

"Whoa," Jia said as she and Ellora stepped away from Rachel. "You're playing with fire, Fort."

But Fort stayed put, matching Rachel's stare. "I'm not afraid of you," he told her, completely lying. "Damian, sure. *He* terrifies me. But that's because he probably doesn't need a nap before doing his job, you know?"

Her jaw tightened so hard he thought she might break it, even as the digging above grew so loud it could have been just yards away. "I know what you're doing, New Kid," she whispered, low and dangerous. "And you're *so* lucky it worked."

And with that, she screamed loudly, then reached down and ripped a deep hole in the dirt beneath them.

Unfortunately, there was nothing on the other side of that hole, and they all immediately tumbled into darkness.

- TWENTY-FIVE -

BEFORE THEY COULD FALL TOO FAR, Fort felt the air around him turn solid as Rachel used it to slow them, then float them down into the darkness until they actually touched ground again. It was impossible to see anything as the firm air that carried them dissipated, since Jia's blue glow had gone out when the fall had surprised her, but Fort could feel something smooth and flat beneath his feet, like carved stone.

And that meant they'd found something made by humans. Or at least by magic.

Rachel ignited a tiny fireball on her palm, which helpfully illuminated the area around them, but also showed just how tired she was. Even if his goading had worked, seeing the exhaustion in her face made Fort feel even guiltier about pushing her so hard.

But he'd find a way to make it up to her later. For now, they needed to figure out where they were before Damian found them. Rachel's light revealed they were standing in a small hallway that ran in two directions, both of which were too dark to see very far.

"You can't take much more of this," Jia whispered to Rachel as she sent more Healing magic into the other girl.

"I can sleep later," Rachel said, then groaned quietly as she closed off the hole above them.

"Look at this stonework," Ellora said, running a hand over the wall. "It's centuries older than *Stonehenge*, even. I can *feel* its age."

"It's a lot easier . . . to build with magic," Rachel said, then seemed to stumble for a moment, only for Jia to quickly catch her, putting her shoulder under Rachel's arm to support her. "Easier doesn't mean . . . *easy*, though."

For the first time, Fort realized he wasn't hearing Damian's digging above. When had it stopped? Had Damian heard them fall? Probably. Those dragon ears were pretty big. That meant he might be waiting to see what happened to them, in case it was a trap.

Or it could be that he was gearing up for one last, big dig, straight for them.

"We can't stay here," Fort said. "Damian wasn't that far behind us."

"Right," Jia said. "So which way do we go?"

She had a point. Fort couldn't see anything down either side of the hallway, and they didn't have time to try the wrong one, not with Damian just above them.

And then the sounds of digging returned, and dust began to fall from the ceiling.

"Ellora, can you check ahead in time to see what we find down each hall?" Fort asked, his heart beating faster with every scraping sound above.

Ellora's eyes went dark again, but she frowned. "There's definitely something blocking me. It's worse than the books, actually. This isn't even a fog, so much as just . . . nothing. I can't see what happens to us in *either* hallway."

Fort banged his hand against the stone wall in frustration. They had gotten so close, if the hallway was any indication. Why couldn't its builders have left up a sign or something? THIS WAY TO THE BURIEL CHAMBER the very least.

209

And then it hit him. A burial chamber. Maybe they could use that?

"Jia," Fort said. "We're looking for a tomb, which means there are probably dead bodies in it, right?"

"That's usually what the word 'tomb' means," Rachel said, but she didn't even seem to enjoy her mocking, as tired as she was.

Fort ignored her, concentrating on Jia. "Is there any way to use your magic and try to, I don't know, animate the bodies? Have the skeletons knock on their caskets or something? If we can hear them, that would tell us which direction to go!"

Ellora gasped, while Rachel looked disgusted. "Wow, have some respect for the dead, New Kid!"

"I respect them, but I'd rather not *join* them," Fort said, pointing at the ceiling.

"Ignore them, Fort," Jia said, looking at him thoughtfully. "They haven't dealt with bones like we have in class, so they aren't as used to dead bodies. It might actually work. Let me see what I can find." She closed her eyes and sent blue light flooding down both corridors.

They all went silent as the light disappeared into the darkness, trying to listen over the sound of the digging above, which was getting louder and closer with every second. For too long, there was nothing, and Fort began to worry that even if Jia found a skeleton, they wouldn't be able to hear it, not over Damian's arrival. But then he caught just the faintest noise off to their right: a very soft scraping of stone on stone.

"That way!" he shouted. "Run!"

Now reenergized by Jia's Healing magic, Rachel immediately pushed past him, leading the way with her light, the others right behind her. Fortunately, the stone was smooth enough that they didn't have to worry about tripping in what little light the flame gave off, so they could move quickly.

That was good, because from how loud Damian's digging was, they didn't have much time left.

The scraping of stones grew louder as they ran, until finally they reached an ornate archway that filled the hallway, covered in decorative words in a language Fort didn't recognize. Beyond the archway, the hall opened up into an enormous room filled with row upon row of stone tombs, each one covered in the same strange writing.

The scraping noise itself was coming from one of the tombs nearest the archway and grew louder as they entered. Horribly, the lid started to push up and off its stone coffin, skeletal fingers reaching from the darkness within, but before it emerged, Jia canceled her spell, and the lid crashed back down on the tomb.

They all breathed a sigh of relief at that—until they heard the ceiling crumble deep in the hallway behind them. A loud, angry roar echoed down the stone walls.

"I'M *COMING* FOR YOU, HUMANS!"

"Wow, he's really just impressed with his own dragon-ness, isn't he," Rachel said as she pulled the stone archway down, blocking the entrance. Even that much magic made her sway again, but Jia was there with more Healing magic.

"There," Ellora whispered, pointing to the far end of the room, where a raised stone tomb shone in the glow of Rachel's flame. "That looks like the tomb of a king."

Running ahead of the others, Fort saw that she was right: This stone coffin had even more intricate carvings than the rest, including a crown, shield, and sword sculpted into the lid, with the words HIC IACET SEPULTUS INCLITUS REX ARTURIUS IN INSULA AVALONIA carved into a stone cross at the bottom.

"What does it say?" Fort asked as Ellora reached the tomb. "I don't know what language that is."

"It's Latin," Ellora said, running her hand over the writing on the cross. "It says, 'Here lies the famous King Arthur on the island of Avalon."

Fort straightened up in shock. *Avalon?* That was where the queen was from that the old man in Cyrus's cottage had told him about. With everything else going on with his father and Damian, he'd almost forgotten about the man's warnings!

"Island of Avalon?" Rachel asked, coming up slowly behind them with Jia's help. "Is this an island? Did I miss something?"

"Glastonbury Tor was surrounded by marshland in the past, so it *looked* like an island," Ellora told her.

"Or the tomb is trapped, and we're going to unleash an ocean when we open it that floods the entire country," Rachel said, then shrugged. "Eh, I guess we'll learn to swim." With that, she turned her magic on the stone lid and started to lift it off.

"Careful," Jia said, supporting her with Healing magic.

"Worry about . . . any *ghosts* that . . . might be in here," Rachel said to her as she floated the coffin lid up and off, laying it gently on the floor.

But as soon as it landed, Rachel's eyes rolled back into her head, and she fell backward into Jia's arms, her fireball flaming out.

"Ray!" Jia shouted, the room now lit only by Jia's Healing

magic, which seemed to be having even less effect than before. That probably said more about how badly Rachel's Elemental magic had wiped her out than the power of Jia's spells.

"Forget all of this," Rachel said drowsily. "I don't even care if it's really King Arthur anymore. Just let me sleep."

"I've got her. You find the book," Jia told Fort. He nodded, took a deep breath, then cast his own Heal Minor Wounds spell to see by as he leaned over the tomb to look inside.

He had no idea what to expect, honestly. A fully armored body holding Excalibur? A perfectly preserved King Arthur ready to wake up?

Instead, all he found was a skeleton lying peacefully, its arms crossed over its chest.

And that was it.

"It's not here!" Fort said, searching the rest of the coffin frantically. But even in the dim light of his spell, he could tell it was empty but for the skeleton.

"King Arthur's missing?" Rachel asked in a daze.

"No, the book of Spirit magic!" he said. "It's not in the tomb. Nothing is except the skeleton!"

This couldn't be happening! Not only was Damian just behind them, but they *needed* to keep the book of Spirit magic away from him, or the world would go to war, and it'd be all Fort's fault. There was no way Damian wouldn't find it on his own if they couldn't, so they had to figure out where it could be. Had Ellora been wrong about King Arthur having it to begin with?

Suddenly Fort was ready for Damian to arrive, just so he had something to take out his frustration on.

Jia gently laid Rachel down on the ground, then moved to join Fort at the tomb. She leaned in and frowned. "Wait, that's odd. You see it too, Fort?"

"The skeleton?" he said, staring at the collapsed archway nervously. It'd been too long since they'd heard the ceiling fall in, and Damian had to be getting close. "Ellora, are you sure you saw the book come in here?"

"They buried him with it, and his sword," she said, looking nervous now. "I saw it, I swear!"

Behind him, he heard Jia grunt, and he turned to find her leaning so far into the tomb that for a moment he thought she was going to climb in.

"There's something off about this skeleton," Jia's voice came echoing out of the stone. "It's not King Arthur, that's for sure. I don't even think it's human."

Uh, *what* now? "Not human? What do you mean?" he shouted. The skeleton didn't look anything like the dwarf or elfin bones they'd seen on display at the Oppenheimer School, in size if nothing else. And not that his light had been great, but from what Fort had seen, the body looked like a normal, human adult.

Something hit the stones in the collapsed archway hard enough to shake the entire room, and red light began to glow in from the cracks.

"We don't have time for a bones lesson here, Gee!" Rachel said, shakily pushing herself up and off the floor. "Tell me you've got something we can use!"

Jia pulled herself back out, looking excited in spite of the imminent dragon. "I think this skeleton's been *changed* somehow, with magic. It looks human on the surface, but everything beneath that is wrong. Let me see if I can change it back to what it's supposed to be. That might tell us more."

The room rumbled again, and the red light grew stronger as Damian dug his way through. "Do it—he's almost here!" Fort shouted.

But Jia had already started. As her magic filled the skeleton, it glowed bright blue, then began to shrink slightly, the individual bones getting smaller, more delicate. Finally, her magic faded, leaving behind a skeleton that now did actually resemble one of the elf skeletons they'd seen in the display room, only shorter, almost more Fort's size than an adult.

"What is—" Fort started to say, but was silenced by the room shaking so hard that the tomb itself began to move.

Except this time, it wasn't Damian's doing. Instead, the tomb slid to one side, revealing a tiny stone staircase directly beneath where it'd stood.

But before they could react, Rachel's collapsed barrier exploded in, showering them with rocks. Fort shouted in surprise and tried to duck, but Rachel was quicker, deflecting the biggest stones with her magic to protect them, while tiring herself out even more.

And then Damian entered the room in his human form, his entire body glowing an angry red. *"No more messing around,"* he shouted, his face furious in the glow of his magic. "I'm done taking it easy on you all. Tell me where the book is, *now*!"

- TWENTY-SIX -

"ELLORA, *FREEZE* HIM!" FORT SHOUTED, readying his own spell.

Even as he said it, Ellora was already moving, and black light shot out toward Damian. But he blocked it by teleporting Jia right in front of him, and Ellora's magic hit her instead, freezing Jia in mid-shout of surprise.

"I guess that's a no!" Damian shouted, pushing Jia aside as the ground rose up around Ellora, locking her in place. "It's getting really annoying, you having that necklace on, by the way."

"Yeah, well, I'm not taking it—hey!" Ellora said as Rachel lifted the necklace up and over her head, then dropped it to the ground. "What are you *doing*?"

"Like it?" Damian and Rachel said at once, both using Damian's voice. "Mind magic can be so useful. Like making people forget for a few minutes how to use their magic."

"What?" Ellora said as yellow magic covered her head now. "No!" She struggled to free herself, but there was nothing she could do as the yellow light faded. "Give it back! Give me back my magic!"

"It'll come back by the time I'm gone," Damian said, turning to Fort. "What about you, Sierra's friend? You want to try me too, like back at the school? Or are you smart enough to give up now, and tell me where the book is?"

"Trust me," Fort said slowly. "No one's *ever* accused me of being smart." He held up his hands, glowing with green Summoning magic. "Let's do this."

Damian's eyes widened. "Seriously? You're joking. What, are you going to teleport me somewhere?"

"No," Fort said with a shrug. "Just distract you."

Damian raised an eyebrow, only for blue light to flood over him, sending him shakily to the ground. Jia quickly moved over him, shaking her head. "I'm sorry about this, Damian," she said. "But you're going to destroy London if you get that book, and you were always kind of a jerk, so I guess I don't feel that bad about putting you to sleep."

Damian struggled to get to his feet, only to fall back against the rubble he'd created a moment earlier. "Oh, right," he said in a daze. "I canceled the Time girl's spell when I made her forget it. Should have . . . thought of that."

"You know what you *should* have thought of?" Rachel said, coming up at his side. "That *no one* takes over my mind!"

And then she punched him right in the gut.

"Ray, no!" Jia shouted as Damian doubled over in pain. "Don't wake him back up!"

The blue light surrounding Damian went out like a snuffed candle, and he grinned up at them. "Thank you for that," he said, then tossed Rachel across the room. She hit the wall hard and slid down to the floor, groaning.

"Ray!" Jia screamed, sending another spell at Damian, but this time, he saw it coming and waved it away, then sent the ground up around her legs, freezing her in place as well.

"That's what I deserve for getting angry," Damian continued. "Dr. Opps was always yelling at me about that. Said I made mistakes when I got angry." He shrugged. "Guess he was right."

The tomb lid came flying at him, and he raised a hand, splitting it in half. Both sides crashed into the ground with a huge noise.

"The stairs! Go!" Rachel shouted, leaning against the nearby wall as she freed both Jia and Ellora from their rock prisons. "Go *now*! I'll take care of him!"

"You?" Damian said, smiling smugly. "Seriously? You're about to fall over."

Someone grabbed Fort's arm, yanking him backward. He turned to find Ellora pulling him toward the stairs, as ordered, and he ran as quickly as he could, knowing Rachel couldn't distract Damian for long.

But as he practically leaped down the staircase into the darkness, barely keeping up with Ellora, he realized there wasn't anyone behind him. Fort immediately slammed to a halt and reversed himself, sprinting back up to find Jia practically carrying Rachel as the other girl sent spell after spell at Damian.

None of them were having any effect whatsoever.

"Come *on*, Ray!" Jia shouted as they moved toward the stairs. "Follow your own advice!" She sent a Healing spell at Damian, but he brushed it off like a bug.

Rachel shook her head and pulled out of Jia's grasp, still looking dazed. "Let me *do* this," she said, and squeezed Jia's hand. "Please go, for me."

"No!" Jia shouted, but Rachel pushed her away and moved to stand between Jia and Damian, blocking his path. Without another word, she reached out with her hands to both sides of the room, then pulled them back to her chest.

As she did, large sheets of stone pulled off the rocks and formed up around her like armor, covering every inch of her except for her face. Now sheathed in rock, and the stone itself helping her to stand, she took a step forward, then another, each one shaking the ground as Damian stared at her incredulously. "What've you got, Dragon Boy?" Rachel shouted, flexing in her armor. *"Bring it!"*

Damian rolled his eyes, then held out his hands toward her. Fire exploded from his fingers, the heat so intense that Fort yanked Jia partly down the stairs to avoid it.

Rachel, though, just covered her face with her arms and continued to push through the fire toward Damian. "You've got *nothing*!" she shouted, her voice shaking enough that Fort knew she couldn't keep this up for long. "You're just a petty jerk, and the only reason you're even good at magic is because you were born a pathetic dragon. You didn't earn any of it, it was all just handed to you!"

"You don't know *anything* about me!" Damian roared, his fire dying out so suddenly that Rachel tipped forward, her momentum knocking her off balance without the force of the

222

flames. As she fell, a wave of solid air sent Damian flying forward, and he drove a glowing red fist into the rock around Rachel's stomach. As his hand touched the armor, the rock split in half, falling away to both sides as the force of his blow sent Rachel flying back toward the stairs.

"No!" Jia shouted, and managed to catch Rachel in her quickly elongated arms, almost falling herself from the other girl's momentum. She gently passed Rachel to Fort, then turned to Damian with rage in her eyes. *"Don't you touch her again!"*

"I didn't want to hurt *any* of you, Jia!" Damian shouted at her. "All you had to do was give me the book and everything would have been fine. So don't blame *me* for this. This is all on you!"

Jia growled, low and threatening, as blue light exploded from her body in every direction. Wings pushed out of her back just beneath her shoulders, and long claws grew from her fingernails. She fell to the ground on all fours as a spiny tail extended from her lower back, and armored scales pushed up out of her skin, then emerged in a wave over the rest of her body, covering her completely.

Fort's mouth dropped open in shock at the sight as he slowly backed down the stairwell, Rachel in his arms. Just above, Jia roared loudly enough to send small rocks falling from the ceiling, now a dragon every inch as big as Damian had been.

"Are you trying to make fun of me?" Damian shouted, his eyes widening with pure rage. "Get out of that form!"

"I will, once *I take you down*," Jia growled, and leaped at him.

As Damian morphed into his own dragon form, Ellora reached Fort's side, and without a word, helped him carry Rachel farther down the stairs. Above them, the room rocked with each blow the dragons landed, feeling like it might collapse at any moment. Fort hated leaving Jia to face Damian by herself, but there wasn't much he could do to help, especially not in a fight between two such massive creatures.

Damian screamed in pain then, and the shaking grew worse as Jia's dragon head appeared in the stairwell. "Go! I've got this!" she roared, then pulled back as stone scraped against stone, and the light from above disappeared. She must have slid the coffin back over the stairs.

"No!" Fort shouted, leaving Rachel with Ellora to run back up and bang his hands against the stone of the tomb. They couldn't leave her behind, not against Damian! As powerful as she was, she didn't stand a chance against an actual dragon. He started to open a portal back into the room, the green light of his spell illuminating the dark just slightly, but it was enough for Ellora to grab his hand and pull him around to look at her.

"She's letting us get to the book, Fort!" Ellora said quickly, glowing an eerie green in his light. "Once we have it, we can use it on Damian and save her. It's the only way to help her now!"

He gritted his teeth, not liking that at all, but he couldn't argue with her point. Instead, he nodded and ran back down to where Ellora had left Rachel, lighting the way now with his Heal Minor Wounds spell. Every crash above them made his chest ache for his friend, but Ellora was right. If they could find the book of Spirit magic, that would stop Damian instantly.

At least, it would if the first spell was not something useless.

They'd only made it a few yards farther down when red light filled the stairwell from above as the tomb went crashing off into a wall. Damian's dragon head snaked down into the stairwell, his shoulders too wide to fit. "I'm getting so *tired* of all this!" he roared, morphing back into his human form as they watched. "Why won't you just give up already?"

Fort growled in frustration but didn't stop moving down the steps. More than anything, he wanted to turn around and fight the dragon, using magic, his fists, whatever he could. But instead, he pushed forward, moving as fast as he and Ellora could go with Rachel between them, probably even too quick for as little as they could see.

And then a fireball exploded past them, lighting the way as it struck the stairs a little ways down. "Don't make me hit you with these!" Damian shouted as the flames singed Fort's clothing but didn't cause much damage.

Even through the danger, part of Fort knew Damian could just use Mind magic on them and immediately put an end to all this. The fact that he hadn't meant he'd rather torture them with fireballs than get the book.

How could Sierra ever have been friends with someone like that?

"Keep moving," Ellora whispered, then groaned in pain as a second fireball passed by her shoulder, burning her.

"Whoops, they're getting closer!" Damian said, sending a third fireball down. "Probably because of how narrow it is in here. You might want to hand over the book before it gets even hotter down there!"

Fort turned to respond but found another fireball heading straight for him. He cursed and dodged as best he could, but in doing so, he missed the next step and dropped Rachel. His momentum sent him tumbling down the stone stairs as Ellora shouted his name behind him.

Each step he hit was another new lesson in pain, and Fort could have almost cried in relief as he reached the bottom, skidding to a halt on a dirt floor not too far from the stairwell. But if the book of Spirit magic was here, at least he could finish this and save his friends.

And then he looked up, and any hope he might have had disappeared.

From the light of Damian's magic above, he could just make out the small, completely empty room in front of him. No book of magic, no tomb of King Arthur, *nothing*.

Above him, Damian began to laugh as he reached the end of the stairs. "Oh no, you've found a dead end!" he said, his laughter growing. "Aw. That's so sad. You've run out of places to run." His hands began to glow red again, fireballs appearing in each one. "No more distractions, no more friends, just your last chance to hand over the book. If not, whatever happens is on *you*."

- TWENTY-SEVEN -

FORT SLOWLY PUSHED TO HIS FEET, facing the wall. In spite of the boy's threats, Fort actually felt more fear for what was to come than for himself. Images of Buckingham Palace on fire and stolen spirits from London's population passed through his head, along with the tsunami caused by the invading army he'd seen in the war to come.

And all of that would happen if he couldn't stop the dragon here and now.

But how? Fort only had two spells: Heal Minor Wounds and Teleport. Well, and one instance left of a Restore Dimensional Portal spell, but that wasn't going to do much, not here—

And then something caught his eye on the wall before him, reflecting the light from Damian's fireballs. Words, barely visible in the darkness, carved in the shape of an arch, just like the one that had led into the tomb.

Only this time, he actually *recognized* three of these words: "gen," "urre'otre," and "platrexe."

The spell words to reopen a dimensional portal.

Maybe the stairs led somewhere after all.

But that didn't matter if he couldn't slow Damian down. There had to be something he could do, even with his limited spells. Send him . . . oh. *Oh!* It was dangerous, and would definitely make the dragon even angrier than he was now, but it still might work.

"I'm not going to fight you," Fort said, raising his hands in surrender as he turned to face Damian, hoping his arms would block the other boy's view of the wall.

Damian snorted. "More lies? You know all I have to do is read your mind, and . . ." He trailed off as he looked past Fort at the wall. "Oh, forget it. I see what you're trying to hide. What's this?"

"No, don't, *please*!" Fort shouted, reaching out to grab Damian's arm, but the dragon just knocked his hand away, moving past him to the wall as if he didn't even consider Fort a threat. Which was fair.

"So this leads to Avalon," Damian said, reading the words, running his fingers over them. He glanced back at Fort. "Sorry,

I know you don't know enough magic to have figured that out. It says that these are instructions, and they invite those with great skill to travel to the dimension of the Avalonians and present themselves to the queen." He paused, then ran his hands over the last few words and laughed. "*And* it says *no humans*! Amazing."

No humans? Hopefully that was just Damian misleading him. Either way, it wasn't something Fort could worry about right now. "So you're going to open it?" he asked, taking a step backward.

"Oh, so that's your genius plan?" Damian said. "I open the portal for you, and then you somehow get past me to find the book?" He snorted. "Nice try. Even if I did open the portal, there's no way you'd ever get past me."

Fort sighed deeply. "You caught me," he said. "Does it help if I promise not to do that?" He took another step back toward the stairs. The room wasn't that big, but there should be just enough space for—

Damian's eyes glowed yellow, and Fort felt the dragon in his mind again, though this time, he seemed to be reading it instead of taking him over like he had Rachel. "Teleportation?" the other boy said finally, the yellow glow disappearing. "That's your big plan, to teleport me somewhere? Anywhere you send me, I can just bring myself right back, Fitzgerald. So please, explain your big plan to me. I can't wait to hear it all."

Fort took one last step backward, his heel now running into the bottom stair. A quick look behind him showed that Rachel and Ellora were just far enough away for this to work. Then he smiled. "I mean, it's not *much* of a plan. And really, I'm actually doing you a favor."

"A favor?" Damian asked, raising an eyebrow. "How is that, exactly?"

"I'm giving you some new perspective," Fort said. "You know, from orbit."

And with that, he opened a teleportation circle directly between him and Damian, one that led to the moon.

Instantly, the vacuum of space sucked Damian straight into the portal, giving him no time at all to react. Fort did regret that part, since he wished he could have seen the look on the boy's face. Still, he didn't exactly have time to worry about it, since he, Ellora, and Rachel were now being rapidly pulled toward the other side of the portal as well, along with small rocks, dust, and anything else not nailed down.

"*Fort?*" Ellora shouted in surprise. "What did you do?"

"Don't worry!" he shouted back as the vacuum dragged him across the floor. "I've got this!"

Just before his foot entered the portal, he quickly slammed it shut, and all the debris heading for it now tumbled down around him as the room went completely dark again.

Fort used his Healing magic to create a light, then pushed to his feet and ran back to where Ellora was bracing herself on the bottom of the staircase, holding Rachel as best she could. "Sorry about that," he said, helping her carry Rachel the rest of the way to the empty room at the bottom of the stairs. "It was the only thing I could think of."

"Where'd you send him?" Ellora asked. "Oh, wait, my magic's back now that he's gone. I can check." Her eyes went black, and she gasped. "The moon?!"

"I figured it'd be a surprise, if nothing else," Fort said, blushing in the dim light. "He should be fine: If Rachel could make her own air, he can too. But it might give us a few seconds to get her up."

"We might not even have that," Ellora said, but Fort was already using his Heal Minor Wounds spell on Rachel.

Her eyelids flickered, and she looked up at him drowsily, then cringed. "I don't think your spell is doing much."

"I know, I'm sorry," he said. "Just get ready with a lightning spell, will you?"

She looked at him strangely, then nodded. "Okay, but—"

Damian reappeared in the middle of the room in a green burst of light, shivering wildly, with his hair askew. *"Fitzgerald!"* he roared, almost as loud as his dragon voice. "You could have killed me!"

"Now!" Fort shouted, and Rachel unleashed her lightning straight at the dragon boy. Far too distracted to stop it, Damian went flying back against the nearby wall as the bolt hit him, taking him down like a Taser. He shuddered a few times, then went quiet, still breathing but unconscious.

"Oh," Rachel said. "I see." She pushed to her feet but almost fell over as she did. "Where's Jia?"

"Right," Fort said, and quickly opened a portal to the burial room above, then leaped through it, hoping Jia was okay.

She'd morphed back into her human body at some point and even seemed to be waking up from whatever Mind spell Damian had used on her. "Did he beat us?" she asked as Fort helped her to her feet, using his Healing spell on her as well.

"Just about," Fort told her. "Come on, we don't have much time."

He helped walk her through the portal back down to the bottom of the stairs, as she turned her Healing magic on herself. When she saw Rachel, though, she quickly switched targets, and moments later, all of them were at least awake, if not feeling great.

"So this is a nice, scenic dead end and all," Rachel said, staring at the wall. "But I guess I was hoping for more."

Fort smiled at her, then brought his Restore Dimensional Portal spell to mind and closed his eyes. Just as it had before, the magic illuminated all the dimensional portals that had been created anywhere within sight, only this time, Fort gasped. While he could see a few portals when he'd used the spell back beneath the old Oppenheimer School, here it looked like the world was on fire. Portals lit up in every direction, extending as far as the eye could see.

Apparently there really *had* been a golden age of magic in the UK.

He concentrated on the portal outline on the wall just in front of him and unleashed his magic. Hopefully that message about "no humans" wasn't real, and whoever lived in Avalon would be friendly, because none of them were in any shape to take on a Dracsi or another dragon.

"Oh!" Rachel said, and Fort opened his eyes to find a glowing green oval on the wall before them, right between the words of magic in the shape of an arch. The light was so bright in the darkness that it almost blinded them, and Fort had to cover his eyes with his arm.

As his sight adjusted, he realized that having used his last instance of the spell, the words he'd been able to read before in the arch now looked like gibberish, and for a moment, he worried that somehow the portal would close, and they'd be stuck there.

And then something flashed green at his side, and Damian disappeared.

Uh-oh. If he was awake, it was only a matter of time until he got his head together and came roaring back. And that meant they didn't have time to think: They had to take a chance on the portal, whether they ended up trapped in Avalon or not.

"Get through the portal!" Fort shouted at the others, and pushed Rachel and Jia through, with Ellora just behind them. With his friends all inside, he started to jump through it as well, as another flash of green light erupted behind him.

Damian in his human form plowed right into him, tackling Fort through the dimensional portal as the dragon boy shouted incoherently. The two landed on something hard and unforgiving, knocking the wind out of Fort.

Around him, Fort thought he saw people gathering, but his attention quickly returned to Damian as the dragon boy punched him in the stomach so hard that he saw spots. "I could have suffocated out there!" Damian roared. He drove his fist into Fort's stomach again, almost causing Fort to throw up from the pain. "Do you even know—"

And then an enormous hammer made of rock slammed into Damian's chest, knocking him back through the portal.

"Do *you* even know, Wyrm Boy?" Rachel shouted, readying the hammer for another hit as Damian picked himself up in the room they'd just left. He roared again and leaped toward the portal—

And bounced off it hard enough to knock himself back to the staircase. He quickly regained his feet and launched a fireball at it, which exploded back at him after slamming into the barrier of black light that now covered the portal. He roared something, over and over, but no sound passed through, not after Ellora had frozen the portal with her Time magic.

Rachel dropped her hammer and stood in front of the portal, laughing loudly. "Look at Mr. All-Powerful Dragon Man!"

she shouted, pointing at him and making exaggerated faces. "Not so tough from that side of the portal, are you?"

"Maybe don't get him more riled up," Jia said, but she seemed just as pleased, watching Damian's silent temper tantrum.

"Thanks, Rachel, and you too, Ellora," Fort said as he slowly began to breathe again. Jia helped him to his feet, sending Healing magic through him, which gave him the energy he needed to confirm that they were, in fact, definitely not alone.

Fort found himself standing in the middle of what looked like a sort of medieval market, with booths and covered wagons showcasing all kinds of unearthly and exotic items for sale. At each little shop stood what looked like a child, all the kids about Fort's size, only with longer ears, skin of every color in the rainbow, and dressed in brightly colored, elaborate clothing.

Not only that, but a group of the children seemed to have them surrounded and were staring at them curiously.

Remembering his first meeting with the Dracsi-caretaking dwarfs, Fort held up his hands in what he hoped was a peaceful gesture. "We're not here to hurt you," he told these new children.

One of them stepped forward, her skin green and hair yellow. She cleared her throat to speak. "Of course you're not, human," she said, giving Fort a pitying look. "You're far too weak for that. What we want to know is if that's a *real* dragon that you've captured." Her eyes lit up as she looked past Fort to where Damian was banging on the time-frozen portal. "If so, what might you be willing to trade for it?"

- TWENTY-EIGHT -

TRADE FOR . . . . DAMIAN?" FORT ASKED, both relieved that the creatures surrounding them didn't want a fight and completely confused. "But he's a person."

"He's a *dragon*," the green girl corrected. "Can't you tell? Look through his magical disguise, human. It's not hard."

"I'll give you ten years of happiness for the dragon, to be used in any order you wish!" another of the creatures shouted, this one with blue skin and black hair.

"I spoke first!" said the green girl. "If you give *me* the dragon, I'll trade you an extra eye for the back of your head that lets you see any moment in the past as clearly as if it just happened."

What was even going on? As the mob all began to shout at

239

once, Fort just stared in confusion, having zero idea where they were, or why any of these strange children thought they could trade for Damian. Was this Avalon?

"Who *are* you people?" Rachel said, slowly recovering as Jia sent more Healing magic into her. "Are you . . . elves?"

Some of the creatures laughed, while others snorted. "We're the Tylwyth Teg," the green girl said, shaking her head. "Some of your kind *have* called us elves, but the polite ones refer to us the Fair Folk, or faeries."

Rachel visibly paled at this but smiled anyway at the green girl. "I see," she said. "Fort, Jia, Ellora? Can I speak to you please?"

Before he could answer, Rachel grabbed Fort by his shirt and did the same to Jia, pulling them weakly back toward the portal, where Damian was still banging on it, trying to break through Ellora's spell. Ellora quickly joined them.

"What's going on?" Fort said. "I know they seem . . . odd, but at least they're not trying to kill us or turn us into Dracsi or something."

"That might be better," Rachel said, her eyes wide with fright. "We're in *trouble* here. There's too much to explain right now, but—"

"Please, I'll give you the color of the sky after a storm has passed for the dragon!" a red faerie shouted.

"I'll erase all memories of embarrassment you've ever felt!" a purple one said.

"I'll *give* you memories of embarrassment, if that's something you enjoy!" another purple one said, and the two glared at each other.

"Don't even listen!" Rachel hissed. Fort put his hands up over his ears, and she quickly yanked them back down. "I mean, don't listen to them, not *me*, New Kid. Here's the summed-up version: The Fair Folk are bad news. Everything is about rules and deals with them. They'll give you a gift, and then expect something in return, and if you don't give it to them, they'll just take it."

"Like what kinds of things?" Jia asked.

"Anything from the smell of your sweat to your heart, and I don't mean figuratively. It's a nightmare to figure out all their rules, so just don't take anything from them, don't follow them anywhere, and *definitely* don't trade with them for Damian, no matter how awful he is. Also, be polite, don't bother anyone, and maybe we'll get out of here in one piece." She didn't look too sure about that last part.

Her panic quickly spread to Fort, and he looked over at the assembled faeries with a lot more nervousness than he had felt before. They, in turn, just stared back at him expectantly, probably waiting for his response to their multiple bids.

"I don't think we're going to be giving up our dragon today, unfortunately," Rachel said to the faeries, her voice shaking a bit. "I'm so sorry. But thank you all for your offers!"

The faeries' faces all fell, and most began to disperse back into the marketplace around them, leaving just the green girl who'd first spoken.

"You made a good choice," she said. "Why take such cheap offers for something as rare as a dragon? You're obviously holding out for something special. What might you be looking for? Your heart's desire? I can show you the stall that carries that, and I won't ask much in return!"

"We're all good, thanks!" Rachel said, wiping her sweaty hands on her pants. "Though we very much appreciate your offer, and *definitely* wouldn't want you to take our saying no as any sort of offense."

The green girl sighed. "None taken, stranger," she said, then turned to Ellora. "How about you? You seem like someone who could use a compass that always points you in the right direction, or a few vials of volcano tears."

"Sorry, no thank you," Ellora said, smiling politely. "We're just looking for a book."

Uh-oh. Fort's heart began to race as Rachel slapped her forehead.

The green girl's face brightened. "A book?" the faerie said. "I know where to find thousands of books! The endlessly unwritten tales might be worth a dragon, or unicorn prophecies are *always* helpful—"

"Oh, none of those, thanks!" Rachel said quickly.

"That's right," Ellora said, giving Rachel an apologetic look. "We just want a book of Spirit mag—"

Rachel clamped her hand over Ellora's mouth. "No we don't!" she shouted. "We're just fine, actually. No need to help us."

But the green girl didn't listen. "Spirit magic, eh?" she said, a smile growing across her face. "The only thing like that is the one the queen has locked away."

Fort's eyes widened. The queen? It had to be the same one the old man had warned him about, if this really was Avalon. "Oh, that's okay," he said quickly, trying to move in front of Ellora.

The faerie pushed him out of the way, knocking him back a few feet with barely any effort. "Oh, it's no problem!" she said to Ellora. "I can take you to her. Come with me!"

She grabbed Ellora's hand, yanking her out of Rachel's grasp with surprising strength. And then, before any of the others could move, the faerie pulled Ellora toward the crowd.

"Ellora!" Fort shouted, and she looked back at them in terror, opening her mouth to shout something, only for the mobs of faeries to close in around her, cutting her off from their view.

"What did I just tell all of you?" Rachel shouted, pulling at her hair.

"Come on!" Fort said, running after Ellora. "We have to catch them!"

"Yes, but we have to be *careful*, Fort!" Rachel shouted from behind him as she and Jia raced to catch up.

Fort threaded his way through the crowd of faeries as politely as he could, remembering Rachel's warnings. He wasn't sure what Rachel knew that had made her so nervous, but considering how uncomfortable the faeries made her, he wasn't sure he particularly wanted to find out.

But as he reached the other side of the crowd, Ellora and the green faerie were nowhere to be seen. "It's like she completely disappeared," he said quietly as Rachel and Jia reached him. "What now?"

Rachel growled in frustration. "That faerie mentioned the queen, right? Then we should probably head for the castle." She pointed up above one of the taller tents in the marketplace.

Fort followed her gaze, moving back to see over the tents, only to jump in surprise as he saw a fortress easily the size of a small city rise so high up that it almost blotted out the sky at that end of the market. How had he not seen that before?

Unlike every other castle Fort had seen, this one sparkled in the sun as if it were made of some sort of crystal but still had some ugly-looking defenses lining its walls, not to mention soldier faeries, each the size of a child, stationed every few yards.

All in all, it wasn't the most welcoming thing he'd ever seen. Not to mention that he'd been pretty severely warned about the queen of this place, and that was most likely where she lived. It was definitely past time to fill Rachel and Jia in on that.

"Remember when I said I saw Cyrus?" he said. "There was something else I didn't tell you about—"

"That's going to have to wait," Rachel said, moving on toward the castle with Jia right behind her. "We need to get to Ellora before that faerie takes something from her, like her lungs!"

Fort quickly followed after them, knowing she was right. "Okay, but I have to tell you something!" he said as they weaved in and out of the masses of people, trying not to even touch anyone. "You really think she'll take something from Ellora just for leading her to the castle?" Jia asked Rachel, and Fort growled in frustration.

"If these faeries are anything like the legends, then yes," Rachel said as they left the crowded market and ran down a mostly empty street, with strange buildings lining each side. One seemed to fade in and out, while another seemed to be made up of the night sky, stars twinkling along the walls.

"Seriously, this old guy was warning me about a queen!" Fort shouted.

"Yeah, the queen will probably be the most dangerous!" Rachel said, glancing back over her shoulder. "The Fair Folk never play fair, ironically, and their deals will always benefit *them*, never you. These are the creatures who stole babies and left changelings in their place."

"Changelings?" Fort said as Rachel and Jia turned a corner just in front of him. "What's a change—"

As he rounded the corner, he tripped on the edge of the stone-tiled street and went tumbling forward.

"Watch out!" Rachel shouted from just ahead, but it was too late. Fort slammed into something soft, sending them both flying. They landed hard on the ground a few feet away, and Fort quickly pushed himself up, then gasped as he realized what he'd hit.

A male green faerie looked up in surprise and anger. "What is *this*?" the faerie shouted, leaping to his feet. "A human *dares* mistreat one of the Fair Folk in full view of the castle?" He pointed at the fortress, which was still a few blocks away at the least.

"Fort, no!" Rachel shouted. "What did you do?"

"I'm sorry!" Fort said to both of them. "I didn't see you, sir, and I never would have run into you if I had."

"Oh, so you're too good to even look out for someone like me?" the faerie asked. "Humans think so little of our kind?"

"No, that's not what I meant!" Fort said. "I don't even think *anything* about your kind!" The faerie's eyes widened at that, and Fort hurriedly continued. "I mean, I never even knew you existed. I don't mean that in a bad way, though. I just mean—"

"The queen shall hear of this!" the green faerie yelled. "Guards!"

"Wait!" Fort shouted, reaching out to take the faerie's arm

before he could move away. "We can figure this out—"

"And now you *attack* me?" the faerie shouted, pulling free of Fort. "I have never endured such disrespect. Guards, guards!"

Two enormous faeries appeared out of nowhere on both sides of Fort and seized his arms.

"A human?" one said, glancing at Fort in surprise.

"I thought your kind were banned from Avalon," said the other.

"And he *attacked* me," the green faerie said. "I demand restitution before the queen!"

"Wait!" Rachel shouted, but it was too late. The two guards disappeared, taking Fort with them.

- TWENTY-NINE -

THE BUILDINGS AROUND FORT FADED from view, replaced by a throne room more opulent and luxurious than anything he'd ever seen, even in pictures. The floor was made from fine jewels, each as large as Fort's head, while the walls and support columns looked like they'd been sculpted of silver or platinum, but so delicately that Fort couldn't believe that the columns could hold up anything, let alone the roof of pure gold above them.

The throne room extended for hundreds of feet behind him, where a long line of faeries waited for their chance to see the queen, apparently. But both thrones at the front of the room now were empty, so Fort wasn't sure if they were waiting for her to arrive, or if she'd just left.

That might be good for him. The last person he wanted to see was this queen. Between Rachel and the old man in Cyrus's cottage, he was practically shaking with nervousness about what she might do. But if the queen had just left, maybe the faerie he'd accidentally run into wouldn't be able to plead his case, and the guards would let Fort go!

A gentle wind passed by, leaving behind the scent of new rain on pine needles, and Fort looked around, trying to find the source. But as the smell grew stronger, the wind picked up, making the candles in the elaborate candelabras on either side of the thrones flicker. The faeries in line behind him all went silent and began to kneel, and the guards pushed Fort to do likewise.

As his knees hit the floor, the wind swirled into the throne on the left, and a figure appeared in the middle of it, lounging with one leg over one of the throne's armrests. She was taller than the other faeries, maybe even taller than a human adult, and her skin was the same dark blue that Fort often saw in the sky after the sun set, just before darkness fell completely. Her eyes shone as she stared at Fort, absently playing with a wooden scepter with a large diamond at the top.

"A human, here?" she said, smiling slightly. "Tell me: Didn't I ban your kind from Avalon under pain of death?"

Fort's eyes widened in shock, but before he could answer,

a familiar voice spoke up from his side. "This human child knocked me over, Your Majesty!" the faerie he'd fallen into shouted. "I demand a thousand years of his service in restitution, and not a minute less!"

The queen turned her gaze on the faerie, and he immediately went silent. "You would make demands upon your queen, my child?" she asked quietly.

"Of . . . of course not, Your Majesty!" the faerie said. "But the laws are clear that I am owed something for his attack."

"Indeed they are," the queen said, spinning her scepter on one finger. "But I don't believe that humans live for a thousand years, my son."

"I'd happily accept one hundred years of living service, and nine hundred of undead service," the faerie said.

"That sounds fair," the queen said, turning back to Fort. "And what say you, human child? Why did you attack this poor faerie?"

Fort opened his mouth to speak, but it was so dry, he had to quickly swallow first. "I didn't mean to, Your, uh, Majesty," he said. "I was looking for a friend, and I tripped going around a corner, so accidentally—"

"Purposely!" the faerie shouted.

"Let him speak, my child," the queen told him. "Go on, human."

"So I accidentally fell into him," Fort told her. "I gave him an apology right away—"

"You *gave* him an apology?" she asked, one eyebrow raising. She turned to the faerie. "You didn't mention that he'd offered restitution, even if it wasn't equitable."

The faerie seemed confused by this. "It was but words, my lady. Nothing concrete."

"Nevertheless, he gave you something in return for his actions," she said, and the air around her began to darken like a storm cloud. "And now, you seek to waste my time with outlandish claims of servitude without taking into account what you've already been given. Where is *my* restitution for that, child?"

The faerie's mouth opened and closed for a moment in fear, before he bowed low. "I offer my apology to *you*, Your Majesty. I can only beg your forgiveness."

"No, I think my forgiveness is worth more than that," she said, and nodded at the guards. "A few years in the dungeon should help you not take other people's time for granted."

The faerie started to object but disappeared instead, along

with the two guards who'd been holding Fort. Somehow, Fort felt even more terrified of the faerie queen without them at his side. A few years for wasting her time? And she'd already said she'd banned humans under penalty of death!

Why hadn't *that* part been on the sign beneath the tomb?

"My children have so much to learn, even still," the queen said, turning back to Fort. "Now, little human, what have you to say about breaking my law? I haven't allowed your kind here since the Pendragon."

All of the warnings from Rachel and the old man jumbled together in Fort's mind, and he had no idea what to say. He knew he shouldn't bargain with the queen, or tell her what he wanted, but she already thought he'd broken her law, so really, was there anything he could say that could make things worse?

"I came looking for the tomb of King Arthur, the Pendragon, Your Majesty," Fort said, hoping his honesty would at least be worth something. "I was hoping to find an item he once had."

Behind him, the faeries gasped but quickly went silent at a glance from their queen. *That* didn't bode well.

"Something of the Pendragon's?" the queen asked, raising an eyebrow. "And why would you care about anything of his?"

"There is a war coming, Your Majesty," he said, clasping

his hands together to keep them from shaking. "Back on my world. And I was, uh, hoping to stop it?"

She smiled. "You humans and your wars. You never cease to amaze me." She turned away, almost like she was losing interest. "The Pendragon failed to fulfill his agreement to me, and thus I claimed him *and* his possessions, even in death." She shrugged. "Unfortunately, undead humans tend to spoil rather quickly, which comes with quite an odor, and seem to be of limited use in such a case. Therefore his belongings are all I have." She looked at him almost lazily. "Tell me why I shouldn't just kill you for breaking my laws, human."

Fort cringed. "We're definitely *much* more useful alive than dead, Your Majesty. I didn't realize that humans were banned from Avalon, or I'd never have come."

"Ignorance of the law is no excuse," the queen said, growing even more bored now. "Still, you are just a child, and I admit I could not *actually* give you the maximum punishment. Perhaps merely three decades in the dungeons will teach you to stay out of our realm?"

Three decades? Fort's eyes widened. He couldn't even imagine being that old! "Your Majesty, I've already learned that lesson—trust me! There's no need for a dungeon!"

"I'm afraid there is, child," the queen said. "We can't be seen to be lenient on your kind invading our realm, now, can we? You humans tend to accumulate like flies, and once you infest an area, it's ever so hard to get rid of you."

She held up a hand, looking away, and two more guards appeared at Fort's side. He knew he had to change her mind, or this was going to be it: Damian would get the book, given that he was a dragon and therefore allowed into Avalon; the world would go to war; and everything would be his fault, all while he waited until his forties to be let out.

"Please, *wait*, Your Majesty!" Fort shouted, and she turned back to him, looking annoyed. "I give you my apology!"

She smiled. "It's been used, child, and I don't want one secondhand. Even if it were still new, breaking the law combined with trying to take what's mine of the Pendragon's holdings is worth considerably more punishment than a mere apology."

"Worth how much?" Fort shouted as the guards grabbed his arms. "Maybe there's something we can trade!"

She looked at him, and he could feel something warm inside his head, like the sun on a hot day. "I see you've had contact with . . . a dragon egg?" she said, perking up a bit. "Fascinating, child. Perhaps there is room to bargain after all. . . ."

And then she stopped and stood up from her chair, and the entire room went dark.

"The Old Ones?" she shouted, and the walls began to shake. The other faeries ran out of the room as silently as possible, and even the guards backed away. "You, human, have had contact with *the Old Ones*?"

- THIRTY -

THE QUEEN'S FURY HAD THE FLOOR shaking so hard that Fort fell to his knees, landing painfully. The guards now fled as the walls began to crumble, and Fort wondered if he wouldn't even need to be sentenced, that he'd just die here and now.

"Answer me, human!" the queen of the faeries shouted. A strong wind blew in out of nowhere, threatening to pick him up off the floor entirely. "What business did you have with the Old Ones?"

"No business!" Fort shouted over the howling wind, shielding his face with his arms. The ground split just in front of him, and he pushed backward, falling onto his behind to keep away from the crack. "They were trying to return to my world, and I tried to stop them!"

"*You*, a pathetic human child, faced the Old Ones?" the

queen roared. "Lies! You would have been destroyed in an instant!"

A powerful gust of wind slammed into Fort, slamming him several yards backward. He landed hard, knocking the air from his lungs, and for a moment, he struggled just to catch his breath as the queen advanced on him, her castle crumbling around them.

"I almost was!" he shouted when he could breathe again. "I was lucky, I promise you. I shouldn't have been able to face them, but I had help. My friends are much better at magic than I am, and they were the ones who really saved us all!"

Suddenly she was looming over him, as if she had teleported to the spot. "Your friends, *powerful*?" she hissed. "You speak of *these* humans?"

Jia, Rachel, and Ellora appeared in the room, their expressions quickly turning from shock to fear as they realized what was happening around them. The green faerie also appeared next to Ellora but took one look at the queen and fled.

"Fort!" Rachel said as she moved to stand in front of Jia, bracing herself against the wind. "What did you do?"

"Look into my mind, Your Majesty!" Fort shouted, trying to push to his feet and failing. "You can see for yourself what happened!"

The queen sneered but leaned forward, and this time, her touch wasn't warm in Fort's head, it was searing hot. As Fort screamed in pain, he saw what she saw: facing Ketas in the courtyard of the first Oppenheimer School, watching D'hea dissolve in the Dracsi dimension as the other members of his family looked on, all of it.

And just like that, the white-hot pain in Fort's head disappeared, and the wind and shaking all ceased in the castle.

"You *did* face them," the queen said, looking shocked. "Just a handful of children, and you kept them at bay, when numerous human adults succumbed to their magic. I never would have considered such a thing!"

"That's right," Fort said, just glad to not be in a dungeon right now. "The adults weren't much use, but *we* stopped the Old Ones!"

Before the queen could respond, Rachel ran over and knelt on the ground between Fort and the queen, facing the monarch. "Your Majesty, you have my utmost apologies for whatever offense we have caused. Please tell me if I can make it up to you in some way?"

The queen looked down at her with amusement, which was a thousand times better than the cold boredom she'd shown

Fort when sentencing him to death, let alone her rage. "You humans *always* offer deals without any idea of the price. You'd think by now you'd know better."

"Some of us do, Your Majesty," Rachel said, giving Fort a dark look. "But we have to protect those we care about."

The queen reached out a hand toward Rachel and pulled the girl's chin up to look at her. Shockingly, the queen smiled. "You are *brave*, young one," she said. "I can see that you know what it is that you offered. You do this to protect your kin?"

"Not kin by blood, Your Majesty," Rachel said. "But my friends are still family. And not just them. We came here to try to keep our people safe from a war that shouldn't happen."

"Is there any other kind?" the queen asked, looking away for a moment. "You children fascinate me. I've seen human adults flee the Old Ones, cowering at the very sight of them, but you stood your ground. Perhaps it's foolishness on your part. It certainly isn't rationality. But maybe what I need is a bit of foolishness."

Fort's eyes widened. He didn't like where this was going at *all*. The old man in Cyrus's cottage had said not to bargain with the queen, and this sounded an awful lot like that was where it was headed.

But if it were a bargain or a few decades of jail, did they even have a choice?

Rachel seemed to have come to the same conclusion. "I would be interested in hearing your thoughts about that, Your Majesty," she said through clenched teeth.

In spite of everything, Fort couldn't help but be impressed by how good Rachel was at all of this. Apparently, her love of Dungeons & Dragons and fantasy really was coming in handy.

The queen looked away again. "You have not yet been long in my kingdom, but even you will have noticed how there are but children here, no adult Tylwyth Teg other than myself." She turned back, her eyes blazing with anger. "That is the fault of the Old Ones, one in particular. I bargained with him to save my people, after Q'baos took over the dwarven kind during the humans' uprising. I couldn't allow the same thing to happen to my people!" She sneered. "But what the Old One didn't tell me was that to spare my people, he'd regress them into children, freezing them at this age *forever*."

Turning the faeries into children? That could explain why they hadn't seen any others as old as the queen . . . and why the elfin skeleton they'd seen back at the Oppenheimer School looked so much taller. It must have come from before that all happened. But why would that work? "What would making them younger solve, Your Majesty?" Fort asked.

"They would no longer be powerful enough to stand against the other Old Ones," the queen said, her rage turning into a sort of sad exhaustion as she fell back into her throne. "He lived up to the letter of our bargain, while dooming my children to never grow older or have children of their own. My people have become frozen in time, ever youthful. But that wasn't the extent of the curse!"

"What more could there be, Your Majesty?" Rachel asked, speaking slowly, like she was watching every word she said.

"*Your* kind," the queen said, the anger reigniting. "After the war that exiled the Old Ones from your planet, my de-aged children tried to reach out to your kind, playing harmless pranks and jokes on them. But somehow, you humans grew angry when you found your *own* children replaced by changelings."

Stealing a human child and replacing it with a changeling was a *prank*? Fort's eyes widened, but he quickly tried to look sympathetic as the queen glanced at him.

"All children have done that sort of thing, Your Majesty," Rachel said, giving Jia, Ellora, and Fort a quick, terrified look.

"It got to the point that I had to close my dimension off entirely, lest the humans try to punish my children," the queen continued as if she hadn't even heard Rachel. "Now we are cut off from everything, an island in the midst of a void, a people frozen in time. And it's all the fault of a bad bargain, an untrustworthy Old One."

"That's truly evil, Your Majesty," Rachel said. "Your children seem to be doing well, though?"

"Oh, they've learned from my mistake," the queen said. "Since the Old One betrayed me, I have raised them to never be tricked again. Now my children know every deal must result in their favor, hardening their hearts to the world, all to keep them safe from those who would do us harm."

Yikes. That explained a lot and almost made Fort feel sorry for the faeries he'd seen out in the marketplace. Not the one who he'd tripped into, but the rest, for sure.

"I have the utmost sympathy for your plight, Your Majesty," Rachel continued. "What did you mean, though, that you might need a bit of foolishness?"

The queen slowly smiled. "Ah, you bring us back to the matter at hand. I like your thinking, child. Come, I shall give you all the test. If you prove worthy, perhaps we can strike a deal."

"What . . . sort of deal, Your Majesty?" Rachel asked, and Fort could see her shake slightly.

"The kind that lets you leave Avalon before you die of old age," the queen said as the destroyed throne room began to re-form around them, with the cracks in the floor pushing back together, and the walls slowly uncrumbling. But even as it restored itself, the room faded around them, replaced by a cliff at the edge of a forest. A river ran over the edge nearby, creating what sounded like a *very* high waterfall.

Now finding himself on the grassy ground, Fort picked himself up to join Jia, Rachel, and Ellora, feeling a tiny bit better standing beside his friends. The trees in the forest behind them grew so closely together that it was hard to see more than a few feet inside it, and there was no telling what they'd find inside if they ran. As for the cliff, from where they stood, they couldn't see the other side, but the sky above it was a deep, beautiful blue.

Still, it was odd not to be able to see what lay beyond the cliff. Fort took a few steps closer, then froze in place as he looked over the edge.

It wasn't a cliff, at least not the way he'd been thinking. There was no other side, and nothing beneath them. The water falling over the side just fell into nothingness, down so far that Fort had to back away to keep from getting dizzy.

This wasn't a cliff: it was an *edge*. And from what Fort could tell, there was nothing at all below.

. . . Well, the queen *had* said Avalon was an island in the middle of a void. Fort quickly backed away, not taking any chances.

"Not many of your kind have been to the brink of the island of Avalon," the queen told them, standing between six large, upright rocks that almost reminded Fort of Stonehenge. "I would not venture much farther if I were you, humans, as if you fall, you will never land, and will slowly die of thirst and starvation as you tumble for all of eternity."

"That's good advice, Your Majesty," Rachel said to her, giving the others a wide-eyed look as Fort took another, very large step away from the edge.

The queen acknowledged Rachel with a nod. "These mark the graves of the six Artorigios, brave humans who ignored my ban on humans and came to Avalon in search of gifts, treasure that only I could grant them. One came for power, a Welsh general, to save his land from the invading Saxons." She put a hand on one of the stones, and the same writing they'd seen in the tomb below Glastonbury Tor began to glow on it.

"Another, a Roman soldier, came in search of truth, to better know himself," she continued, and a second stone lit up. "A third wished for the world, a fourth to learn the minds of humankind, and the fifth to live forever." The others all showed the same language in turn, until she moved to the center and laid her hands on the sixth stone, the final one, right in the middle of the others.

"But it was the sixth, the final Artorigios, the Pendragon, who came closest to fulfilling his debt to me. And yet, he still failed, just like the rest."

"What did *he* wish for, Your Majesty?" Fort asked.

"Peace," she said, staring at the memorial. "And to get it, he, like the rest, was willing to give me anything I asked for. And yet, all failed to meet their end of the bargain." She turned around and gestured at the ground before them. The earth beneath their feet began to rumble, and Jia and Rachel held each other to keep from falling over. Fort almost *did* fall, but Ellora reached out and caught him just before he did, and he gave her a quick, thankful look: They were *way* too close to the edge of the world to want to accidentally tumble over it.

As the earth shook, a seventh stone rose from the ground, this one only half as large as the rest but standing in front of them all, closer to the cliff's edge. The ground stopped shaking as it finished rising, thankfully, and they all moved in closer to see.

The queen raised a hand over the stone, and it began to glow as she slowly lifted her palm up.

Out of the stone, the hilt of a sword appeared.

The queen raised her hand higher, and the sword pulled out farther in response, revealing a blade covered in words of the same language that covered the stones.

But before the blade emerged completely, the queen dropped her hand, leaving it halfway submerged in the stone. "This is *Caliburn*," she said, staring at the sword warmly. "Forged by the ancient Avalonians out of a human spear and a Tylwyth Teg sword as a sign of the unity we once shared." She sneered. "It is now all that's left of *that* cause. Caliburn is our greatest weapon, one that is no less dangerous for the wielder than their foes. Only the worthy may bear it, for its power is too great for anyone lesser."

"The sword in the stone," Rachel breathed, a huge smile spreading across her face. She blushed at a quizzical look from the queen. "We, um, call it Excalibur."

"Only an Artorigios may wield it," the queen said. "And solely to an Artorigios will I grant your fondest wish: the book of magic that you seek." She nodded at Fort, then spread her arms to them. "My deal is thus: Use this blade to destroy the Old One who betrayed me, Emrys, the Old One of Time magic. Touch it to him, and with even but a scratch, you will grant me my vengeance for taking my people from me. Promise me this, and I will grant your boon. I will give you the book of Spirit magic." Her hands once again dropped. "Fail, like the six Artorigios in the past, and you will belong to *me*, just as they now do, both in life *and* in death."

- THIRTY-ONE -

FORT JUST STARED AT THE SWORD IN the stone in shock. To get the book of Spirit magic and stop a war, one of them had to be *worthy* of the sword? What did that even mean? Who decided who was worthy or not?

Would Fort himself be considered for trying to stop the war, even if it was going to start because of him? Or would he be blamed for everything that came from rescuing his father, which only happened because he'd wanted to save his dad?

Not that he'd considered the consequences of any of it. And he'd ended up hurting a lot of people in the meantime and setting things up for the world to go to war. Maybe he couldn't have foreseen all of that, but he certainly could have thought things through more.

Beyond the whole worthiness thing, they also had to make

a bargain with the faerie queen, the very thing the old man in Cyrus's cottage had warned him *not* to do. But what choice did they even have? If none of them agreed to take down this Old One of Time magic—not that they'd ever even *seen* an Old One of Time magic—then they wouldn't get the book, either.

Still, it wasn't like the Old Ones were anything but monsters. If touching one with Excalibur ended up destroying it, it wouldn't be the worst thing. One less Old One trying to destroy the world would actually be a pretty good thing.

That was assuming they could take the queen at her word, though.

"Your Majesty, we mean no offense by asking, but where is this Emrys?" Rachel asked. "If he is in another dimension, then we won't be able to reach him."

The queen gave her a long look. "You think if I could sense him that I would not have taken my vengeance? He *hides* from me, and has for millennia, knowing I would doom him with a touch. Do not agree to this lightly, children. Six of the greatest human warriors I have found have attempted to do this same task and failed." She paused. "But none of them had faced an Old One before, and you three have. This decision is in your hands."

"How long would we have, Your Majesty?" Fort asked.

"Time is meaningless to Emrys," the queen said, shaking her head. "It is his to control, and your challenge will be to find a way to overcome that. But as for our agreement, I will not wait longer than one turning of the four seasons on your world."

Fort's eyes widened. One *year* to find an Old One? That didn't seem like anywhere close to enough time, especially not if that Old One had Time magic. For all they knew, this Emrys monster could be living in the past or future. How would they ever actually find him?

"You have until then to use Caliburn, or it will return here, and bring *you* along with it," the queen continued. "If you agree to this, I will grant you the book of Spirit magic that the Pendragon returned with here, after he perished, as well as grant you forgiveness for the crime of entering my land." She stared down at each of them in turn. "Refuse, and I will be merciful. I will only sentence you to a few decades in our dungeons for you to learn your lesson."

Jia and Ellora gasped, while Rachel groaned softly. Even having heard the queen's "merciful" punishment already, it still hit Fort in the gut. They couldn't spend half their lives in a dungeon, especially not while the world they'd left behind went to war. There really was no other choice.

But maybe there'd be something good that came from this. If they did have Caliburn, or Excalibur, whatever it was called, they could use it against Damian, and maybe even the other Old Ones, if it was actually powerful enough to destroy one. It could be a huge advantage overall.

That's it, son! Fort heard his father say in his head. *Think positively. Anyone would love to have a magic sword, but only you will get to stop a* war *with it. What better excuse could you have? And there's no one more worthy than my Forsythe!*

Fort winced at his imaginary father's words. Yes, his real dad would say that. But that didn't make it true.

But there wasn't any other choice. And Fort couldn't leave it to his friends. The old man had said that Rachel specifically shouldn't take the sword, but even if he hadn't, this was all because of what Fort had done, so he couldn't just leave Jia or Rachel, or even Ellora, to fix it.

"I'll take the agreement, Your Majesty," Fort said, stepping forward. "We're only here because of me, so I'll find this Emrys Old One and, um, get your revenge, if that's what it takes."

But before he could move, he felt a hand on his shoulder. "Fort, this isn't just on you," Rachel said quietly. "The three of us were all there, getting your dad back. And none of us could ever let the war happen, no matter how it started. You don't have to do this. We can flip a coin or something—"

He smiled thankfully at her, then gave her a quick hug. "Thank you," he said, "but I really do need to try."

She patted him awkwardly on the back. "Okay, let's not make a scene or anything. I was just being polite."

"The sword will determine if you are worthy to wield it, child," the queen told him. "If it finds you unworthy, it will erupt into flame, burning you in its wrath. Attempt this at your own peril."

It was going to *burn* him if he wasn't worthy? That might have been important to mention before he'd volunteered! Still, there was no way he could back out now, especially not with the possibility of fire. He couldn't let his friends take that risk without at least trying himself.

"I understand," Fort said, and wiped his now-sweating hands on his shirt, hoping he didn't look too nervous. What did worthy mean to a sword anyway? Was it about how brave he'd be, or how well he could sword fight? Or would it judge him based on everything he'd done?

The sword looked oddly threatening, sticking halfway out of the stone, and Fort stared at it anxiously, then forced himself close enough to take it. Gritting his teeth, he slowly reached out toward the hilt, his hand shaking so much he had to steady it with his other hand.

Take it, my once and future king! his father shouted in his head, and Fort winced, quickly grazed his fingertips against the hilt, then yanked his hand back.

Nothing happened.

Behind him, he heard Rachel, Jia, and Ellora all let out their held breaths, and he gave them a relieved smile over his shoulder. It hadn't burned him! That meant at least the sword considered him worthy. Who would have thought?

Me! said his father's voice. *I would have thought!*

Not me, Fort thought himself, then turned back to the sword, reached out, and grabbed it.

It immediately lit on fire.

A flame of pure white spread up from the bottom of the blade to the hilt faster than Fort could move. As it reached his hand, pain shot up through his fingers and into his arm, like nothing he'd ever felt.

Fort screamed in agony, releasing the sword instantly. He desperately cast Heal Minor Wounds on his hand, cradling it to his chest.

And then Jia was there, spreading cooling Healing magic into his burned hand, and it began to restore itself, the blackened flesh changing back to a healthy color, and the pain finally extinguishing.

He turned to stare at the sword in the stone before him, its fire having disappeared as soon as he dropped the hilt.

He wasn't worthy. The sword didn't think he was good enough to hold it. As painful as the flames had been, the sword's decision almost hurt more.

Everything he'd ever done had been judged and found not to be good enough. He squeezed his unburned hand tightly, digging his fingernails into his palm, trying not to think about it, trying not to lose it in front of everyone.

Why would the sword have found him worthy? A war was going to erupt around the world because of him!

"Ray, we can't do this," Jia said to Rachel as she continued healing Fort. "Who even knows what worthiness is?"

"The sword does," the queen said, looking down at Fort with something that could have been pity, feeling like another kick in his gut. "Who will attempt to wield it now?"

Rachel sighed deeply, then stepped forward.

"No, don't!" Fort shouted, as Jia dropped Fort's now-healed

hand and moved to block Rachel from the sword.

"Fort's right," Jia said, spreading her arms out wide. "I'm not letting you do this!"

"It'd just be a little burn," Rachel said, but her expression made it clear she wasn't as brave as she sounded. "What's there to lose? I have to try."

"No!" Jia said, louder this time. "I'm not letting us all burn to a crisp just to prove some point!" Her eyes lit up, and she quickly turned to the queen, bowing low. "Your Majesty, is that what this is, a test? You wanted to see if we were wise enough to *not* take the weapon, and if we chose correctly, you'd give us the book?"

The queen's eyes narrowed, and the sky darkened around them, the wind picking up out of nowhere as rain began to fall. They all had to duck behind the memorial stones just to avoid being blown off the edge. "This *is* a test, young one, but you are incorrect about its meaning!" the queen roared. "I *will* see Emrys destroyed for what he did to my people. We shall have our revenge for his deceit!"

"Right," Rachel said, and pushed off the stone she was hiding behind. "Enough of *this*. I'm going for it."

"Ray, *no!*" Jia shouted, but Rachel was already moving, driving into the wind toward the sword. With Fort just behind her, Jia followed Rachel and tried to grab for her, but the wind tossed her and Fort backward, almost deliberately.

The memory of the pain in his hand made Fort try again, but the wind plowed into him harder the second time, knocking him back into one of the stones, pinning him there. A moment later, Jia crashed against the stone next to him, trapped as well.

Somehow, though, the wind allowed Rachel to reach the sword. She held out her hand to grab it, then paused, giving Jia an almost apologetic smile. "Did you really think I'd give up a chance to pull the sword out of the stone, Gee?" she shouted. "I mean, come on."

Then she wrapped her hand around the hilt.

Fort flinched as she did, imagining what the white flame would do to her, what pain she was about to experience.

Except, no flame emerged.

Instead, Rachel, looking as amazed as Fort felt, slowly pulled the sword straight out of the stone, then held it up to the queen.

"I guess a deal is a deal, Your Majesty," she shouted as the rain and wind whirled around her. "Give us the book, and I'll take down the Old One of Time."

- THIRTY-TWO -

CALIBURN JUDGES YOU WORTHY, SO therefore the bargain is *complete*!" the queen shouted, the wind dying down and the rain gradually stopping as her mood seemed to improve.

Fort and Jia rushed over to where Rachel stood, Fort barely able to comprehend what he'd just seen. Jia, though, leaped in for a hug that almost sent them both tumbling to the ground.

Then she pulled back and smacked Rachel hard in the shoulder.

"Don't *ever* do that again!" Jia shouted. "What were you thinking?"

"I just told you that I wanted to pull Excalibur out of the stone!" Rachel said, beaming as her face turned red. "When else would I have this chance?"

"What if it burned you, too, like Fort?" Jia asked, pointing back at him.

Rachel shrugged. "I don't know. I half expected it to. We'll probably never know what the sword was looking for. Maybe after six guys kept failing, it finally realized it should have been a girl all along?"

Fort forced a smile, knowing that she was being nice, not pointing out that the sword had found her worthy for a reason and hadn't done the same for him. And honestly, he couldn't look at Rachel and feel jealous of her, not with everything that came along with the sword. Plus, if anyone would be able to use it well, it was Rachel.

No, the part that really bothered him was that the sword had just confirmed everything he'd ever felt guilty about. Turned out that yes, it *was* all Fort's fault, from his father getting taken to a world war starting, and even a magical weapon knew it.

"Your Majesty," Rachel said, bending down on one knee and holding the sword's tip into the ground before her. "I beg your forgiveness, but I would ask you further questions about our agreement."

"You have my forgiveness, then," the queen said. "You may proceed."

"You said you would give us a year to find this Emrys," Rachel said. "When we find him, and I . . . use the sword on him, what will happen? What does it do?"

"It will protect you from his magic, and that is all you need to know," the queen said. "If you are successful, the sword will return to me under its own power."

This seemed to throw Rachel. "So I shouldn't take it to a lake and throw it in?"

The sky around the queen seemed to darken. "Do not bring that woman up to me, child. You will find I am less merciful when angered."

Fort blinked in confusion, having no idea what was going on. He vaguely remembered something about a Lady of the Lake from the King Arthur stories, the one who gave King Arthur his sword, maybe. But why would the faerie queen not want to talk about that? Who was the lady, and what had she done to anger the queen?

At some point, Fort was going to have to track down a copy of the King Arthur legends and catch up on everything, if just so he didn't offend anyone else.

"We will fulfill your quest, Your Majesty," Rachel said, nodding her head to the queen. "Will you grant us the book of Spirit magic in return, then, as agreed to within our, uh, agreement?"

As the sky returned to normal behind her, the queen lifted a hand, then plucked something out of thin air and handed it to Rachel. "Your boon, as promised. This was left here by the Pendragon and does not belong in my realm." She tilted her head. "In truth, I am happy to see it go. It creates too many . . . temptations, and I would be a poor queen if I ever used it upon my people."

Rachel accepted the book and nodded. "I promise, you'll never see it again." She looked at it for a moment, then shuddered and tossed it a bit too hard at Fort, who managed to catch it, after fumbling it momentarily.

He glanced down at the cover. *The Forbidden Art of Spirit Magic.*

Yikes. Not exactly the friendliest title.

"And now, my end of the bargain is kept," the queen said. "If you ever return, I will assume you have failed in your part of our agreement, and therefore you will remain forever. Do we understand each other?"

Rachel coughed. "Yes, Your Majesty. Could you, uh, take us

back to the portal we arrived through? The one in the market-place?"

The queen looked down at her coldly. "Of course not. I closed that portal the moment I became aware of it. I would not allow my children to enter your world, especially with a dragon waiting on the other side."

What? She'd closed the portal? How were they going to get home, then? That had been the last use of Fort's Restore Dimensional Portal spell! "Your Majesty," he said, "we might have a problem—"

The queen turned to him, and Fort took a step backward, shrinking under her intensity. "You would ask *more* of me, human?"

Fort violently shook his head. "No, not at all! It's just that you closed our only door back to our world, and—

"You arrived here with no way home?" the queen sighed, rubbing her head. "You are no better than my own children. I will send you home."

And with that, Rachel, Jia, and Ellora all disappeared. Fort waited for a moment for the memorial stones to fade away as well, but when they didn't, he looked up at the queen in surprise.

Had she changed her mind? Was she going to throw him in the dungeon by himself until he was fifty?

"Calm yourself, child," the queen said, shaking her head. "Your brave friend was found worthy of Caliburn, so you will all be sent home. But before you go, I wished to speak to each of you alone, and offer you . . . a bargain."

Alarms began sounding in Fort's head as the queen moved closer to him. Between Rachel and the old man, he knew he couldn't accept any agreement, no matter how tempting it was.

"Meaning no offense, Your Majesty, I don't believe I'm interested," Fort said, hoping Rachel would have been proud of him for how he spoke to her.

"I believe you will be," the queen said, and turned her palm over. Inside it, where nothing had been a moment before, now shone a bright green jewel, sparkling in the sun. It was almost as big as Fort's palm and had to be worth more money than he'd ever seen.

With a jewel like that, Colonel Charles could send him home, and his aunt wouldn't have to worry about money anymore. It'd solve so many problems for him!

"I, uh, don't need any money," he said, having trouble getting the words out. "But thank you, Your Majesty."

"Oh, this isn't a treasure to be sold," the queen said, picking the jewel up and holding it in the sunlight, sending beams shining into Fort's eyes. "This is worth far more than any gold or silver."

Fort nodded, believing her, but knowing he couldn't make a deal. Whatever the stone was worth, the queen would want something of equal or greater value, and that wasn't anything Fort could afford.

"I'm sure it is, Your Majesty, but—"

"This stone," the queen said, looking Fort in his eyes, "will grant you your heart's desire. Do you know what that is, child?"

He blinked, not sure he understood the question. Did he know what his own heart's desire was? Of course he'd always thought about what it'd be like to be rich, or not have to do chores and save money for months to buy video games.

But those weren't his heart's desire. If there was one thing he wanted more than anything else, it was the only thing he'd been thinking about since the attack in D.C.

"I just want my father to be safe," he said quietly.

"Then safe he shall be," the queen said, holding it out to him. "Place this in his hand, and the stone will ensure your father's protection no matter the danger. No harm shall fall him, neither mental nor physical, if you place this magical stone upon him."

Fort's mouth dropped open as he stared in wonder.

"And for this," the queen continued, "all I'd ask is a simple favor, to be given at a time of my choosing."

Part of Fort's mind screamed out the warning the old man had given him earlier.

And under no circumstances should you accept any *deal to save your father!* he had said.

But the rest of Fort couldn't stop looking at the stone. It would make his father safe . . . forever?

"I can see you are conflicted," the queen said, and moved the stone closer to her own eye, appraising it. "And far be it from me to hold you up for any longer, not when you and your friends have an Old One to find. So take the stone with you. If you use it, then a favor you'll owe me. If not, then there is no agreement."

And with that, she handed Fort the stone with a smile. He looked down at it in wonder.

"I only owe you if I use it," he said, almost not believing it.

"That's the deal, child," the queen said as the stone monuments around him disappeared. "That's the deal."

- THIRTY-THREE -

A CIRCLE OF FAMILIAR-LOOKING STONES faded into view, replacing the monuments at the edge of Avalon's island. This was Stonehenge, or at least that was Fort's assumption from all the photos he'd seen, as a semicircle of stones surrounded him, many with a horizontal stone on top of them.

As Fort appeared, he noticed Jia, Rachel, and Ellora all doing the same, as if they were just now arriving as well. Had the faerie queen made bargains with them, too? Or had they all turned her down separately?

He quickly placed the stone in his pocket, just in case the others had all said no. The last thing he wanted to hear was Rachel or Jia telling him why it was a terrible idea to owe the queen a favor. It wasn't like he didn't already know that.

But if it meant his father would be safe—from Colonel

Charles, the Old Ones, anyone—wouldn't it be worth it?

"I didn't realize she'd send us here," Ellora said, her eyes going black. "Maybe I wouldn't have used it to fake Damian out if I'd known."

"Can you even see anything around us now that we have the book?" Fort asked, holding up the book of Spirit magic.

She sighed, shaking her head as her eyes returned to normal. "I'd hoped I could see if Damian was tracking us, but no, you're right. The book fogs it all up. But I don't think we have much time."

Fort looked at Jia and Rachel, wanting to ask about the faerie queen, but not knowing how to bring it up without answering the question himself. Finally, he gave up and just brought up the other uncomfortable, awkward elephant in the room. "If Damian's coming, I need to learn Spirit magic to use on him, then. That way we can keep him from destroying London before we figure out how to stop the war."

Jia nodded quickly, but Rachel just stared at the book anxiously. "What about Excalibur?" she said, holding up the sword. "Maybe I could use it against Damian, to stop him somehow. Then we wouldn't have to use the magic."

"We don't even know what the sword does," Jia pointed out.

"And the faerie queen said one scratch would destroy an Old One. Do you really want to do that to Damian?"

Rachel sighed loudly. "No, I guess not," she said, then looked around hopefully. "Unless the rest of you think we should? *Fine*, okay, Spirit magic it is." She gave Fort a suspicious glance. "But the first sign of it making you evil, I'm going to fireball you right in the chest."

Fort couldn't help but smile. "Just like when we first met. Jia, you should watch me too. I don't trust this magic any more than you two do."

Jia nodded, and both her hands and Rachel's began to glow with their respective magic. "Ready," Jia said.

"Let's do this," Rachel said, looking disgusted.

"You'll see—it'll be okay," Ellora said quietly. "I think this could change the world if we use it right. Just give him a chance."

Fort nodded and opened the book. A familiar poem appeared on the first page:

One for the body, bones and skin,
One for the spirit, its spectral kin,

One for the mind, thoughts and dreams,

One for the world, from dirt to streams,

One for all space, wide and vast,

One for all time, future and past.

Seven from six, the rest unearthed.

One saves all, if proved their worth.

Right. That was the prophecy Damian apparently was following, the one that appeared in every book of magic. When Fort had first arrived at the Oppenheimer School, Dr. Opps had warned him not to take it seriously, since all the other students wanted to believe it was them. Apparently, students believing they were the chosen one was a common problem, but that wasn't something that had ever even occurred to Fort. He *knew* he was nobody, and besides, he'd never be as powerful as the other students, since he hadn't been born on Discovery Day.

Even a magical sword knew he'd never be worthy. So saving everyone was already out.

Besides, believing in the prophecy was dangerous. Look what it had done to Damian, convincing him that he could defeat the Old Ones if he learned the six types of magic.

Hopefully, he was still waiting beneath Glastonbury Tor and would never know what happened to them—

A green glow out of the corner of Fort's eye caught his attention, but by the time he looked up, it was already too late. Hardened air slammed into his chest, sending him flying into one of the nearby stones, the book dropping where he'd stood.

As Fort looked up, he found Damian standing in the middle of Stonehenge, his face contorted with anger.

"Thanks for bringing me the book of Spirit magic," he said, his voice bitter as he glared at them. "Normally I'd give you a chance to walk away from this, saying that I didn't want to hurt you." He slowly smiled, revealing some incredibly sharp-looking fangs even in his human mouth. "But after all the trouble you've given me today? That'd be a lie: I actually kind of *do* want to hurt you."

And then he attacked, flying into the air straight at them. . . .

Only to freeze in a burst of black light.

Fort just stared in surprise for a moment, then slowly picked himself up off his feet. Jia and Rachel were both staring as their magical light faded from their hands, apparently having been prepared for a fight. Fort turned to Ellora as well, but found her looking just as confused.

"That . . . wasn't me," she said, and continued on, but Fort didn't hear the rest as Stonehenge faded out around him, replaced by a now-familiar-looking cottage.

"What did I tell you?" Cyrus said, sitting at the long wooden dining table in the middle of the cottage's main room. "As soon as you get the book, come here. Now get everyone here already: Me in the past can't keep Damian frozen for *that* long."

- THIRTY-FOUR -

STONEHENGE FADED INTO VIEW ALL around him as Fort found himself back in the present, Damian still frozen in midair. The others were staring at Ellora in surprise, so she must have just shared that this wasn't her doing.

That meant he had time to get them to Cyrus's cottage.

Or he could ensure that London wouldn't be destroyed, once and for all.

"Ellora, can you unfreeze Damian?" Fort asked, walking back to where Damian had knocked the book of Spirit magic out of his hands.

"Um, what?" Rachel shouted. "Did the faerie queen take your brain in exchange for something? You want to release him?"

"I can, yes," Ellora said. "And I agree, you should use Spirit magic on him."

Fort nodded as Rachel ran over, shaking her head violently. "Whoa, no way, New Kid. We said we'd use it to stop the war. Damian's not going anywhere. We don't need to use it on him!"

"Cyrus did this," Fort said, nodding at Damian as picked the book up. "And he just told me it was only temporary. He can't keep him frozen forever."

"Then Ellora can!" Rachel shouted. "Or all those other kids. They can let the dome go now, because we did what we set out to do: We stopped Damian!"

"Unless we take him out of time altogether, there's no way to know for sure he won't get free," Ellora told her. "Damian is too powerful. Our spells don't seem to work on him as well. It could be that dragons have some sort of natural resistance."

"Don't D and D me at a time like this!" Rachel shouted, but Fort barely heard her. Ellora saying they'd have to take Damian out of time brought to mind exactly why he needed to do this.

Damian had to be stopped. So did the coming war. If not, then his own father would have to be sent out of time as well. And there was no way he could let that happen.

"Same as before, keep an eye on me," Fort told Rachel and

Jia. "I'm just going to change his mind about wanting the books, that's all."

"And if that's not the first spell?" Rachel shouted. "What then? What will you do to him?"

"Whatever it takes!" Jia shouted, moving to Fort's side to face her. "Rachel, we can't take a chance on London. If it starts a world war, so many people will be hurt, or killed! Including my . . ." She trailed off as she rubbed her eyes and took a deep breath. "You saw what happened to Chicago, Ray. Just like I saw Hong Kong. I *can't* let that happen, not if I can stop it. And we can, using this." She pointed at the book.

"We could do a lot more with it too," Ellora said quietly. "Change world leaders' minds, make them help the poor and feed the hungry."

Rachel whirled on her. "Not *now*, Ellora!" She turned back to Jia and Fort. "I get it, I really do. I'm all for changing the world and saving everyone. But you two don't understand how *evil* that power is! And I don't want you to find out. I don't want *anyone* to find out!"

"That's why you have my permission to take me down if I use it wrong," Fort said. "We need to do this, Rachel. If we're going to save my dad, and Jia's parents, we *need* to!"

She groaned loudly, rubbing her forehead, then finally nodded. "I really will take you down, Fort," she said quietly, her hands glowing red. "So *be careful*, okay?"

"I will," he said, relieved that she had finally come around, while still feeling just as nervous as she was about the whole thing. Just because he didn't have a choice didn't mean he had to like it.

He opened the book past the poem, to the first page. For a moment, he was worried that the first spell wouldn't be what he needed, just like Rachel had said. That had happened with the book of Summoning magic, and while Teleport had turned out to be incredibly useful, at the time, all he'd wanted was a dimensional portal spell. What if the first Spirit magic spell was about making someone's bad day better, or—

Create Devotion in a Living Creature, he read. *Be warned—this spell will ensure loyal obedience to any command of the spellcaster but has been shown to affect the temperament of the spellcaster the more it's used. Spirit magic as a whole is intricately tied to the force of magic itself, and given what was hidden there, the user should be taking the utmost care whenever attempting any Spirit spells—*

The book went on, but Fort didn't care as he felt an odd sort of energy fill him. Summoning magic had felt kind of itchy, and Healing magic made him cold, but this wasn't anything like those two: It almost made him feel . . . *powerful*.

The spell words, "gen ly'la," appeared in his head, and some part of him wanted desperately to shout them out to the world, to turn them on the nearest person and see what happened. That made him even *more* nervous, but somehow, the warmth of the magic comforted him, told him everything would be okay.

And besides, he did have a perfect target for the magic.

Fort looked up at Damian in the sky and quietly whispered the words, grinning in spite of himself. Orange light surrounded the dragon boy, then slowly faded, leaving Damian still frozen.

"Close the book, Fort," Rachel said to him, a spell at the ready. "You got your one spell. *Close it.*"

He nodded, though part of him was annoyed. Nothing had gone wrong, and the magic had been so comforting. Why did she care so much? She had no idea what it was like to have the power he did now.

He could even use it on her, ask her to relax a bit, and then he could learn more spells. Why not? It was obviously nothing bad.

"Fort?" Rachel said. "Did you hear what I said? You haven't closed the book yet."

He rolled his eyes but closed the book. He *had* asked her to watch over him, so he'd have to do what she said, for now at least. And then when everyone realized there was nothing bad about Spirit magic, he could dive into the rest and learn it *all*.

"Did it work?" Jia asked as he closed the book.

"Only one way to find out," Fort said. "Ellora, will you release him?"

Rachel turned to face Damian now as Ellora unfroze the boy. Immediately Damian's momentum kicked back in, sending him straight at them, an attack at the ready. He landed just in front of Fort, glowing with multiple types of magic.

"Stand down, Dragon Boy!" Rachel shouted. "Drop the magic or I'll make you wish you'd never left your cave!"

Damian sneered, then slowly looked up. His eyes locked on Fort, and the sneer immediately faded, along with his prepared spells.

"Forsythe!" he said, almost as if in surprise. "I didn't mean . . . I'm so sorry that it looked like . . . I apologize! I never meant to attack *you*. I would never!"

Fort just stared back joyfully, enjoying how this was going *way* more than he'd even hoped.

"You should probably call me sir," Fort said. "Or, you know, Your Majesty."

"Anything you want, Your Majesty, sir!" Damian said, bowing low. "Is there any way I can possibly help you? I can't believe I was even considering taking your book of magic from you. I have to make up for that, *please*! Anything you need, I'm your servant, sir, Your Majesty, sir!"

"Fort, stop this, now," Rachel hissed, and he looked over to find a nauseous look on her face. "You don't need to humiliate him."

"He was going to do far worse to us!" Fort shouted back. "I think he could stand a *little* humiliation."

"I *was* going to do worse, and I do deserve all the punishment for it," Damian said, his face contorting wretchedly. "Please, tell me what I can do to make up for it. I'll do anything!"

"Fort, seriously, get this over with quickly," Jia said, not looking much better than Rachel.

Fort sighed loudly, not understanding why they were so against a little payback. The magic had just felt so good, and now he had Damian groveling in front of him. Why was that so bad? Maybe he *should* show them what the magic felt like, just so they could see it wasn't as bad as they thought.

And then Damian looked up at him with true despair in his eyes, and a small, quiet part of Fort felt true revulsion. What *was* he doing? Humiliating Damian just for kicks, all without the other boy having any sort of control? This wasn't who he was. This was sick!

"Don't . . . don't try to steal the book of Spirit magic from me, okay?" he said, not even able to look at Damian now, even as part of him couldn't believe he was letting Damian off the hook. "Just . . . just go back to the Carmarthen Academy and turn yourself over to William."

Damian nodded, his sneer coming back a bit. "He was the one who tried to keep me from getting the book of Spirit magic." For a moment, he looked tentatively excited. "Shall I interrogate him for you, sir, Your Majesty? Stick him under the earth for a few months or teleport him to the Arctic until he tells us everything he knows?"

"No!" Fort shouted, even more of him now terrified of his own power over the other boy. "Do *none* of those things. In fact, *he's* in charge." He glanced over at Ellora. "William will know what to do, right?"

She nodded. "He should be able to see the future and figure out what has to be done to keep . . . what we saw from ever happening."

"Good enough," Fort said. "That's the plan, then, Damian. You listen to William, and do whatever he tells you. Got it?"

Damian looked disappointed for the briefest of moments, before nodding. "I will, Your Sir Majesty!" he said, enthusiastic once more. "Anything to make up for my awful behavior earlier. Are you sure there's nothing else I could do too? Destroy your enemies, or fly you around the world?"

Fort had to swallow the bile in his throat. How hadn't he seen this right away? What was *wrong* with him that he'd enjoyed this, even for a second? It wasn't about humiliating Damian . . . the dragon boy had no choice in the matter. It was like kicking him over and over when he was already unconscious. Just brutal, and cruel.

"No, just what I said," Fort said. "Please . . . just go. And I'm sorry, Damian. Really. I am."

Damian looked at him in shock. "You have nothing to apologize for, *ever*, Your Majesty, sir! But I will go, if that makes you happy." He gave Fort a long, deep bow, then disappeared in a blink of green light.

Fort turned to the others, feeling just as sick about it all as they looked. "You were right," he told Rachel, not even wanting to hold the book anymore. "That was *not* okay. Any of it. I felt it in my head, pushing me to learn more, and to . . . to use it on more people."

Rachel's eyes widened, but she nodded and let out a huge breath. "The fact that you told us that actually makes me feel better. I'd be more worried if you were hiding it and planning on using it when we stopped watching you. I'm just glad you were able to fight off the magic."

For a moment, there was silence, and Fort tried to forget how easily the magic had almost taken him over. It'd been so *easy* to listen. Did he really want to hurt Damian that badly? Sure, the dragon was a jerk, but humiliating him, or worse, using the magic on Rachel, just because she was telling him to stop? He'd asked her to watch him for that exact reason!

"So, wait," Jia said, interrupting Fort's guilting session. "Did we just stop London being destroyed? Does that mean the war won't happen now?"

They all turned to Ellora, who frowned, her eyes going black. "It's so hard to tell, since the book of Spirit magic is involved," she said. Her eyes went back to normal as she gave them a miserable look. "But I'm still seeing a war in the future. That means if London doesn't set it off, something else does."

"*No!*" Jia screamed, while Ellora's words felt like a punch in Fort's gut. All of that and they still hadn't stopped the war? Everything they'd promised to the faerie queen, having to face down Damian, and all of it was for nothing? Even the dome above them would be useless, causing panic but nothing more.

"I told you this might happen," Ellora said, staring at the ground. "This is why we needed the book, just in case!"

"There *has* to be another way," Rachel hissed, her eyes on Jia as she paced away, her arms wrapped tightly around her body as she muttered to herself, something about this not being the deal. "Come on, Ellora: You can see what's coming, so tell us how to fix it!"

Ellora pointed at the book in Fort's hands. "There *is* no other way. It's either Spirit magic to make sure the world's leaders never *want* to go to war, or . . ." She trailed off, staring at Fort sadly.

Or she'd have to remove Fort's father from time completely.

"Then it's the book," he whispered, his chest hurting like something was squeezing his heart tightly. "I used it once; I can do it again."

Even as he said it, disgust filled him at what he'd felt while casting Spirit magic. It'd been so tempting to keep going, to make Damian do whatever he wanted, or start in on his friends without even having a reason to. Would he be able to resist a second time?

And why was it so *tempting* to open it again right now?

It wasn't like he had a choice, anyway. He'd have to use it, because the only other option was sending his father away. And he couldn't do that, not even for a year, let alone *forever*.

Still, he hated how a part of him rejoiced that he'd get to feel the power again.

"We can't do whatever we're going to do out here," Rachel said finally, turning to Fort. "We'll need to go somewhere safe. Just in case things . . . get out of hand."

He nodded, trying not to think about how warm and comforting the Spirit magic had felt. "Cyrus did want us to come to him when we got the book," he said.

The others all looked at him in confusion. "Where *is* he, anyway?" Rachel asked.

"Oh, just some magical cottage in the woods with a weird old man that he keeps yelling at," Fort told her. "So nothing really new for today. Let's go."

- THIRTY-FIVE -

AS THEY TELEPORTED TO THE COT-
tage, Fort realized he hadn't really taken a close
look at it, given how Cyrus had been vague and
confusing at the time. Now that he was here with his other
friends, it was like seeing it for the first time.

The cottage itself looked like it was either hundreds of
years old, or built in the last few years; there was no way of
telling. The stone was so expertly laid in the walls that it felt
like the product of modern architecture, and yet, from the
ways the trees surrounded it, Fort couldn't imagine it hadn't
always been here.

A strange door knocker made of what looked to be iron
hung from the middle of the old wooden door. The knocker
was in the shape of a small imp, hanging upside down by its
tail, and honestly was a bit *too* lifelike for Fort's taste.

Still, Cyrus was waiting, and Fort wasn't going to waste any more time before getting answers from him. He reached out, lifted the door knocker, then yelped in pain as something stabbed his fingers. The knocker dropped back against the wood, hitting with a loud bang.

And then the door knocker itself groaned as well.

"Easy there, boy," the imp said, turning to look at him. "I'm not as young as I used to be."

"I've got this!" Rachel shouted, pushing her way past Fort before he could even object. Even with everything they'd just been through, she couldn't hide her excitement at the talking door knocker. "Hello, sir! Are you actually alive, or just magicked to be that way? Do we need to answer some kind of riddle to get past? Who cursed you to be like this?"

She put a hand up to touch it, but the imp bared its teeth at her, revealing what had stabbed Fort in his hand. "Polite people don't ask such personal questions!" the imp said. "And what makes you think I'm magic?"

"You're a talking door knocker," Rachel pointed out. "I'm not sure science has really gotten that far with believable artificial intelligence yet."

"Well, maybe it should think harder," the imp said, crossing its arms. "And frankly, I don't enjoy this attitude you all have going. Time was, prospectives would have the good courtesy to be *afraid* when I came alive. But you lot all seem practically jaded. What's the world even coming to?"

Prospectives? What did that mean?

Something clicked on the other side of the door, like a lock turning.

"Hey!" the imp shouted. "I haven't let them in yet."

"That's okay," said a familiar voice, and Cyrus opened the door with a smile. "I can vouch for them all."

"Cyrus!" Jia shouted, and leaped forward to hug the boy as the door knocker sighed dramatically. Rachel quickly followed, while the imp continued its complaints.

"Oh, so that's how we're doing things now?" the imp said from behind the opened door "Vouching for people? No care for security nowadays, is there? This is just sad, that's what this is."

"Are you sure you vouch for all of us?" Ellora asked, stepping into the doorway.

Cyrus smiled at her. "It's been too long, Ellora. I'm sorry I couldn't help get you all home before now."

"That's okay," she said. "It wasn't like you had a choice in the matter."

Cyrus looked uncomfortable at that, nodding and moving past her. "Nice to finally see you in person, Fort," he said, looking half-excited, half-unsure about where they stood. "I know we've spoken in time visions, but now that you're here . . . I owe you an apology. I just wanted to say, I'm so sorry for how we left things. I never should have told you not to go after your father. I should have realized that nothing would stop you, no matter what kind of warning I gave you."

With everything that had happened since the Dracsi dimension, Fort had almost forgotten about their argument. But it was still kind of touching that Cyrus seemed worried about it, and that he cared enough to apologize. "You were right," Fort said, shaking his head. "I should have listened to you. You knew what was coming, and I . . . I didn't want to hear it." He nodded up at the dome. "I know this is all my fault."

Cyrus shook his head too. "You just set things in motion. You're no more responsible for it happening than a piece of yarn is for the sweater it becomes."

Fort nodded, not understanding what *that* meant at all, but happy to put it behind him. "So we didn't really get a lot of time for questions when I was here last," he said as Cyrus waved him and Ellora inside. "What *is* this place?"

"Protection," Cyrus said as the door closed behind them all. "I happened upon it before I went to the Oppenheimer School and kept it secret just in case."

But Fort barely heard him, staring in wonder around the room. In the time visions, he almost couldn't believe the dining room was in the same cottage as before: From the outside, the cottage didn't even look big enough for *one* room this size.

But doors led off in different directions, now that he was inside. Not to mention that outside, the cottage was clearly just one floor, but inside, a wide staircase led up to another hall leading to more rooms, from what Fort could see.

How was this possible? It had to be magic, which made him even more curious about it. Who had built this place? The old man? And how?

"Where did this come from?" Jia asked, her eyes wide with amazement as well.

Cyrus just shrugged, gesturing for them to sit down. "It's not really important. Take a seat! The tea should be ready in a moment, and I've got food if you're hungry." He paused, his eyes unfocusing. "Which I see that you all are. Let me bring you something."

He clapped his hands, and plates filled with warm bread and

pastries floated out from a table next to the fire to land on a dining table in the middle of the room, while a kettle of tea began to pour itself into several cups.

"Magic plates? Tea that serves itself?" Rachel shouted, almost exploding with excitement. "I love this place!"

"Yeah, okay, but what kind of magic is this?" Jia said, staring at a plate with a chocolate pastry floating by her.

Cyrus wrinkled his nose. "It's actually not, to be honest."

Not magic? Fort reached for one of the steaming teacups floating by him and picked it out of the air. It came free of whatever was holding it without any difficulty, and he waited for it to start yelling at him like the door knocker, only the cup stayed silent, seemingly nothing more than a regular, normal teacup.

"Not magic?" Rachel said, putting her sword on the wooden table, where it clanked for some reason, not at all the sound he'd have expected from wood. "Explain, Future Boy."

Cyrus stared at the sword for a moment, his eyes wide. "That's . . . quite a sword, isn't it?"

Fort gave him a surprised look back. "You didn't see this coming? But your friend warned me—"

"No, I did," Cyrus said, his eyes still on the sword. "I just . . .

didn't realize it was so . . ." He seemed to snap out of it abruptly and smiled at them as he grabbed a floating cup of tea. "Right, the cottage. I can show you how it's all done, if you'd like, but it's much nicer all around if you just let it do its thing."

"*Show us,*" Rachel said, and she and Jia both leaned in toward him curiously, while Ellora sat down in a corner seat away from the others.

Cyrus sighed. "Oh, fine." He snapped his fingers in a quick pattern, then sat back and waited.

The wood on the table below them disappeared, revealing what looked like transparent plastic filled with various lights and projectors. The thatched roof above them turned into thick plastic sheeting, as did the floor, which had previously looked like it was made of stone.

The floating teacups now hovered along with some sort of glowing device on the bottoms. Whatever it was, it seemed to hold them in the air with no difficulty, but the technology to do such a thing was far beyond anything Fort had ever seen. Even the plates were pulled from the cupboards by what had been invisible robotic hands, and the food emerged from some sort of science-fiction-looking dispenser.

"It's all future tech," Cyrus said, sounding almost sad. "Isn't it kind of sad? The man who built this place went to a lot of trouble to make himself comfortable by using things he found in the future. But he didn't want anyone in his time to know where it came from, so he disguised it all to look like magic."

"Future technology?" Jia said, tapping one of the floating teacups.

"*Who* built this place, Cyrus?" Rachel asked, grabbing her sword again. "I think we're going to need a name."

Cyrus winced. "He went by a lot of names, but the one you'd know best would be—"

"*Merlin,*" said a voice as the old man stepped out from one of the doorways, raising his arms majestically but dropping them as a confused look passed over his face. "At least, I *imagine* that's how you know me. It's always so hard to remember what year I'm in."

- THIRTY-SIX -

ORT STARED IN CONFUSION AS RACHEL leaped to her feet in excitement. He couldn't have just heard right. Had the old man really said his name was Merlin? It couldn't be the *actual* Merlin . . . could it?

Granted, they'd just found out King Arthur was real, and Rachel had Excalibur sitting on the table next to her. Could this really be the magician who'd raised Arthur? Or at least *one* of the Arthurs?

"You're not *serious*!" Rachel shouted at the man, getting up close as if she couldn't believe he was real. "Are you really him?" She began to run in place nervously, waving her hands as if she was meeting her favorite celebrity. "Am I dreaming? I'm just imagining this, right? Tell me I'm right!"

But as if in answer, the old man's image seemed to glitch out for a moment, turning bright blue, before reappearing solidly before them again. He smiled as he returned. "Ah, child. Who's to say what's real and what isn't?"

"*I* am, actually," Cyrus said to the man, sounding annoyed as Rachel just stared in shock. "And you're *not* real, not here." He turned to the others, blushing a bit. "I'm sorry about this. I tried to turn off his hologram before you got here, but somehow he keeps coming back to life."

"Life finds a way," the hologram of Merlin said, moving to stand at the head of the table. With the fire from the kitchen behind him, they could now see the flames through his transparent body.

This made Fort even more confused. The old man wasn't actually here? Was he a part of the high-tech cottage too somehow?

As Fort stared, he realized the old man was looking right back. "Is something wrong, young man?"

"Oh, ah, no, sorry," Fort said quickly. "I didn't mean to be rude."

"I should hope not," Merlin said. "Rudeness deserves our full attention, so only attempt it when you are sure you mean to be."

Cyrus sighed loudly. "I'll go try to turn him off again." He stood up and left for the other room, and they heard him start kicking something over and over.

Meanwhile, Rachel looked devastated at the reveal of the hologram. "So what, are you some kind of program?" she asked. "You're not the real Merlin."

"Why, of course I am, young lady," Merlin said. "This isn't a recording. I'm speaking to you from the distant past, using technology from the far future. Why let time get in the way of a good conversation, I always say!" He laughed at his own joke, but Fort didn't really get it.

"Except I keep turning off the communicator, and he still won't go away!" Cyrus yelled from the other room.

"Ignore that cranky fellow," Merlin said, sitting down at the table with them. "Now, I see we've got the Avalonian sword." He smiled at Rachel. "A female Artorigios? About time. So you're on the hunt for Emrys, the Old One of Time, eh?"

Fort's eyes widened. How did *he* know that?

"Oh, Forsythe, you'd be surprised by how little I don't know," Merlin said, seeing what Fort was about to ask before he asked it, just like Cyrus and Ellora had done. The old man turned back to Rachel. "Besides, I didn't need magic to know this. I've trained *every* Artorigios to face Emrys, so now it appears to be *your* turn, Rachel."

"I'm going to be your *apprentice*?" Rachel said, then began making a sound like a teakettle going off.

"Do you know where the Old One is?" Fort asked when she didn't seem capable of speaking any further.

"Obviously," Merlin said with a wink. "But only those who are prepared to face him will get that from me." He looked at Jia. "You, my child, have a different goal, don't you?"

Jia looked at him strangely. "I'm not really clear who you are, honestly."

"No one important," he told her. "But what I can do is help you with your own magic. I can teach you how to merge disciplines and create your own spells without the use of books. And that—"

She gasped. "That would mean no one would have to go to war over the books of magic. There'd be no need!"

Merlin smiled slightly. "One would hope. Besides, I know about your deal, and I'd prefer you were ready for it."

Jia went pale as Merlin moved on. What deal was that? Had she taken the faerie queen up on something too?

But Merlin had turned to Fort, keeping him from any further

wondering. "And as for you, my boy . . . well, there's nothing I can do for you, unfortunately."

Fort blinked, not especially surprised, but still a little hurt. "That's, um, okay. I didn't need anything."

"I didn't say that," Merlin told him. "But what you'll need isn't something I can teach you myself. Still, I might be able to provide some guidance. Come back here when your dragon problems get worse, and I'll see what I can do."

Dragon problems? But Damian was under his Spirit magic. What future problems was Fort going to have with him?

"You're not going to be around to do any of this!" Cyrus shouted from the other room. "I'm going to figure out how to turn this thing off, and that'll be the last any of us have to hear from you, old man!"

As strange—*very* strange—as all of this was, Fort actually felt most surprised by how annoyed Cyrus was acting. He'd never really seen his friend so irritated, or even anything besides laid-back. What was it about Merlin that was putting Cyrus in such a bad mood?

"You know, you once told me that King Arthur wasn't real," Fort shouted to Cyrus in the other room.

Merlin snorted.

"He's not," Cyrus said, coming back in, glaring at the hologram. "Not the version you know from stories, at least." He flopped into his chair, looking frustrated. "I don't think the communicator that's running him even has power. I *hate* this future tech."

"You say that now," Merlin said. "But wait until you're my age. It's just the thing for these old bones, getting waited on hand and foot."

Cyrus dropped his head into his hands. "Isn't it time you left, Merlin? We have some things to take care of here."

Merlin's eyes seemed to go unfocused for a moment. "Ah, of course!" he said, turning to Fort. "The future war over the books of magic, right. I remember now." He lowered his spectacles to take a better look at the book of Spirit magic in front of Fort. "Dangerous magic, that. The Pendragon so feared the book that he insisted it be returned to Avalon with him when he passed. He didn't trust even his most loyal men to have its power. Are you sure you're up for it?"

Fort glanced at Rachel, but she still had her eyes locked on Merlin.

"I hope so, sir," Fort said to the old wizard. "If you have another way to stop the war from happening, though, I'd love to hear it."

Merlin sighed. "It's either that or your father, I'm afraid. Your friend Ellora isn't wrong about that." Ellora sat up straighter in the corner, a slightly vindicated expression coming over her face. "But choose wisely between the two, as both actions lead to futures you won't necessarily like."

The playfulness of the past few minutes crashed to a halt with that, and Fort nodded silently, his hands resting on the book. With all the strangeness of Merlin's cottage, he'd almost let himself forget what would happen if he didn't fix things using Spirit magic. "I've made my choice, sir."

"Then I hope it works out for you," Merlin said, then stood up. "Now, children, I expect to see you all back here when the current crisis is finished. We'll have quite a bit of training to do, Jia and Rachel, and even you, Forsythe, will have some tasks if we're going to get you into shape for the storm that's to come."

"Don't tell them anything else!" Cyrus shouted, standing up as well and jabbing a finger right through the hologram's chest. "They can't know or they'll mess it all up!"

"Oh, my boy," Merlin said, giving Cyrus a mysterious look. "You of all of them should learn to behave yourself. We both know you've got a lot to learn."

"That's none of your business, old man," Cyrus said, giving Merlin a death look.

The old wizard just laughed. "Well, don't do anything *I* wouldn't do, my boy." With that, he began to fade in and out. "And now, the boy's right. I *should* let you get back to things. You'll have some hard times ahead of you, but I have faith that you'll all come out okay." He threw a look at Cyrus. "Well, most of you."

Cyrus sighed loudly. "Just go, *please*?"

Merlin winked at him, then disappeared in one last glitch.

For a moment, they all were silent, probably thinking about the old man's words as Fort was. Rachel and Jia were going to be trained by Merlin, Rachel to fight an Old One, and Jia to learn magic without spell books? And Merlin even wanted Fort to return, after this was all over? What did it all mean?

"It all means that we've wasted *way* too much time on him," Cyrus said to Fort. "William and the others won't be able to keep the dome up for more than another twenty minutes or so, and once the dome goes down, there's going to be a lot of very angry soldiers coming after everyone. So can we *please* get back to saving the world now?"

- THIRTY-SEVEN -

CYRUS HAD A POINT: SINCE STOPPING Damian hadn't changed the fact that the world would go to war using magic they acquired from studying Fort's father, they couldn't worry about anything else right now. After they'd fixed things, they could think about Merlin and the Old One of Time.

"What exactly do I need to do to make sure the war never happens?" Fort asked Ellora. "Who do I need to use Spirit magic on to fix things for good?"

"Lots of people, unfortunately," she said, and began ticking them off on her fingers. "The TDA leadership. Your president. Our prime minister. China's president. Japan's president. Brazil's president. The president of the EU." She paused to take a breath, but Fort put up his hands in surrender.

"That's a good start," he said, wincing slightly. Even with just that list, this was going to take a while, no matter how fast he teleported around. After all, he'd need to break into some of the most highly secure places in the world.

And that wasn't taking into account how much Spirit magic he'd have to cast. The magic had nearly taken over his mind after one spell on Damian. Who knew how hard it'd be to resist after using it on dozens of world leaders?

But if it came down to resisting versus losing his father, he'd find a way to be strong enough.

"Cyrus, I know Ellora said there was no other way, but just to be sure, you don't know of anything else we can do either?" Rachel asked, her excitement from meeting Merlin now having faded before the coming use of Spirit magic. "I *really* don't want to do it this way."

"Ellora's right," Cyrus said, shaking his head. "It's either this, or remove Fort's father." He gave Fort a pitying look, and Fort had to turn to the floor to hold himself together.

"Is there any way to keep Spirit magic from affecting Fort when he uses it?" Jia asked. "I think that's what Rachel's most afraid of."

"That, and destroying people's free will," Rachel said quietly.

"From what I've seen, Spirit magic has that effect on any

human who uses it," Cyrus said. "Other beings, creatures more resistant to magic in the first place, can use it more easily."

"Like dragons?" Rachel said, wincing. "Not that I'm suggesting we give it to Damian. That would unleash a *whole* lot of trouble."

"Damian should be able to use it without giving in to it, yes," Cyrus said.

An image of Damian burning down Buckingham Palace, then destroying London in the form of a giant monster made of Spirit magic flashed through Fort's head, and he sighed. "Not from what we've seen. Maybe it'd be easier for me if I knew what was coming, so I could brace for it. Is there any way to see ahead?"

He looked over at Ellora, who shrugged. "It's involving the book, so it's too foggy for me to see. Cyrus?"

He tilted his head thoughtfully. "If you add your magic to mine, I might be able to break through the chaos." He sighed. "Guess there's only one way to find out."

The first Spirit spell went easily enough. Fort teleported back to the Oppenheimer School with Ellora, then waited while Ellora froze Colonel Charles, Agent Cole, and even Dr. Ambrose.

When she was done, he used Create Devotion in a Living Creature on all three, relearning the spell between each one.

"You will never give magic to adults," Fort commanded them, and they all nodded, eager to follow his orders. "And if any other country wants their book of magic back, you will give it to them!"

Colonel Charles seemed to struggle with this last bit, his face contorting at the very idea, but eventually he fought through it and smiled, promising he'd do as Fort said.

"And even more importantly," Fort continued, "you're to give my father all the best care he could possibly get, and *never* threaten to expel me or my friends, or take any of our memories away ever again."

Again they made their promises, and Fort let out a huge breath. "So far so good," he told Ellora. "I mean, I'm really tempted to make Colonel Charles beg me for forgiveness, but I'm able to resist it, so that's a good sign. Who's next?"

Over the next half hour, they made their way down her list, stopping to look up any presidential house or office they needed pictures of, so that Fort could teleport them in and out. It turned out to be a whirlwind tour of the most powerful places on earth, from Zhongnanhai in China's Imperial City to Strasbourg, France, and the president of the European Parliament's office in the Louise Weiss building, to Buckingham Palace and 10 Downing Street in London.

The final stop was the Oval Office, which Fort didn't need a photo reference for (not to mention he'd accidentally teleported inside it when he was first learning Space magic). After using his magic on everyone present, including the president, vice president, and the joint chiefs, Fort sent them all out of the room, first asking the president to grab him a soda while he sat down behind the desk to see how it felt.

"What are you doing?" Ellora asked him, looking worried.

"Just resting," Fort said, smiling widely as he put his feet up. "That was a *lot* of magic in a short time. Did we get everyone?"

"I think so." Her eyes went black, and she slowly began to smile. "*Yes*, we did it, Forsythe! I can't see any war in the future, not anymore! We actually stopped it from happening!" She began to shake slightly and rubbed her arm over her eyes. "I can't believe it, after all this time—"

Fort nodded slowly, glancing at some of the paperwork on the president's desk. "Yeah, it's pretty great, I guess."

This seemed to take her aback. "What do you mean, you guess? We saved the world!"

"From the war, maybe," Fort said as the president brought him his drink. "Oh, thanks, Mr. President. Can I get some snacks, too? Popcorn maybe?"

"Of course, sir!" the president said, and quickly left the room.

"Wasn't that the whole reason we did this, to stop the war?" Ellora asked.

"Yeah, but I'm starting to wonder if you and William didn't have a point," Fort said. "I mean, what are we doing here? I've got the magic to completely change the world, make everyone care about each other, end violence, that kind of thing. Isn't it almost worse to *not* do it, if I have the power?"

Ellora seemed even more unsure now. "But before, you were against that. I think the magic might be changing you."

"Maybe it is, maybe it isn't," Fort said with a shrug. "But am I wrong? I could make it so no one ever goes hungry again. I could make sure all the homeless have shelter, everyone has a job, no one hurts anyone else. Maybe the magic's just opened my eyes, you know?"

Ellora slowly nodded. "I wanted to use it for that from the start, but I still don't like this. This is why you wanted Rachel to watch over you, to make sure the magic didn't affect you."

"Eh, she'll never know," Fort said. "Not unless it works. And then she'll be too happy to care."

"I don't think she will be," Ellora said. "Listen, I think we should go back to the cottage and talk this through. Just so we're sure *you're* sure."

Fort smiled. "We'll just start small. That way we'll know if it works, and *then* we can talk it through. Deal?"

His hands glowed orange for the slightest of moments, as did Ellora's head. And then the light disappeared, and she matched his smile. "Okay, fine, deal," she said. "I'm not even sure why I'm arguing with you."

Fort nodded. "Me either."

The first thing they did was have the president order all nuclear warheads to be disarmed, just to see how it went. A few military generals tried to argue, but Fort used his magic on them as well, and it was smooth sailing after that.

When that worked so well, they teleported to Moscow and ordered the same of the president of Russia and his military. "And make sure never to attack anyone again!" Fort shouted as they teleported away.

"This wasn't exactly starting small," Ellora told him. "Not that I'm complaining!"

"Well, it was working, so I figured, why hold back?" he said. "I bet Rachel feels completely differently about all of this when she sees what we accomplished. What's next?"

The next few hours became a blur, teleporting from corporations to dangerous dictatorships, doing whatever they could as quickly as possible. Soon, they'd set up regular shipments of food to poverty-stricken countries, freed the people from some of the most dangerous leaders in the world, and even made sure hungry kids had free school lunches back in the U.S.

"Maybe we should head back to the cottage, just so they don't worry about us?" Ellora said as they lay on top of George Washington's head on Mount Rushmore, resting between visits. "They're *definitely* going to be wondering where we are by now."

"Oh, it'll be fine," Fort said, and his hands glowed orange again. "Honestly, I don't want to hear it from Rachel if we go back now."

Ellora laughed. "Right? She's such a rule follower. Lighten up, Rachel!"

"Maybe she'd have a point," Fort said, looking at his fingernails. "Do *you* think I'm losing control here, Ellora?"

She snorted. "Of course not! You're completely in control.

If you want to stay out here forever, fixing the world, I'm with you!"

He touched his chest with his palm. "Aw, thank you! That means a lot. But maybe we *should* go back and bring Rachel, Jia, and Cyrus in on this. Feels mean to leave them out, huh?"

"But what if they don't think it's a good idea?" Ellora asked.

"Then I'll *make* them, " Fort said, his hands glowing orange. He grinned again, then opened a portal back to the cottage. "And anyone else who tries to take this power away from me. After all, I'm the one saving the world. They should all be *bowing* before me!"

A few feet away, a translucent Fort dropped to his knees, feeling like he was going to puke. "This is what I become?" he whispered to an equally translucent Cyrus, who stood next to him, watching the future Fort and Ellora teleport back to Merlin's cottage. "Rachel was right—I *can't* handle the magic! Either it completely changed who I am, or this was somehow . . . inside of me all along." He dry-heaved at the thought. "But whoever this is? It's *not* me. It can't be!"

- THIRTY-EIGHT -

SPIRIT MAGIC IS THE MOST POWERFUL of all the types, in some ways," Cyrus said quietly, tired after fighting against the fog of the book of Spirit magic. "And it has a greater hold on the wielder than any other kind, by its nature. Humanity just can't control it, Fort. No one has been able to. Even King Arthur fell victim to its charms eventually. But that doesn't mean you still couldn't use it to stop the war—"

"I don't *want* to use it!" Fort shouted. "I thought that I'd be able to stop before, but look at what that version of me just did! Look at what *I* did! How do you know I'd stop *this* time, when I didn't here?" He gestured at the spot where his future self had stood.

"Because now you know what's coming, like you said back in the cottage," Cyrus said. "So you can prepare yourself."

"Can I?" Fort shouted. "Future me just used Spirit magic on a *friend*, and was about to use it on three more, including one who hated the very idea of it, not to mention *you*. What kind of monster does that?" He gritted his teeth, not able to wipe the memory of Ellora agreeing with everything he said out of his mind. "I know I wanted to do good, and I still think all those things would help the world. But right now, it just all feels so wrong, so disgusting!"

"You stopped a war and saved countless lives, Fort," Cyrus said. "No matter what you did, *that* was a good thing—"

"But to do it, I took away people's free will!" Fort shouted. "I put them through the same thing Rachel went through with the Old Ones. Did you see their faces, how they all looked at me?" He thought back to Damian bowing to him and how he'd liked it at first. "How far do I go, Cyrus? What comes next? You can see it, can't you? *Tell me.*"

Cyrus looked away. "You don't want to know."

"No, but I *need* to," he whispered. "Show me. Please, Cyrus. *Please.*"

Cyrus sighed, and Mount Rushmore changed to what looked like a throne room, one covered in red wallpaper and velvet curtains. Buckingham Palace, the same spot Damian had burned down in another future vision.

And there, in one throne at the end of the room, an older Fort sat with a crown on his head looking incredibly lonely. Chad, Bryce, and Sebastian all stood by his side, but clearly under his Spirit magic from their expressions.

As for the rest of his friends, they were nowhere to be found, Spirited or otherwise.

"You take over, Fort," Cyrus said at his side, as Fort just stared in horror. "You've got good intentions, but too many people try to stop you, and you can't resist the magic. So you take over *everything*. You name yourself king and eventually turn on everyone, friends and enemies alike, until it's just you alone."

"This can't be real," Fort said, staring at himself with the worst disgust he'd ever felt.

"It is," Cyrus said sadly. "You protect all the people of the world, but only by making them follow your every order."

Another wave of bile hit Fort, and he almost threw up. Whoever this version of him was, he couldn't let him come to pass. He couldn't allow *any* of this to happen!

But if he didn't use the magic, that left only one other way that they knew of to stop the war: sending his father out of time. And he couldn't do that, either.

As of right now, though, he couldn't stand to watch his future self as king, not for one second longer. "I can't look at this anymore," he whispered. "Take us back."

Cyrus immediately reversed time back to Mount Rushmore, and as the awful scene disappeared, Fort balled his fists and tried to slam them into the ground, only for his hands to pass through it. Why did this have to be so *difficult*? Two impossible choices: one that left the world completely under the control of magic, the other taking his father away from him forever. Why did it all have to be on him? Was it so wrong to want his father back?

But no, he had to save the world from a war that was his fault, in a lot of ways. And to do that meant either losing his father or becoming someone awful, almost less than human.

What good would it do to keep his father around if his dad had to see him like that, adored by the most powerful people in the world not because he'd earned their respect, but because he'd forced them to? Alone, friendless, and ruling a world that didn't have any choice in the matter?

You'd never do that, Forsythe, he heard his father say in his head. *You're not that person.*

No, he wasn't. Not until he used the Spirit magic.

And if Fort had any choice in the matter, he never would be that person.

"So what will you do?" Cyrus asked him finally.

Fort slowly pushed to his feet, not looking at his friend. "I've seen enough. Take us back to the present. I can't do this. I don't know *what* I'll do, but I can't use Spirit magic." He choked a bit, then swallowed hard.

Cyrus nodded and closed his eyes. And then they immediately flew back open.

"I can't get us back," he said, his voice on the edge of panic. "Something's stopping me."

The fear in Cyrus's tone cut through Fort's depression enough to catch his attention. "What? What could be stopping you?"

Cyrus gave him a wide-eyed look full of terror. "I think someone froze our bodies in time."

"Indeed, my friends," said another voice, and a third person appeared, just as translucent as they were.

They turned to find a familiar-looking boy in a black hoodie with the same color hair as Cyrus.

"Someone did, in fact, freeze you," William said with a smile. "Perhaps it is time we engaged in a quick conversation?"

THIRTY-NINE

WILLIAM?" FORT SAID, NOT BELIEV-
ing his eyes. "What are you *doing* here?"

"Not much fun, is it?" William said, los-
ing his fantasy language as he glanced around. "You know,
being stuck in time, having no way to get home." His face
grew darker as he turned back to them. "I spent years like
this, you know. *Years.* All because our teachers, our government, wanted power."

"William, unfreeze our bodies," Cyrus said, his eyes glowing
black, and his tone more dangerous than Fort had ever heard it.
"You know what I can do, even from here. Do you really want
to challenge me?"

Fort glanced at his friend, and a chill went down his spine.
While the boy next to him still looked exactly like Cyrus,
the expression on his face wasn't one Fort had ever seen, not

between all the smiles and confused looks Cyrus normally favored. This was a deadly serious Cyrus, and for some reason, he almost made Fort more nervous than William did.

"Oh, I would never face you in direct combat, my old friend," William said, smiling.

And then his hands began to glow with an orange light.

"No!" Fort shouted, leaping at the boy, knowing he had to stop him somehow. But here in the future, he plowed right through the insubstantial Carmarthen student, not even touching him.

"Ah!" William said, looking behind him for a moment. "While that was *very* impressive, it was, I might add, a bit too late, for it is already done."

Fort quickly pushed to his feet but felt horror rush through him as he found himself staring at Cyrus, awash in orange light, giving William an absolutely adoring look.

"William!" Cyrus said, his face now just ecstatic. "I'm so glad you're here. How can I help you?"

"Oh, now you want to help me?" William said, again speaking normally as his anger grew. Fort slowly moved back to stand next to Cyrus as William glared at his friend. "You mean, like you didn't help any of us back at school? How you decided to go to the American school instead, leaving us all at the mercy of our teachers?"

Cyrus's joyous mood disappeared, and he fell to his knees, clasping his hands in front of him. "Please forgive me, William," he pleaded, sounding completely dejected. "I cannot begin to apologize enough for what I did!"

William stared down at him for a moment. *"Try."*

"I'm so, so sorry!" Cyrus said, tears now falling down his cheeks as Fort turned to William, feeling hatred for the boy for the first time. Yes, he knew how Spirit magic could change you, make you want to do things exactly like this: He'd felt that way when using it on Damian. But that didn't make it okay. That didn't excuse it in any way.

"William, stop this," he said, having no idea what he'd do if the other boy refused.

"I don't think so, Forsythe," William said, watching Cyrus with a grin as Fort's friend babbled on, apologizing in every way he could think of. "Imagine how *you'd* feel if Cyrus had abandoned you to a life like this, with no idea if you'd ever get home."

"I'm unworthy of your forgiveness!" Cyrus wailed, his head now on the ground as he tore at his hair. "I only wanted to fix the future, to see them once more, but that's no excuse! I never should have left you all. You're right to hate me. *I* hate me!"

"William, *please*!" Fort shouted. "This isn't right! It's the magic that's making you do it." He paused, realizing something. "How do you even have the book of Spirit magic? Why did you freeze us?"

William sighed and snapped his fingers. Instantly Cyrus went silent, looking up at William for further instructions, but William ignored him, addressing Fort instead. "It's because of you, Fitzgerald. I *had* to do this. Did you think I wouldn't see this coming? See that you would *fail* to save the world, when you had every chance of doing so? Stopping the world from going to war, that's great . . . but you had the chance to fix *everything*, and you didn't take it!"

Fort just stared at the other boy in shock. "I saw what it'd turn me into, what I'd do to everyone!" he shouted. "If you're here, you must have seen it too, at least part of it. I would have taken over the world, declared myself king!"

"Yes!" William shouted. "Exactly! You would have ruled, just like King Arthur had to, to make sure that there was peace! Do you think the people in charge now feel bad if they force people to do what they say? That's all they do, Forsythe!

Your colonel, my teachers, both our governments . . . they all tell people what to do, and force them to do it if the people refuse. How is that any different?"

"Because I'd have taken away their choice!" Fort shouted. "It's not *right*, William!"

"Maybe not," William hissed. "But it's necessary."

"What are you going to do?" Fort asked, dreading the answer that he knew was coming.

"Oh, I believe I will answer the call and save the world of my birth," William said with a smile. "But first, perhaps a taste of *revenge*." He turned back to Cyrus, and this time, Fort fought the urge to leap at William, fight him off Cyrus somehow, since he knew he'd pass right through the other boy.

"Don't do this," Fort whispered. "Please, William. He's my friend."

"He was mine once too," William growled, his eyes on Cyrus. "Maybe I'm doing you a favor. This way, he can't betray you like he did me."

And with that, he leaned down to Cyrus's level.

"Would you like me to keep apologizing, William?" Cyrus asked, and he sounded so hopeful that it broke Fort's heart.

"No, that's okay, Cyrus," William said. "Actually, I'm going to unfreeze your body, okay? And when I do, I want you to use your magic to send yourself somewhere . . . sorry, some*when* in time. Don't tell anyone, and make it a long way from the present, okay?"

"No!" Fort shouted, but both William and Cyrus ignored him.

"Of course, William!" Cyrus said, eager to please. "When should I come back?"

"Actually, stay there," William said quietly. "And don't come back until I send someone for you. Do you understand me? Send yourself to some random, distant time, and don't return until you hear from me."

"Got it!" Cyrus said, as William's hands glowed black.

"Cyrus!" Fort shouted, and his friend looked up at him in confusion, as if he'd forgotten Fort was even there.

"Fort?" Cyrus said as he faded out. "I have to go. I'll see you in—"

And then he was gone.

"There!" William said, his eyes covered in black light. "The evil are vanquished, and the good have won the day once more. With the threat of Cyrus now diminished, and all of your friends under my Spirit magic spell, I believe no one remains to stand against me." He paused. "I also put Ellora under. I knew she wouldn't go along with it, once we got to this point." He cleared his throat and resumed his narration. "Now, forsooth, Forsythe! Let us travel back to the present, as the world won't save itself!"

- FORTY -

MOUNT RUSHMORE FADED OUT, replaced by the clearing where Merlin's cottage stood. Or used to stand.

Now all that was left of it was ashes, some large pieces of melted plastic, and the occasional metal beam. It'd been utterly destroyed, apparently by fire. And before Fort could even comprehend that, he found the culprit.

"Welcome back, Fitzgerald," Damian said, his voice low and threatening even in his human form. "Like what I've done to the place? Consider it payback for putting me under that Spirit magic."

"Now, now, Damian," William said. "We're all friends here, aren't we?" He turned to gesture to where Ellora, Jia, and Rachel all waited silently, not moving, right next to the other Carmarthen Academy students. Fort recognized Simon,

341

as well as a few others from the video. "Or we will be, once I use my magic on Forsythe. Don't we all share the common goal of saving the world?"

"Yes, Your Majesty!" they all shouted in unison, gazing at him adoringly, even Damian.

Fort inwardly screamed, not able to understand how this had happened, and so quickly. How could William have gotten to the book of Spirit magic and used it on everyone? How much time had even passed?

Granted, he'd been frozen in time, so no matter how much later he'd arrived back in his body, he wouldn't have noticed. But Cyrus had said William could only keep the dome going for another twenty minutes or so. They couldn't have—

And then he noticed how light it was and looked up. The dome was gone, replaced by a gray, cloudy sky.

"Thanks for sending me Damian, by the way," William said, patting the dragon boy on the shoulder. "And especially for telling him to do whatever I said. That made things so much easier, since his teleportation spell got us here instantly, and then he kept all your friends busy while I had a chance to study the book of Spirit magic in sped-up time." He smiled at Fort. "Anything to say before I use it on you, Forsythe?"

"Don't *do* this," Fort said, knowing it was useless. If he'd spent that long with Spirit magic, he had to be completely taken over by it now. "Please, William! The magic changes you; I felt it myself. You have to give it up. We'll destroy the book and figure out another way to stop the war."

"Really?" William said, looking annoyed. "That's what you're going with? I thought you'd try to kiss up more, honestly. But if you're not even going to try, I'm going to have to use magic on you. You know, just to be safe." He winked, since they both knew he'd have used it no matter what.

Fort gritted his teeth and opened a teleportation portal as fast as he could, but it was still too slow: The Spirit spell hit him before he could move, his head filling with orange light. And suddenly he had no idea where he was going.

Why would he *ever* want to leave the presence of William?

"Ah, now I see you're within your right mind, my friend!" William said. "You may address me as Your Majesty, of course, since a ruler must be respected by his followers."

"I respect you *so much*, Your Majesty!" Fort shouted, bowing low before the magnificence in front of him. "You're like the sun shining on a rainy morning, brightening my day just with your presence, and—"

"Oh, stop that," William said, glaring at him, and Fort straightened up quickly, completely embarrassed. But then the other boy grinned, so he let out a sigh of relief, just thankful not to have displeased his king. After all, more than anything, Fort just wanted to bring William happiness.

"How may I serve you, Your Majesty?" he asked.

"Well, we don't really have the time to waste, but personally, I'd like a great, big apology from you, Forsythe, for doubting me when I said we should use Spirit magic to fix the world," William said, smiling smugly. "I already got one from your friends, obviously."

"Again, we can't tell you enough how wrong we were," Rachel said, looking distraught.

"So, *so* wrong, Your Majesty," Jia added, just as upset.

"I cannot even begin to tell you how mistaken I was," Fort said, dropping to his knees to stare at the ground, humiliated. "I offer no end of apologies, Your Majesty. Is there any way you might grant me your forgiveness?"

William considered for a moment, then leaned in and whispered in Fort's ear. Fort immediately nodded, then turned to his friends. "I wet the bed until I was eleven!" he declared proudly. "Our Majesty told me I should say that to you all!"

"I didn't tell you to say that last part!" William said, groaning. "Eh, forget it, we can go into more humiliation later. For now, we have things to do. Oppenheimer students, *kneel before me*."

They quickly did, while Damian and Ellora looked on jealously. "Rachel, present me your fine weapon, would you?" William said. "A ruler deserves a king's sword, after all. And there's no finer one than the sword of King Arthur. Perhaps seeing it in my possession will convince our people that I am the good king returned, here to save Britannia in its darkest hour!"

She held out Excalibur with a big smile on her face. "It's all yours, Your Majesty!"

He gave her a patronizing look, then grasped the handle.

The sword immediately lit on fire.

"HEY, OW!" William shouted, dropping the sword and clutching his charred hand. "What was that? What did you *do* to it?"

"Your Majesty, I'm so confused!" Rachel said, leaning over to grab the sword from the ground as Jia hurriedly healed William's hand. "We were told that only the worthy could hold it, but who could possibly be more worthy than *you*?"

Fort frowned, almost thinking he'd detected just a hint of sarcasm in her voice, but glancing over, he found Rachel staring at William in awe, so he must have been mistaken.

William, though, didn't seem pleased, and his displeasure made Fort more upset than anything he'd ever felt, even worse than when he'd lost his father. "Must be broken then," William said, glaring at Excalibur. "I'll have to find another sword. The government dug up a bunch of them, so there should be plenty to choose from. You take it, Rachel, and knight the three of you in my name."

Rachel nodded. "Of course, Your Majesty." She tapped the sword to both of her shoulders, then moved to stand in front of Jia, giving the other girl a long look. "I knight you Sir Jia," Rachel said, gently laying the sword on Jia's shoulders one at a time, lingering with it on each one.

Jia's eyes widened, and she slowly nodded at Rachel.

Then the Destruction girl moved to stand before Fort. "And you, New Kid, I knight Sir Fort," she said, giving him another very loaded look.

"Can we hurry this up?" William asked. "Now that the dome's down, things are going to move quickly."

"Of course, Your Majesty," Rachel said, and tapped the sword to Fort's shoulders in turn.

As soon as the blade touched him, his mind cleared instantly, like the sun had burned off the fog in his brain.

FORTY-ONE

THE SPIRIT MAGIC WAS GONE, AND Fort found that instead of worshipping William, all he wanted to do was punch the other boy in the stomach. What had happened? He looked up at Rachel in shock, and she almost imperceptibly shook her head, trying to tell him something.

That was what it was like being under Spirit magic? He'd felt it a bit, back in the Dracsi dimension, but then he'd been prepared, and the Old Ones had been more concerned with their sibling at the time, not Fort. Now it just felt like such a *violation*. He'd lost all control over himself, including his feelings. To think that he'd ever been more upset about William than his own father!

His hands began to shake as anger filled him, but an intense look from Rachel made him realize he had to calm down. He could see from her gaze that she felt exactly the same way, but she was pretending to be under the magic to keep William ignorant of the fact that they were free. He'd have to follow her lead.

But how had she kept her own mind against his spell? He watched as she returned Excalibur to her side and realized it had to be the sword. After all, William's spell had been canceled at its touch, and the queen of the faeries *had* mentioned something about Excalibur protecting her from magic. So, holding Excalibur, she probably hadn't been under William's spell at all and had been acting this whole time.

That meant she had a plan. And if it involved Fort not teleporting William into the sun just yet, then he'd hold off, at least for now. But still, they'd need help. With Ellora and the other Time students there, not to mention Damian, they were *vastly* outnumbered, not to mention underpowered. So Rachel using surprise did seem like the smartest plan.

If they could just get the book of Spirit magic away from William and use a spell on *him* . . .

"Are we *finally* ready?" the self-proclaimed king asked, and Rachel turned to him and bowed low.

"We're your loyal knights now, devoted in every way to Your

Majesty," she said, holding her sword's hilt out to him. "You have my sword now, and forever—"

"Yeah, keep that thing away from me," William told her, then pointed at Fort. "You, teleport us to the throne room of Buckingham Palace. I'm going to use Spirit magic on the royals to start, then move on to Parliament and the military. You don't need a photo, right?"

Not to teleport you to Jupiter, no. "No, Your Majesty," Fort said, trying to fake the adoring gaze he'd just been giving William. "I saw Buckingham Palace in the future, when Damian destroyed it."

At least *that* wouldn't be happening, not with William in control.

"Well?" William said, waving at him to hurry.

Fort hid his anger as best he could and quickly opened a portal to Buckingham Palace, then bowed to William, letting the "king" go first.

William leaped through the portal with a grin, Damian right behind him. They heard shouting, some scuffling, even Damian roaring before everything went quiet. Fort threw Rachel a look, but she just shook her head slightly, saying it wasn't yet time. He frowned but hoped she knew what she was doing. If nothing else, she could try to free Ellora, as it'd be nice to have at least one Time-magic user on their side—

And then William peeked his head back through the portal, almost scaring Fort out of his skin. "The royal court has been assembled!" the fake king said with a smile. "Come, join us, my friends!"

The rest of them, including William's fellow students, followed him into the portal, having no idea what to expect. At least it wouldn't be on fire, if nothing else.

On the other side of the teleportation circle, they found themselves in the same long, luxuriously decorated room that Fort had seen in Ellora's future vision. Beautiful red tapestries and elaborate wallpaper ran the length of the room, culminating in some velvety red curtains behind two red-and-gold thrones.

Various guards and officials lined the hall, all on their knees, while a man and a woman in formal clothing, each wearing elaborate sashes covered in medals, stood next to the thrones, bowing low. William led the group of magic users slowly toward the end of the hall, waving and nodding in greeting to everyone he'd used his magic upon.

Finally, he reached the thrones and turned to face them all

before sliding slowly into the seat, as if he was lowering himself into a hot tub. "Ah, that's the stuff," he said as he made himself comfortable. "You know, I always wondered if I was related to one of the Arthurs. I probably am, wouldn't you say?"

The assembled gathering all agreed loudly, with a few yelling, "Long live the king!"

"Yes, I *would* like to long live," William said, then beckoned to Damian. "Dragon, now that I'm sitting on my seat of power here, I'm finding myself less interested in getting back up again. How about instead of traveling to the various ministries and Parliament and such, you just teleport them all here one by one? Much more efficient that way. But let's get it moving; I don't want anyone panicking and ordering a missile strike just yet."

"Of course, Your Majesty," Damian said, then opened a portal and disappeared through it. A moment later, he returned holding a woman up by her suit coat and presented her to William.

"Prime Minister," William said, his hands glowing with orange light. "So nice to finally meet you in person. How much did you know about what your government did to us at the Carmarthen Academy?"

"Everything, Your Majesty," she said as the light filled her head. She tried to bow but couldn't as Damian hadn't yet put her down. "I cannot begin to express how *awful* I feel about that. What can I do to make it up to you?"

"I'd think giving a speech to the public revealing everything would be a good start," William said. "I'll need you to inform my new subjects around the world that I, the future king of the world, have come to fix everyone's problems. They should lap that up." He paused for a second, considering. "And after that, you should make a list of the most humiliating things you can think of, then just start working your way through them. You know, still on television. That should be a good way to start earning my forgiveness."

"Gladly, Your Majesty!" the prime minister said as Damian dropped her to the floor. She quickly picked herself up and bowed again and again, backing out of the room. "Thank you, Your Majesty! Your greatness is truly—"

"Who's next?" William said, bouncing on his throne with excitement, and Damian opened a second portal.

"Be ready," a voice said in Fort's ear, and he turned just enough to see Rachel at his side.

"What's the plan?" he whispered.

"Jia paralyzes him, and then I smack him over the head with the flat side of the sword," she whispered. "Hopefully it'll cancel all of his magic like it did his spells on us."

"I can teleport you right next to him," Fort said, a bit surprised she wouldn't be using the sharp end of Excalibur. He wasn't sure he'd be able to resist, if it were him.

"On my signal, then," she whispered, and Fort readied himself. All they'd need was a distraction, and Rachel's plan *should* work.

Just then, Damian emerged through his portal holding a man in a military uniform. But as he did, his eyes lit up with the yellow light of Mind magic, and he turned to point at Rachel and Fort. "Your Majesty! Your knights are plotting against you! I can hear it in their thoughts!"

- FORTY-TWO -

RACHEL WINCED. "GUESS THAT'S THE signal! Jia, *go*!"

Jia immediately cast her paralysis spell on William, then turned to face Damian. Before she could, though, Simon reversed time, freeing William, while another Time student quickly froze Jia.

As fast as it all happened, Fort almost couldn't believe how easily they'd been countered. But if this was going to be their only chance, he wasn't going to just throw it away, not now. He quickly opened a portal between Rachel and William, ready to open another if Damian or a Time student tried to stop her.

"Looks like there's a revolution coming!" Rachel shouted as she leaped through the portal, then swung out with the flat of her blade.

William flinched in surprise and fear as the sword swung

toward him, then disappeared into thin air. The sword passed through the spot he'd been, while from across the room, Fort caught Ellora's hands glowing black out of the corner of his eye.

"Don't you touch His Majesty!" Ellora shouted as William reappeared, having jumped forward just a few seconds in time.

"Oh, come on!" Rachel shouted, aiming her sword at Ellora, who sent another Time spell at her. The magic hit the sword and fizzled out, making Rachel stare at it in surprise, then grin. "Whoa, I do love this sword. That's all you've got?"

"Try *me*," Damian said, transforming in midair into his dragon form as he leaped at her. One strike on her hand from his enormous claw sent the blade spinning across the floor toward Fort.

For a moment, he considered grabbing it. But the memory of the sword's flame burning his hand was too strong, and he couldn't bring himself to try again. Fortunately, that wasn't the only weapon they had here. If he could just get the book of Spirit magic away from William, he might be able to use it on the king himself.

Except Fort had seen what he'd become if he started using it again. Could he take the chance, even with the world falling apart?

As it turned out, he didn't have a choice.

"Your Majesty!" Damian shouted. "Fitzgerald is going to take the book of Spirit magic!"

Fort cursed, really wishing he had one of Colonel Charles's mind-blocking amulets right now.

"Of *course* he would try to steal it," William said, sneering. "But you had your chance, Forsythe. Damian?" He held up the book, then grinned. "You really should learn to keep your plans to yourself, Fitzgerald," he said as the book disappeared in a glow of green light.

Damian growled, the book reappearing in his claws. "I will protect it with my *life*, Your Majesty," the dragon promised.

That didn't bode well. Even with Damian under William's spell, they weren't going to have much of a chance against him, especially not without Jia. And William had all of the Time students on his side, even if they hadn't yet started moving against Fort and Rachel.

It was almost like none of them really wanted to act unless ordered to by William. Sure, they'd protected him when Rachel had attacked, but that was it. Was this actually a weakness in the magic? If it meant William had to order them to fight, Fort might be able to use that.

But first, they'd need the book themselves. And for that, they'd need a weapon.

"Why are you people even *doing* this?" William shouted at Fort and Rachel. "I'm just trying to save the world, you *jerks*! Would you rather have the same terrible people in charge, ruining everyone's lives like they did ours, like they're doing to you at your school? How do you not see how awful they all are?"

"William, the magic is making you just as bad as them!" Fort shouted as he dove for the sword. But instead of taking it himself and burning his hand again, he kicked it back to Rachel, just as Damian in dragon form dove for it too, his teeth snapping out toward the blade.

Rachel reached it first, picked it up, then slammed the flat of the sword against Damian's snout.

As she did, Fort wondered what Damian would do, freed from William's Spirit magic. Whose side would he be on? Were they unleashing a monster even worse than the one they had now?

But instead of waking up from the magic, Damian shrieked in pure agony, the sound so loud that everyone immediately covered their ears. As he screamed, he writhed in pain, shooting plumes of flame in every direction, forcing several of the other Time students to jump forward in time to avoid being burned.

Damian's tail struck out, striking Simon right in the chest, knocking him into the nearest wall, where he hit hard and slid to the floor, dazed. The dragon's flames struck the curtains and the wall hangings, immediately setting them all on fire, but Damian didn't even seem to notice, his pain was so intense.

And that was when Fort got the worst feeling of déjà vu he'd ever had. He'd seen this *exact* scene before, when William had shown them the future back at the Carmarthen Academy. This Damian was destroying Buckingham Palace exactly as they'd seen him do it before. But how could that be? Damian wasn't even using the book of Spirit magic! William had told them exactly what to do to stop this, and yet, here it was, happening again right before Fort's eyes! How could . . .

Oh. *Oh.*

William *had* told them exactly what to do. And now he'd gotten the book, just like he'd wanted.

They hadn't been stopping this. They'd been *causing* it. This had to have been William's plan all along. Even Ellora had said William had shown her this future, not that she'd gone here herself. He must have shown her, and them, a possible future, *if* Fort and his friends were gullible enough not to ask any questions and just get the book of Spirit magic for him.

But why would William want to see London destroyed? Fort could understand him wanting the book of Spirit magic, given how much he wanted to change things, but this was still a city full of innocent people. Why would he let it, or even Buckingham Palace, be torn down?

"That's enough, Damian!" William shouted, and Damian's eyes filled with orange light. The order seemed to cut through the agony he was feeling from Rachel's sword strike, and he shuddered, quashing more flames. "I know this was the future I promised everyone, but I do kind of like this place. Best to keep it in one piece."

Rachel looked at Fort with wide eyes, and he knew she'd figured it out too. "All this time, you were lying to us?" she shouted, getting even more angry, if that were possible.

"Call it what you want," William said with a shrug. "You didn't see what I saw, all those years in the future."

"And what's that?" Fort asked. "Yourself on a throne?"

William smiled at that. "No, actually. Not at first. No, what I saw was this large reptile here destroying the world!" He pointed at Damian, who looked pained at being pointed at in such a negative way by his idol. "I was the one stuck in the near future, so I saw everything. Sierra would bring us back, and she and Damian would read Ellora's mind to find the book of Spirit magic. They'd get it, and use that to find the Time book, wherever our teachers took it. And then he'd call the Old Ones, challenging them to a fight!" William snorted. "A fight, against the embodiments of magic! And he thought he'd *win*!"

"Um, did he?" Fort asked.

"Of course not!" William shouted. "What he did was bring all the Old Ones back here, and then lose to them pretty much *instantly*. And where did that leave humanity?" He shuddered violently. "You *really* don't want to know. So I knew I'd have to stop him."

Could that be true? Had William actually stopped Damian from letting the Old Ones return? It wasn't like he had any reason to lie at this point, but after what he'd done to them, Fort also had no cause to believe him either.

Even if William *had* saved the world, it definitely didn't justify what he was doing to it now.

"Why bring us into this?" Rachel demanded. "You couldn't start a world war all on your own?"

"If I hadn't needed you, trust me, you wouldn't be here,"

William said. "But to get to the book of Spirit magic took either one Damian or three of you. But you don't have to worry about the war. When I take over everyone using Spirit magic, there'll be no one to start it."

"You can't do this," Rachel whispered. "You can't take away everyone's free will!"

"Really?" William said. "Because actually, it looks like I can, and pretty easily." He looked around at his adoring subjects, then frowned. "You know what? I think I've changed my mind."

Changed his mind? Was he actually going to turn away from the Spirit magic and let them go?

"I don't think I like this place that much," he said, crinkling his nose. "I'll find a different castle to live in. Damian? Take this one down."

"Yes, Your Majesty," Damian said, and let loose another huge barrage of flame, straight into the walls.

"No!" Fort shouted, teleporting the dragon's next fiery attack out over the California desert. "William, call him off! There are innocent people here!"

"Innocent?" William said, staring at his subjects. "I wouldn't call them that. They've all done horrible things in their lives."

He turned to a group of older men in suits to his right. "Wouldn't you agree, gentlemen? Getting stuck here in this fire would almost be fitting for you, I'd say."

"Agreed, Your Majesty!" one shouted, and the others all nodded.

Fort didn't even know what to say, had no idea how to help. He could try to teleport them all out—

"Jia!" Rachel shouted, and Fort turned to find Damian's next blast heading straight at the Healer, who was still frozen in time. He quickly opened a portal beneath Jia, and she fell through a moment before Damian's flame plowed into the spot she'd been standing. Jia landed right next to Rachel, and Rachel quickly tapped her with Excalibur, freeing her from her Time prison.

"Damian!" William shouted. "Hurry this up. If I remember right, and of course I do, the Americans will be showing up any moment now." He laughed. "Invading my city? They need to be taught a lesson. I won't even take them over. They don't deserve to see my new world order. Let them instead see what kind of spirit the British people have!"

Damian, still apparently in pain from where Rachel had slapped him with her sword, nodded vigorously to William. "Yes, Your Majesty!" he shouted, unleashing even more fire.

Fort dodged another burst of flame, having no idea what to do. If this was all happening exactly as they'd already seen it, did that mean there was nothing they could do to stop William from destroying London?

Even if so, he had to try! "Rachel, use your sword on Damian again!" Fort shouted. "We need that book to stop William!"

The fires spread toward the ceiling, which began to creak and moan, making things even more dangerous inside the palace. "Take them down!" William shouted at the other Carmarthen Academy students. "I won't have these *children* disobeying me!"

And just like that, the remaining Time kids turned on them, with Ellora in the lead, looking angrier than Fort had ever seen her. Whatever advantage they'd had before William had ordered the Time students into the fight was now completely gone.

Jia managed to get a Sleep spell off on one of the Time kids, but that was it before the rest were upon them.

"You're ruining His Majesty's plan!" Ellora shouted, throwing Time spells at both Fort and Jia, which Rachel slapped down with her sword. "Who do you think you are?"

"Speaking for myself, I'm an American," Rachel said, then

leaped forward and smacked Ellora's arm with her sword. "And we've never really had much time for royalty."

Ellora's eyes widened as her mind was freed of the Spirit magic, and she turned to Fort in disgust. "Augh, that was *awful*! Rachel was right; we can't use that magic on anyone!"

"Oh, way too late, Time Girl," Rachel said with a snort. "Can you freeze Damian? We need that book back!"

But before she could, Simon blipped out, as did the other Time students. Ellora swore softly, then disappeared as well, all of them now moving too fast to see, just a bunch of shadowy blurs between the flames.

Someone slammed into Fort from behind, and he fought back, discovering that it was one of the government officials. "All hail the one true king!" the man shouted, making a fist while pinning Fort to the ground. Fort started to defend himself, but the man fell unconscious as Jia hit him with a Sleep spell as well, snoring before he even landed on Fort.

"Gee!" Rachel shouted. "Can you get the whole room at once with that? It could take down all the Time students!"

"On it!" Jia shouted as a host of royal guards ran toward her. Rachel pushed them back using solidified air, giving Jia the time she needed to put them to sleep. But before she could get to the rest, Fort's body froze, black light covering him. Somehow, he could still see and hear, which meant whoever had done it had just frozen everything below his neck.

"I should have left you frozen in your dumb school!" Simon shouted, reappearing at his side. He raised a glowing black hand to Fort's face. "And don't expect to be saved now, Fitzgerald. Tim and Amelia are keeping Ellora busy. Even Rachel's sword can't stop my spells, not when I'm this close." He grinned evilly. "What say I send you back to watch the war for a few years, like I did? Serves you right for trying to stop us from changing the world."

And then he unleashed his magic, and Fort flinched, expecting to be whisked back to the tsunami, or maybe the futures that Jia or Rachel had seen . . . only nothing happened.

Fort opened his eyes and found Simon staring at him in surprise. And then, almost casually, he collapsed to the floor, a large rock still glowing with red Elemental magic on the floor beside him. "I don't even need the sword to take *you* down, Clock Kid!" Rachel shouted from a distance.

As Simon's magic faded with his consciousness, releasing Fort, Jia sent a wave of Healing magic though the rest of the hall, sending all the various civilians, guards, and even the well-dressed couple near the thrones to sleep. As they all slid to the floor, Ellora and the other Time kids reappeared as well, Ellora's arms being held by a boy and girl as the three of them fell down, snoring.

Another wave of fire, though, revealed that Damian hadn't been affected. A blue glow faded around him, apparently having protected him from Jia's Sleep spell. Not only that, he had William held protectively in one of his claws.

"You're all so lucky I have more important things to do than deal with you now," William shouted as Damian roared, sending more flames into the roof. "Otherwise I'd have my personal dragon here show you exactly how much better at Healing magic he is than you are!"

"You're all traitors!" the dragon roared at them. "I'll burn you all to the ground before I let you take this book!"

"Shush, Damian," William said. "We've got places to go. Take me to the skies above the city!"

Damian nodded, looking almost embarrassed, then burst through the collapsing ceiling with a flap of his massive wings, sending even more debris tumbling toward the floor.

"We need to get everyone out of here!" Fort shouted.

"I could try to fly them all to safety," Rachel said, sounding a bit tired, but Fort shook his head.

"You've done enough. I've got this." He raised his hands and opened a portal on the floor of the room before Rachel could object, then pulled it up above his head, teleporting everyone away.

The entire group of officials, royalty, guards, Time students, and Oppenheimer School students all landed gently on the floor of the bell tower of Big Ben.

"Seriously, back here?" Rachel said, sighing. "You need to get out more, Fort."

"I've been a bit busy," he told her. "Plus, I wanted to be up high. We need to see if we can find William before . . ." He trailed off as he caught something orange out of the corner of his eye.

He ran to the railing around the clock tower, with Jia and Rachel just behind him. Even having seen this before in a vision, the sight of what was happening over London still rocked Fort to his core, and he wanted desperately for it not to be real.

Throughout the city, orange light streamed into the air from far too many sources to count. As the light rose, it merged together, forming a sort of giant, humanoid-looking monster.

A monster with William and Damian floating in the dead center of it, glowing with Spirit magic.

"Why is he doing this?" Fort shouted. "How is destroying a city going to save the world?"

"He mentioned something about the Americans," Jia said. "But I can't believe even Colonel Charles could get here so quickly, not with the dome just having come down."

"Look," Rachel said, her voice filled with terror as she pointed down. Fort glanced over the railing's edge to see an elderly couple on the bridge below, the orange light draining out of them, rising into the air to form William's creature. As the light left them both, they disappeared.

Others tried to run, but it was too late. No matter where they went, the light trickled up from their bodies into the sky, taking everything they were with it.

"He's taking their *spirits*," Fort said, completely in disbelief.

"What?" Jia said. "Can he do that?"

"Apparently," Rachel said. "He did say he sped up time to study Spirit magic."

"But we still don't know *why* he's doing this," Fort said, slamming his fist down on the railing. "These are his people! Even messed up from the magic, he still says he wants to help them. Why take their spirits?"

And then he saw it, and his blood turned cold.

Green portals were opening on the streets below, at least a dozen of them. And from each portal emerged squads of what looked exactly like TDA soldiers, their weapons drawn as they ran toward William's Spirit monster.

Jia was right: Colonel Charles couldn't have gotten here in time. So he'd found a shortcut.

- FORTY-THREE -

HOW IS THAT POSSIBLE?" JIA SHOUTED. "How can they teleport? We destroyed the book of Summoning, and Damian's under William's spell!"

"Please don't tell me you messed with my mind when I burned it the second time, Fort," Rachel said, but he shook his head.

"It's gone, I promise. The only other person who could be doing this *would* be Damian, obviously, or . . ." He trailed off, but Rachel completed his thought.

"Or *Gabriel*," she said, clenching her hands into fists. "If Colonel Charles let *him* come back to the school, the colonel and I are going to have a long talk."

"Looks like you're going to get your chance," Jia said, and pointed to the streets below. Fort and Rachel both looked over again, and even from a distance, they could still make out the colonel's uniform at the front of one of the squads of soldiers.

"Fort," Rachel said quietly, "get us down there. *Now.*"

Already ahead of her, Fort opened a portal to a point on the street just in front of William's monster. As one, he, Jia, and Rachel stepped through and found themselves facing the first squad of soldiers, who immediately raised their Lightning rods.

"Turn back!" Rachel yelled at the TDA forces, waving her sword in the air. "We will take care of this!"

"She's got a weapon!" someone shouted, and a lightning bolt came sizzling toward them.

Rachel batted it away with her sword and growled loudly. "Did you not *hear* me? I said, go away! You can't handle this, not like—"

"Behind you!" another of the soldiers shouted, and Fort whirled around to find William's giant Spirit foot crashing down toward them from above. He quickly opened a portal, and the three of them fell right through it a moment before the foot landed, cracking the street in half and knocking the TDA forces to the ground.

They emerged on a roof just above where they'd been but

quickly teleported again as William crashed his giant hand through the roof of the building they'd landed on.

"There might still be people inside there!" Rachel said from the next roof, pointing at the building, where more orange rivers of light were rising out. "Fort, get them out! Jia, use your magic to help whoever needs it. I'm taking that thing down!"

Fort nodded and opened two more portals, one back to the building they'd just been standing on, and the other to a building closer to William's height on the monster for Rachel. Fort ran through the first and found a mostly empty office building, thankfully. But the remaining people who hadn't yet had their spirits stolen by William were now trapped beneath the collapsed roof.

The first two he found, he was able to teleport back to Jia on the last roof for healing, but the rest were going to take more work: If he shifted the rubble too much, it might collapse in other spots, causing more injuries.

As Fort looked around for a way to save them, again, he couldn't understand why William would do this. He'd wanted to help fix the world, not hurt his own people! How much of this was the Spirit magic taking him over, and how much was it just magnifying something within himself?

Part of Fort didn't want to know that answer, since it'd mean he'd have to think long and hard about what he'd seen himself do in Cyrus's future vision.

"Help!" someone screamed, and Fort ran over to find a woman with an enormous concrete beam pinning her lower half to the floor. "Please, I can't feel my legs!"

"Don't worry," he told her, readying his spell as carefully as he could, hoping to avoid any further collapse. "I've got you."

"You?" she said as he carefully opened a teleportation portal just below her. "But you're a kid—"

And then she teleported to the roof, and he moved on to the next.

Outside, he heard lightning sizzling almost constantly as more TDA forces reached William, but they didn't seem to do much good. He had to get back out there to help, but the farther he advanced into the building, the more people he found, and he couldn't just leave them there.

When he finally teleported what he hoped was the last person to Jia, she stuck her head back through the portal. "Fort, get back here! Rachel needs help!"

He leaped through the portal and quickly saw that things had gotten much worse: Easily half the buildings around

William had been destroyed now, including the building where Fort had sent Rachel.

"You need to get me over there!" Jia shouted, grabbing Fort's arm and whirling him around to point at a different building, where Rachel was swinging her sword at William's giant hand. She barely missed, and William took advantage of that by punching right through the building beneath her. She managed to catch herself on solid air, but another blow was heading toward her, and she wouldn't have time to get her sword up.

"*Now!*" Jia shouted, and Fort opened a portal again, but instead of sending Jia through it, he instead made it big enough to fit William's entire hand.

The giant fist passed through the portal and out the other side, which Fort had placed directly in front of the Spirit monster's head, hoping to at least send the creature reeling. But the fist passed right through the Spirit creature's head, and William pulled it back out of the portal, laughing.

"You think that's where its brain is?" he shouted, and his voice echoed throughout the city. "*I* control it, just like I do this country. And I refuse to let you foreign invaders hurt us!"

Someone grabbed Fort's leg and yanked him down, hard. He groaned as he hit the roof and quickly looked up to find one of the people he'd saved reaching out to strangle him, the woman's eyes glowing orange with Spirit magic. "Invaders!" she shouted. "You dare fight against our leader?"

"Oh come *on*," Jia shouted, sending Healing magic through her former patients, including the one attacking Fort, putting them all to sleep.

But as they fell asleep, each of their bodies began to dissolve into orange magic, and a moment later, the roof was empty. Everything they'd just done had been for nothing. Fort gritted his teeth, looking up at William in disgust. "Let's get out of here," he said, and teleported them back down to the ground, where Rachel had just landed.

"Oh, hey," Rachel said when she saw them appear, leaning over her sword to catch her breath. "How are we doing?"

"Not exactly great," Jia told her. "You're okay?"

"Never been better!" she said with a smile, then stood up straight, grimacing at some pain in her back. "Okay, new plan. Fort, you teleport me straight at William, and I'll sword him. That way—"

"That way *what*, Cadet Carter?" said a voice, and they all turned around to find a full squad of TDA soldiers aiming their Lightning rods at them.

And Colonel Charles was in the lead.

"That way *we* will end this, because no one else can," Rachel finished. "What are you even doing here, Colonel? He can take over your soldiers if he wants!"

"Not my squad," the colonel said, pulling a necklace out from under his body armor. "Sierra made these, so they should work against this new kind of magic as well."

Rachel screamed in frustration. "You don't even know if that's true! *This* is what's wrong with you! You insist on holding us back when *you* have no idea what's even going on. But we do! Let *us* fix this, while you rescue whoever you can."

Colonel Charles slowly smiled. "I'm sorry, but students aren't allowed to take field trips without permission." He raised his hand and pointed at Rachel. "Squad, take them!"

Rachel laughed. "You think your Lightning rods are going to work on us? I've got a sword that deflects spells, big man! Just try it!"

"If you insist," the colonel said as the man next to him aimed something right at Jia and fired.

Rachel swept her sword through where the magic would have been, but instead of lightning or fire, a small dart hit Jia in the stomach. She glanced down at it in confusion before her eyes rolled back into her head and she collapsed to the ground, where she began to snore, completely knocked out.

"Oh I forgot: Tranquilizer darts aren't magic," Colonel Charles told Rachel as she ran to Jia's side. "Isn't that funny?"

"You *monster*!" Rachel shouted, throwing up a shield of fire as the soldier readied another shot. His dart passed straight through her fire to hit her in the shoulder, and she too passed out, right on top of Jia, Excalibur falling to the ground next to her.

"And now it's just you, Fitzgerald," the colonel said, turning to Fort and raising his hand. "I can't say I won't enjoy this. You've disobeyed my orders for the last time!"

- FORTY-FOUR -

FORT FRANTICALLY LOOKED FROM THE soldiers to his friends, not sure he could reach Jia and Rachel in time to cast his only Healing spell on them, or that it'd even wake them up. But what else could he do? He couldn't just leave them there!

"Take him!" Colonel Charles shouted, and Fort realized he'd missed his chance. "And then get me that British kid, *now*!"

As the soldiers shot their tranquilizer darts at Fort, he threw up a portal in front of him just in time, sending the darts sailing through to the opposite portal, just behind the squad. The tranquilizers hit the soldiers at the rear, and each of them collapsed, unconscious.

"No!" Colonel Charles shouted as Fort teleported Jia and Rachel away to the only safe place he could think of, back to Big Ben, then eyed Excalibur still lying on the ground. He *could* teleport the sword right into his hand, but again, he'd just be burned: There was no reason to think he was any more worthy now than he had been back in Avalon. If anything, he was a lot *less* worthy after what he'd seen his potential future self do with Spirit magic.

But without it, he had no chance against William, let alone Damian.

Before he could decide, one of the soldiers sprinted through the portal he'd left open, leaped for him, and tackled him to the ground. The soldier pinned Fort down, then dug a tranquilizer dart out of his belt and aimed it at Fort's arm.

Just as the soldier struck, though, Fort opened a portal beneath them, dropping them both out over the River Thames, the quickest, softest landing he could think of. As they fell, the soldier dropped the tranquilizer dart in surprise, but Fort managed to grab the man's protective mental necklace off his neck a moment before they hit the water.

Their momentum sent them plunging into the river farther than Fort would have thought, but he quickly opened a portal for himself, leaving the soldier to swim back up to the surface. As he passed through his portal back to the street, a bunch of river water came with him, but that didn't matter. He couldn't afford any delays, not with Excalibur just sitting out on the street, waiting for someone to take it.

Only he was too late. The colonel was already reaching for the sword.

"You children think you know *everything*, don't you," the colonel said, sneering at Fort as his hand paused just over Excalibur's hilt. "You have no *idea* how to protect a country. Everything I do, I do to keep people safe. And look what you three have accomplished here. London's destroyed, and there's a rampaging child threatening to take over the world. Why couldn't you leave this to the adults, the ones who know better than you?"

"Let me know if you find any adults like that," Fort said quietly.

Colonel Charles snorted, then reached down to take Excalibur. "Well, *I* know I've got Rachel's magic sword, so we'll see what—OW!"

The sword immediately lit on fire as he touched it, and the colonel dropped it back to the ground, staring at it in surprise as the flames died out.

"The sword doesn't think you're worthy, Colonel," Fort said, trying not to smile. "Let me tell you, I'm just *shocked*.

But I can't stay and argue. I have to go take that monster down."

"Don't you take one step, Forsythe!" the colonel shouted, cradling his burned hand to his chest.

"Okay, I won't!" Fort said, and instead pulled a teleportation circle down over himself. "See? I can follow orders!"

Fort emerged on a roof closer to where William was standing, turning what citizens of London he hadn't already used for his monster into his willing army. Each person he used his Spirit magic on then ran screaming after the TDA soldiers, roaring about foreign invaders. Fort sighed. Now he'd have to worry about the soldiers *and* London's citizens, making Colonel Charles's decision to come even more of a pain than it'd been before. And that was saying something.

"William!" Fort shouted. "You need to stop this! You're not making the world a better place—you're *destroying* it!"

William and his monster slowly turned to face Fort, with Damian floating below him. William laughed. "Oh, Fitzgerald, I almost didn't see you there. Shouldn't you be serving me?"

An orange glow appeared around his head, and Fort winced, hoping Sierra's necklace in his hand would hold it off. The necklace began to grow hotter as he held it to the point it was almost too warm to hold, but just as Fort thought he'd have to drop it, William canceled his spell, looking annoyed. "How are you doing that?" he shouted. "How can you block my magic?"

"Come down and I'll show you!" Fort shouted at him.

Instead of answering, William swept his massive monster hand over the roof Fort was standing on, forcing him to teleport to another. "You don't have to do this!" he shouted at William. "I know you wanted to help people, to make them want to help each other! But the magic changes you, William. I felt it myself and saw what would happen to me if I chose your path. It controls you, just as much as your teachers did!"

"*Nothing* controls me now!" William roared. "No magic could change who I am and what I want. But I'll destroy this world before I leave it in the hands of the evil monsters running it now!" He drove his foot down into the street so hard that the blow reverberated up through the building Fort stood on, knocking him to the roof as William's Spirit hand came flying down at him. He teleported just in time, but he was quickly running out of buildings that were still standing.

"Think about your friends!" Fort shouted. "What would they say? Ellora would never want this!"

William laughed, low and ugly. "That's why I never told her!

None of the others knew the full truth, other than Simon. He was the only one who saw things clearly, just like I do. Sometimes you need to tear things down to rebuild them right."

Fort teleported again just before getting hit, now on his last building within reach of William. Clearly, trying to reason with William wasn't working. The Spirit magic had either already changed William to the point he wasn't going to listen, or he just wasn't ever going to hear Fort out anyway. And that meant there was only one way he could stop the self-proclaimed king.

But it was going to *hurt*.

"William!" he shouted, changing tactics. "You're *no* true king! You know who was worthy of Excalibur? Rachel. Sounds like *she* should rule all of Britain!"

"That sword should be mine!" William roared, whirling around to face Fort again. "*I* am the one who's come to save Britain, just like Arthur was going to. I'm his rightful heir!"

"No," Fort said as William readied another blow. "You're just an angry boy who wants revenge. Believe me, I know how it feels."

"I *am* the king!" William roared. "And you *will* bow before me!" Fort braced himself to teleport again, but instead of attacking with the Spirit monster, this time William sent Time magic flying at Fort. The spell struck the medallion in his hand, which disappeared in a flash of black light into the future or past. Not that it mattered, since either way it left Fort vulnerable to William's Spirit magic.

And just like that, William's hands glowed orange. Before Fort could move, William shot the light out toward him like a lightning bolt. He had no time to dodge or jump. . . .

But he was ready for it anyway.

Just before the spell hit, he pulled a flaming Excalibur from a portal and cut through the magic like it was butter.

"What?" William shouted, drawing back. "You can't hold that sword. You're not worthy!"

"You're right, I'm not," Fort shouted back, cringing at the pain as he cast Heal Minor Wounds into his hand over and over as the flame burned him. Opening another portal to Big Ben, he quickly sent two Healing spells back through it, hoping that'd be enough to wake Jia and Rachel up. "But why don't we see if *you* are?"

And with that, he opened a teleportation portal aimed directly at William, right in the heart of the Spirit monster.

Everything they'd done to save London and stop a war had failed. In fact, by trying to stop those things, they'd just made them happen in the first place. But whatever it took, Fort wasn't going to let William take people's spirits from them.

It was all so clear now. This had all started because of Fort's actions, and now it would end that way too. And if he made it out okay, then his very next step was to head back to his father with Ellora, and . . . and remove him from time.

There was no other way to fix things. And he owed it to his father, in all ways, to not let a war come about at his expense.

Don't feel bad, Forsythe, he heard his father say in his head as he wiped his sleeve over his eyes. *It's what I'd want you to do.*

I hope that's true, Dad, he thought back, and then leaped through the portal at William.

"No!" William shouted, and tried to block with his Spirit monster, but the sword cut right through the magic, not even slowing Fort down. Damian tried to snap at him with his jaws but flinched at the sight of the sword as well, dropping away into the city below, the book of Spirit magic falling from his claws in his moment of surprise. And then Fort reached William and swung out with the side of the blade, hoping to cancel the other boy's magic.

But instead, William put a hand out to defend himself,

and the sword nicked his palm just enough to cut him, barely enough to even draw blood.

Instantly the Spirit monster shuddered violently, as if it were going to come apart at its seams.

"What?" William shouted, looking down at his hand in surprise. "What did you do to me? *Where did my magic go?*"

Before Fort could respond, the Spirit monster exploded, sending magic radiating out in a million different directions. The force of the explosion knocked William out and almost did the same to Fort, dazing him to the point he could barely even tell they were both falling rapidly toward the ground.

- FORTY-FIVE -

THE WIND RUSHING BY HIM WOKE Fort up enough to know he had to do something to save himself, and William, too, but the explosion of Spirit magic made it incredibly hard to think clearly, and he couldn't bring the Teleport spell to mind. Excalibur tumbled from his hand, the ground coming up fast. . . .

And then the air beneath him suddenly turned solid, slowing him down as he fell, until he touched the ground with barely any speed at all.

"Nice catch," Jia told Rachel as she knelt down beside Fort, sending Healing magic through his body. Instantly his mind cleared, and he tried to jump to his feet, not willing to let William get ahold of himself again, but Jia pushed him back down.

"Hold still—I'm not done," she commanded. "Rachel has him; don't worry. Just relax."

She turned to his hand that had held Excalibur and began healing the burned marks as well, which Fort had almost forgotten about. Somehow, his hand had stopped hurting during the fight with William, and though the pain came racing back now, he wasn't sure how it could have possibly slipped his mind.

"You know the sword's fire went out, right at the end there," Jia told him, smiling slightly. "Looks like it changed its mind about you."

Fort's eyebrows shot up. "You're joking."

"I mean, *I'm* still not going to touch it, but I'm glad to see it's got good taste in people," she said with a shrug. "Seems like you just barely passed its test, though, so I wouldn't do anything to make it mad."

"Give me back my magic!" someone shouted, and Fort turned his head slightly to see William struggling against some rock bindings that Rachel had magicked into place. "What did you do to me, Fitzgerald? I can remember all my spells, but they won't work! I can't cast any of them, not even my Time spells!"

"We didn't do *anything*, King Artless," Rachel shouted back, Excalibur back in her hand and pointed at him. "Keep yelling at me, though. Any excuse to knock you out."

"It must have been the sword!" he said, focusing in on her weapon. "It had to be. It stole my magic from me somehow! That's not fair. Give it back!"

What? Fort just stared at him in confusion. That couldn't be possible. How could the sword take away someone's ability to do magic? It was just supposed to defend against spells . . . wasn't it?

Jia helped Fort to his feet as Rachel stared at the sword. "He might be right," she said, looking at Fort. "The queen wouldn't tell us what it did."

"Maybe that's why it was so painful to Damian," Fort said, shaking off the remaining fog in his head. "He's *made* of magic. If it takes magic away, it could have killed him!"

They all went silent for a moment at that, until Rachel nodded. "So what you're saying is, next time, hit him harder?"

Jia rolled her eyes. "Come on, Ray. Did you see where he dropped the book of Spirit magic, by the way? We need to find it before anyone else does."

Rachel cringed. "Wherever it started, William's explosion could have thrown it a lot farther away. It might be anywhere, covered in rubble, too."

That was pretty awful news. But they couldn't worry about it now, not with the TDA forces looking for them. "Either Colonel Charles or the British military will find it, and then we'll just take it back from them," Fort said. "But for now, we need to get out of here."

"I still need to know what my sword can do," Rachel said. "I don't want to accidentally nick someone and take away their magic forever. We need to test it."

"On who?" Jia asked.

Rachel smiled. "Simon's still sleeping back at Big Ben."

"Don't move!" Colonel Charles shouted as he and his TDA squad raced toward them, and Rachel turned, readying her sword. But she, Fort, and Jia were all exhausted now, and the last thing they needed was to face down innocent soldiers.

"Let's get out of here," Fort said, glaring at the colonel as he teleported the three of them back to Big Ben, leaving the powerless William to the TDA.

Everyone was fortunately still asleep back in the bell tower when they arrived. Wasting no time, Rachel walked over to where Simon snored, picked up his hand, then poked his finger with the tip of her sword.

"Want to wake him up?" she asked Jia, who frowned.

"Are you sure? Because if it wasn't actually the sword that

took William's magic, Simon could give us some problems."

"Come on, Ms. Risk Taker," Rachel said, smiling at her. "How else will we know?"

Jia shrugged and used her magic to wake Simon up. He quickly pushed to his feet, then stared down at himself oddly. "Why didn't that work?" he mumbled.

"Why didn't what work?" Rachel asked innocently, sharing a secret grin with Fort and Jia.

"I tried to speed up my time!" he said, sounding confused. "You wouldn't have even seen me, and I was going to . . ." He paused as Rachel tapped her sword against her hand. "Ah, I mean, I was going to help bring all of these people back to where they belong, since I'm always ready to help!"

"Nice try," she said, then continued around the bell-tower room, helping Jia wake everyone else. Apparently, with William losing his magic, his Spirit spells were canceled, as everyone woke up in full control of themselves.

As Jia and Rachel saw to the others, Fort moved to Ellora's side. He gently tried waking her using his Healing spell, which seemed to do the trick: She stirred slowly, then yawned widely and looked up at him. As soon as she saw it was Fort, her eyes widened, and she bolted awake. "Where's William? What happened? Is he—"

"He . . . destroyed the city," Fort said quietly. "Everything we saw in your vision, it all came true. Because we made it happen."

She just stared at him, and tears began to run down her cheeks. "That can't be true," she whispered. "We did everything we could!"

"There's still a war to stop," he told her. "And there's only one way to do that. Will you come with me to see my . . . my father?" He almost choked on the last word but managed to get it out.

"Are you sure about this?" Rachel asked Fort, while Jia looked away uncomfortably. "We could still try to find a different way."

He shook his head. "We couldn't stop the London attack. That means the war is coming if we don't do this. I have to, Rachel. I just . . . I *have* to."

She nodded and moved to Jia's side as Fort helped Ellora to her feet. "You're sure you want to do this now?" Ellora asked. "It can wait at least a few days, if you need the time."

He paused, wondering if that would help, then shook his head. "We can't risk it. Who knows what Colonel Charles will do if we don't do it now?"

Not to mention that the longer they put it off, the more likely it was that Fort would find a reason *not* to do it, that not having his father wasn't something he could live with.

No, if it was going to happen, if the world war was going to be stopped, it had to be *now*.

And with that, he opened a portal to the Oppenheimer School.

- FORTY-SIX -

THE MEDICAL WARD AT THE OPPEN-heimer School was quieter than Fort had ever heard it. It helped that all the staff were frozen in time by Ellora, and the Time girl herself now waited in an adjacent room to give him some privacy, along with Rachel and Jia. But still, the silence was almost palpable as Fort sat down next to his his father's bed.

Maybe it was because he had no idea what to say.

"Hey, Dad," Fort said, taking his father's hand as tears started slipping down his cheeks. "I feel like I was just here, talking to you like this." He almost laughed. "Probably because it was just last night. Feels like a lifetime ago."

He paused, hoping there'd be some kind of response, but all he heard was the soft beeping of the various machines his dad was connected to.

"So guess what?" he asked, rubbing his arm over his eyes. "I'm messing everything up, *again*! I know, pretty hard to believe, huh? First I lose you, then I find you but almost lose Gabriel to the Old Ones, and have to leave his brother with them. And then it turns out everything I did just leads to horrible things in the future." The tears fell more quickly now, but Fort barely noticed. "A war. A war over magic, and it's all because I brought you back."

In his head, he heard his father's voice. *That seems a bit harsh, everyone going to war over me coming home.*

Fort snorted, which was odd, since the voice was just his imagination. "It *is* pretty harsh," he agreed. "All of it is. Everything I do just seems to make things worse. But I'm *trying*, Dad, I really am. I want to do good. Which is why I'm here. There were two ways to stop the war, but only one where I can still live with myself."

He sniffed loudly and laid his head down on the bed, next to his father's hand. "I have to send you away," he whispered. "You won't even notice; don't worry. Maybe someday we can bring you back, when all of this is over. But for now . . . I have to say good-b—" He paused, trying not to throw up. "I have to say good-bye."

And with that, he broke down completely, unable to continue, pushing his face into the bed so the others wouldn't hear him from the other room.

When he finally brought himself back under control, he took his father's hand again. "I can't believe I have to do this," he said, then shook his head. "Maybe I won't even remember that I did, because Colonel Charles is probably going to erase my memories of all of it, so I won't even know I rescued you. Maybe that will actually be for the best."

He waited for a response in his head, but his imagination seemed to have gone quiet.

"I hope you understand why I have to do this," he whispered, and squeezed his dad's hand. "I wouldn't if I had another choice. But the only thing worse than you not being here would be you seeing what I become using Spirit magic."

"Fort," Ellora said quietly from the doorway. "We don't have much time. Colonel Charles will be back soon—"

"I know," Fort said, standing up and looking away. He ran his sleeve over his face, then turned back to her and nodded. "Give me one more minute, okay? Can I have some privacy?"

She nodded and left the room. Through the window, Fort could see Rachel, Jia, and Ellora all turn their backs, giving him just a moment.

That was good, because there was one last thing he had to do.

"I shouldn't do this," he said, reaching into his pocket and taking out the green jewel the faerie queen had given him. "But I can't risk it. I *have* to know you're safe, even if I never see you . . . again. And she said you would be. The faerie queen will protect you, even outside of time. At least, I have to believe she will."

You don't need to do this, he heard his father say in his head. *Merlin warned you about making deals with her.*

"I don't even care," Fort said. "If nothing else . . . I have to know you'll be okay."

And then he put the jewel in his father's open palm and closed the man's fingers around it.

Not sure what to expect, he stood back up, sniffing loudly. But nothing happened, and the jewel just sat in his father's hand. Did he have to say something, ask the queen to—

The jewel burst into a brilliant green light, so bright it

blinded Fort. He yelped in surprise and heard his friends do the same from the other room.

"What did you do?" Rachel shouted from the doorway. "I can't see enough to come in!"

"I don't know!" he said honestly. "The faerie queen offered me a deal, and—"

The light faded as quickly as it'd come, and Fort blinked rapidly, just trying to see. A blur of something moved in front of him, and he momentarily wondered if Colonel Charles had already made it back.

But then the blur cleared its throat. "Fort?" it said. "Is that you?"

And then Fort's eyesight returned, and he stared in amazement at his father sitting up in the bed. "Dad?" he said, not even able to believe it.

Something bit into his neck just at that moment, and he reached up to swat away whatever bug it was, only to find a dart sticking into him. The room suddenly turned sideways, and Fort collapsed to his father's hospital bed as people began shouting all around him.

From the corner of his eye, he saw a green, glowing portal, with Gabriel standing in the middle of it. Next to him was his father, holding a tranquilizer gun, as were the soldiers on either side of him. Everyone seemed so angry, which Fort didn't understand.

He wasn't sure how, but he could figure that out later. Right now, he just needed to sleep and hope that this wasn't all just a dream.

- FORTY-SEVEN -

FREEZING-COLD WATER SPLASHED ON Fort's face, and he instantly woke up, sopping wet. For a moment, he had no idea where he was, but the green paint on the walls gave it away.

He was back in the Oppenheimer School, tied to a chair.

And Colonel Charles was sitting across from him, calmly staring at him as he placed an empty bucket on the floor.

"What did you do to your father, Fitzgerald?" the colonel asked. "Ambrose ran some tests. She said that all the abnormalities have disappeared."

It took a few seconds for that to filter through the fog in Fort's brain, but when it did, he woke up immediately. "He's okay?" Fort shouted. "My dad is going to be okay?"

"I asked you, what did you *do* to him?" the colonel said again. "Ambrose said she had some ideas that might be beneficial to the TDA, but she'd need to do further research. Now that's all out the window."

"I . . . just healed him," Fort said, shaking his head. "That's it."

"Healed him?" Colonel Charles asked. "You mean what we'd done a hundred times since you brought him back? Why don't you quit wasting my time and just tell me the truth?"

"Maybe it was the power of love," Fort said, smiling weakly. "I don't know. But it *is* the truth. All I did was use my Healing spell on him, and he woke up."

The colonel stared at him in silence for a few moments. "He has no memory of the other dimension," he said finally. "We've used some of Sierra's mind amulets on him and have found literally nothing from that time. Did you wipe his memory somehow?"

"With Healing magic?" Fort said. "I wouldn't even know where to start."

"Ambrose thinks you could have used Healing magic to make him forget, to restore his brain to an earlier version without those memories," the colonel said, then rubbed his forehead. "But whatever. You know . . . I get it. I do. I understand why you all think you're so right about everything. You've got the power, and we don't." He glanced up at Fort now. "But look at what you caused. If you'd just sent us into the UK like I'd asked, London would still be standing."

Fort's mouth dropped open. "We made some mistakes, yes, but I *did* try to send you, and the Carmarthen Academy students took you down immediately! They showed us this future, and told us how to stop it. We couldn't have known—"

"That you were just causing it in the first place?" the colonel said. "Maybe not. But the governments of the world know, and they all are demanding their books back. The president has already refused, which is good, because otherwise I'd have had to take them away myself. We're not giving them back, not to anyone."

Fort felt his body go cold at the colonel's words. "You're going to start a war if you don't. Trust me on that."

"Then I start a war," the colonel said, still strangely calm. "I'd do that and more to protect my country, Fitzgerald."

That was almost worse without the anger and rage he'd had back in the briefing. Why *was* he so composed now? "Then you shouldn't have the books at all," Fort told him.

"Fortunately, that's not your call," the colonel said. "Someone had to take the fall for the UK, you know. So Oppenheimer is finally gone for good. Agent Cole will be running the school from now on, under my command." He shrugged. "Not that it will matter to you, of course."

"What do you mean?" Fort said, the chill getting worse.

"As promised, you're expelled," Colonel Charles told him, a small smile playing over his lips. "I'm here to wipe your memory. This . . . discussion is basically just a formality. I didn't think we'd get much out of you. Whatever that jewel we found in your father's hand was, there's no magic left in it now. But we'll still study it and see what we can find."

"You're sending me home?" Fort asked, dreading the answer. "What about my father?"

The colonel sighed. "Ambrose tells me he's no longer useful, and we can't have a civilian adult on the premises. So he's going with you. Neither of you will remember this, but you'll have your family, at least." He gritted his teeth for the moment, a familiar anger rising up again, only for him to take a deep breath and calm himself. "You don't deserve it, but maybe *he* does. If someone could give me back Michael . . ."

He trailed off at this, and Fort waited quietly for him to continue, inwardly not able to believe what was happening. His father was coming home? Even without their memories, he'd have his father back? After everything, losing him to the Dracsi, rescuing him, then finding out that a war was started in the future because of it all . . . his dad was going to be okay and come back to live a normal life with him?

Fort didn't deserve it. He knew that, without a shadow of a doubt. Not after everything he'd done.

But there was no way he wasn't going to take it anyway.

Silence filled the room for an uncomfortably long time before the colonel finally spoke again. "I'm guessing it's useless to ask you where that Time student who was with you sent Rachel's sword?"

Fort raised an eyebrow. "I don't know what you're talking about. Ellora sent the sword away?"

The colonel nodded. "She grabbed it from Rachel when we arrived, and it started burning her, but she used her magic on it and it disappeared. And then she blipped out herself. We have no idea where she went."

"I don't either," Fort said, his mind racing. Ellora had escaped and taken Excalibur with her? She must have been trying to keep it out of the TDA's hands. "What about Jia and Rachel? Are they okay?"

"Rachel is expelled as well," Colonel Charles said, sighing

again. "Such a waste, but she's lost respect for authority, and we can't have that. Such a good soldier before you came along, too." He shook his head. "Jia, though, we're keeping around, as relations with China are bad enough already. We're hoping that leaving her here will buy us some time to keep the book of Healing."

Rachel was being expelled too? Out of all of them, she was the one who seemed most suited to the school, and Fort couldn't imagine what she must be going through right now. "You can't blame Rachel. This was all my plan. I brought her along when she didn't want to go. She shouldn't be expelled, not for things I did."

The colonel laughed. "She said the same about you." He stood up from his chair and pulled a silver amulet out from under his shirt. "Enough of this. Time to forget everything, Fitzgerald." He smiled. "You were a mistake from the start, and all you've done is make the world a more dangerous place. You're so lucky that you'll get to forget all of this, while those of us charged with protecting you clean up your mess."

Don't say anything, Fort thought. *He can still not send Dad home with you.*

"You're right, sir," Fort said, forcing himself to look sad. "This is all my fault. And I wish I could make up for it all." That was the truth, so at least he could say it with a straight face.

"Wishes are for children, Cadet," the colonel said, then touched the amulet. "It's about time you learned that."

He reached out and grabbed Fort's arm, and the magic flowed through their connection, straight into Fort's brain, as one by one, the colonel began to erase Fort's memories.

- FORTY-EIGHT -

RIDING TO HIS AUNT'S APARTMENT IN a car with his father would never have been something special, not before the D.C. attack. But now, staring at his real, healthy father in the front seat next to his dad's sister, Fort couldn't imagine anything more perfect.

The empty streets around them were more than a bit disturbing, though.

"It's just the curfew," his aunt had told him when they left the airport. "There's been one ever since London was destroyed. I had to get special dispensation to even pick you both up at the airport. No one really knows if it's safe to go out, you know?"

"I'm personally in favor of more staycations, I think," his father had said, and his aunt gasped, realizing what she'd said. But in spite of everything, Fort found himself laughing. His father joined in, as did his aunt, and they all kept laughing until tears started to fall.

Once they'd reached her apartment, Fort saw a few people peek out their windows, but that was the only sign of life he could find. It was almost eerie, how empty the city was.

But even that couldn't ruin this day for him. His father was coming *home*.

"I still can't believe you're okay!" Fort's aunt said to his father as she carried Fort's suitcase up the stairs to her apartment. "I only wish your memory had returned quicker after the attack. I can't even imagine what it must have been like, not knowing who you were while you recovered. If only you'd had your ID on you, they could have reached out to me!"

"There's a lot I still don't remember," Fort's father said, his arm on Fort's shoulders. "Nothing much after D.C. until I saw Fort standing in front of me, which, let me tell you, was a sight for some very sore eyes." He smiled down at Fort, who couldn't help but beam back up at him. "Probably came from all the weight lifting my eyes did."

Both Fort and his aunt groaned.

"When we all thought you were . . . missing," his aunt said, "the bank took your house. But maybe we can find a way to get it back, so you two can go home?" She blushed at this. "I mean, you're always welcome to stay here! But I just figured—"

"Oh, we know," Fort's dad said. "And going home does sound nice. But right now, I'm just happy to be back with my son and my sister. It's been a long eight months!"

As they went into his aunt's apartment, Fort decided it looked exactly the same as the last time he'd been there. His aunt didn't have a lot of money, and what she'd gotten after the attack had all gone to Fort's multiple schools, so his behavior had just made things even worse for her. Yet through it all, she had never stopped trying to help, to make his life feel normal again. And for that, he'd always be grateful to her.

"I haven't had a chance to fix up your room yet, Fort," she said as they reached the kitchen. "I'm really sorry about that. Between finding out you were expelled and that your dad was okay, it's just been a whirlwind!" She smiled at him. "And don't think I've forgotten about what they said. Sounds like you need a talk about following rules."

Fort's father laughed. "I think we can just enjoy being home for a few days at least. Give my boy here a break. I can't even imagine what you both went through."

"And definitely don't worry about my room," Fort told her. "I'm fine with whatever."

"When you left, I meant to use it as a little gym," she said, blushing again. "So I'm sorry about the stuff in there. Haven't even had a chance to get in there in the last few weeks. Let me order some food, and I'll move it all while you two eat."

"Oh, that's okay," Fort told her, grabbing his suitcase. As much as he never wanted to leave his father's side again, he had to get into the room quickly, before she did. There was still one thing he had to do. "I'm not really that hungry. I'll just go unpack and move the gym stuff out of the way, if that works?"

"Of course, honey," she said with a nod. "That'll give me a chance to catch your father up on this new world." She sighed, running her hand through her hair. "It's terrifying, honestly. The government says they're considering instituting martial law, and no one knows anything about this Gathering Storm organization, but apparently they took credit for London, too. But how could they make these monsters? And there was a *dragon* of all things, flying around to different cities just a few days ago!"

"Well, we're together now, and that's what matters," Fort's dad said, his forehead wrinkling as he smiled. "I'm sure someone in the government knows what's going on and is trying to fix it."

Fort chose that moment to drag his suitcase over to his aunt's second bedroom, not able to contain his response to his father's words. As he reached his old room, he stopped outside, making sure they hadn't followed him.

Then he slowly opened the door, slipped inside without turning on the light, and closed the door behind him. Finally, he flipped on the lights and almost screamed in surprise at the sight of a glowing yellow girl sitting on his bed.

"You know, this isn't the best hiding spot for this," Sierra said, patting the enormous dragon egg sitting on the bed beside her. "At least put it under the covers or something."

Fort grinned at her. "I didn't really have a free moment since I got it, if you remember."

"I don't, actually," she said, bouncing on the bed. "Probably because I was *frozen in time* for most of your little adventure?"

"My little *adventure*?" he said. "Oh, you mean the one where your best friend Damian tried to kill me, Jia, and Rachel? Oh, and where London basically got destroyed by one of Cyrus's old classmates?"

"Don't high-road me, Fitzgerald," she said, glaring at him. "The only reason you didn't have your memory erased is because I jumped in and protected you from Colonel Charles's spell. If it weren't for me, you'd think you just failed out of some random boarding school and would have no idea of what had gone down in the last few months."

"You could have warned me about that, by the way," Fort said, beginning to unpack the bag the TDA had handed back to him when they'd sent him home, the bag he'd packed before going to the school and never seen again until now. "I thought I was really going to forget it all!"

His eyes lit up at the sight of his favorite hoodie, which he'd assumed was gone forever. Granted, that was because he thought he'd still be at the Oppenheimer School, and that wasn't exactly happening, but still.

"Eh, you're not that great an actor," she said, lying back on the bed to watch. "Colonel Charles would have figured it out right away."

"I noticed you glossed right over what I said about Damian," he said, picking up the dragon egg and carrying it gently into the closet. That wasn't much better as a hiding spot, but at least his aunt wouldn't see it if she came in. He'd have to think of somewhere safer for it tomorrow.

"I'm not going to lie, Fort," Sierra said, staring down at her feet. "I don't know *what* to say about him. Wherever he is now, he's hiding his mind from me. Which is smart, because I have a lot to say once I find him."

"And Cyrus is still lost in time somewhere," Fort said, not letting the good news of his father's return make him forget that his friend was still missing. "Hopefully, William's spell over him broke when he lost his magic, so Cyrus can make his way back."

"I'm sure he will," Sierra said. "And Jia and Rachel are both okay, since I know you're about to ask. Jia's still at the school, like you thought. But she said that Colonel Charles is watching her pretty closely." She smiled. "Fortunately, Dr. Ambrose is helping her study in private. Jia's still working on creating new spells by mixing the spell words she knows, so I expect she'll burn the school down soon enough."

"And Rachel?" Fort said, not sure he wanted the answer.

"She's . . . a bit depressed, obviously," Sierra said. "Not thrilled about being home, but she's still got her memory too. I got to her just in time. She's worried about whatever Ellora did with Excalibur, and that she still has to track down the Old One of Time magic within the next year." Sierra frowned. "Also, she said something about how Merlin was going to train her, but his cottage burned down, so now she has no idea how to find him. You all really did get up to some strange stuff in a short time, didn't you?"

"You've got no idea," Fort told her. "Could you find Ellora for Rachel? She *is* going to need that sword."

"I'll do my best," Sierra said. "And what about you?"

Fort paused. "What *about* me?"

"You took the faerie queen's bargain too," Sierra said, nodding at his bedroom door to where his father and aunt were in the kitchen. "Aren't you afraid of what she'll make you do?"

Fort felt his stomach drop at the reminder but forced himself to ignore it. "Nope," he said. "Because I've got no power. All I can do is teleport and heal minor wounds. Whatever she wants from me won't cause too much trouble. And besides, I'm done with all of this anyway. I'm out of the school, and my dad's home. So it's time to just live a nice, normal life—"

"Rachel said you better be ready to teleport her to wherever Merlin is, once she finds him," Sierra said.

"A nice, normal life with some teleporting here and there," Fort said with a sigh. "At least that means I'll still get to see her, and maybe Jia, too." He already missed them both, even having been gone for just a few days now. But after everything they'd been through, not having them around to talk to and share what it was like having his father back . . . their absence just felt like a huge hole in his life.

"Oh, Jia for sure," Sierra said. "She's on fire about learning magic without books, so that the world doesn't go to war." She sighed. "Remember when it was just about fighting evil monsters, and not worrying about humans, too? That was nice."

Fort snorted. "That's why I'm done with it all. Everything that went wrong in the last few months, it's all been my fault. At least if I'm here, not at the school, I won't make things worse. And maybe living a regular life will be kind of nice for a change."

"Maybe," Sierra said. "And maybe I'll try holding Excalibur once I find Ellora. I bet I'm worthy."

Fort almost choked. "Don't you dare. You'll get burned so badly!"

Sierra gasped. "It would *never* burn me. I'm sure it'd love me!"

"The fire would be seen for *miles*!" Fort said, imagining the carnage and shuddering.

She stuck out her tongue at him. "You could stop me if you were still in all of this, you know."

He smiled at that. "I trust you to not actually touch it.

Besides, who said I won't be around? I'm not leaving *you* to get up to no good, not without me giving you my thoughts at least." He tapped his head. "But other than that, yeah, I think I'm done. I just can't take any more of it—the danger, the Old Ones, the surprises, none of it."

Sierra winced. "No more surprises, huh? Uh-oh."

He looked at her in shock. "'Uh-oh'? What do you mean?"

"Well, you might not want to open your closet, if you're done with surprises," Sierra said, and backed away slightly.

Fort felt the blood drain from his face as a loud cracking noise sounded from behind his closet door.

"Don't look now, Mr. No Surprises," Sierra said with a huge grin. "But I think you're about to be a *dad*!"

ACKNOWLEDGMENTS

Aww, Fort's going to be a dad! That's so cute. I'm sure it'll all be fine, and he'll be able to live out the normal life he wished he could have for the last three books. How hard can it be to raise a dragon, after all? Not to mention this Timeless One thing . . . and the favor he promised the faerie queen.

But how bad could *those* things end up being?

cough

On a happier note, I want to thank you all for reading, as I'd just be telling these stories to myself without you. And the reason they're as good as they are can be chalked up to the following people: Corinne, my partner in all things, Michael Bourret, my agent, and especially my two editors at Aladdin, Liesa Mignogna and Anna Parsons, who both could easily pull any number of swords from stones.

I also need to give huge thanks to Mara Anastas, my publisher at Aladdin; Chriscyntheia Floyd, my deputy publisher; the marketing team of Alissa Nigro and Caitlin Sweeny; Cassie Malmo and Nicole Russo in publicity; Elizabeth Mims in managing editorial; Sara Berko in production; and Laura DiSiena, the designer of the book; Michelle Leo and the education/library team; Stephanie Voros and the sub rights group, too; Christina Pecorale and the whole sales team; and Vivienne To, whose talent is the reason everyone's picking these books up to begin with!

See you in the pages of *Revenge of Magic: The Timeless One*!

THE ADVENTURE CONTINUES IN

THE TIMELESS ONE.

TURN THE PAGE FOR A PEEK....

FORT FITZGERALD HAD TRAVELED TO other dimensions, flown with dragons, and fought off ancient horrors. He'd saved the city of London from a boy under the spell of Spirit magic; he'd held the sword of King Arthur—one of the Arthurs, at least—and made deals with the queen of the faeries.

One thing he'd never done, though, was raise a pet.

Sure, he'd always wanted one. He'd begged his father for years to get a cat, but his father had always refused, saying he was a dog person. So Fort eventually tried a different approach and asked if they could get a dog, only for his father to claim he'd always been a cat person, and just not into dogs. It'd been an ongoing battle that Fort had no chance of ever winning.

Well, at least until now, ever since Fort had arrived home after being expelled from the Oppenheimer School to find a surprise in his old room at his aunt's apartment—a surprise that Fort needed his friends to help him with *urgently*.

And so, the same night he arrived back at his aunt's place, without even having had enough time to unpack or, more importantly, actually spend time with his newly returned father, Fort opened four circles of green light in the cavern beneath the original Oppenheimer School—teleportation portals to four separate places.

Fort stepped through the first one, carrying a large green duffel bag that a few hours earlier had been filled with clothes but now had strange mewling noises coming from it. He winced at the sound as he looked around the cavern, barely lit by the glow of the portals.

This wasn't going to cut it, he decided. They'd need a bit more illumination, so he cast Heal Minor Wounds but didn't release it from his hand. The blue magic of the spell played off the surrounding rocks, giving just enough light to see by.

Behind him, the teleportation circle led back to his bedroom at his aunt Cora's apartment, and Fort looked at it with a long sigh. As excited as he was about the little newcomer in the duffel bag, a huge part of him wished he could be in that apartment, spending every possible minute that he could with his dad.

They'd barely had any time together, between getting his father released from the TDA after days of debriefing and medical checks. And then they'd been watched on the military transport the entire way home, until finally they'd been handed over to Fort's aunt.

Even now, he worried that he'd walk back through that portal and find out it was all a dream, that his father was still gone, taken by the Dracsi. Fort had to constantly remind himself that his dad was home, awake, and *safe*, and that he wasn't going anywhere. The reminder sent a shudder of relief through Fort.

Granted, it wasn't like everything else was okay. Cyrus was still missing after a fellow Carmarthen Academy classmate of his, William, had used Spirit magic on the silver-haired boy, forcing Cyrus to send himself somewhere else in time. Not to mention that Fort, Rachel, and Jia only had a year to find the Timeless One—the Old One of Time magic—and defeat him using Excalibur, or they'd be prisoners of the faerie queen of Avalon for the rest of time.

Oh, and where was Excalibur now? No one knew. Ellora, another Carmarthen Academy student, had jumped away in time with it, in order to keep the sword out of Colonel Charles's hands. That had been a smart move at the time, but now they had no idea where or when she was, or if she'd be coming back with the sword.

At least Merlin, a mysterious old man who seemed to be the mythical wizard from the King Arthur stories, had offered to train Rachel and Jia to fight the Timeless One. He hadn't mentioned training Fort, which had stung a bit, but Fort tried not to think about it with all the other things to worry about. Still, all the training in the world wouldn't help Rachel and Jia without Excalibur.

And yet, for all of that, Fort had his father back. Even just reminding himself that his father was here, home with family, made the rest of it feel like it wasn't so bad, that they'd be able to work it all out. It also didn't hurt that he was about to see his friends again after missing them for a few days, including one whom he hadn't seen for even longer in person—

Sierra Ramirez passed through the second portal from where she'd been hiding in the UK, looking tired but still thrilled, her eyes on the duffel bag in Fort's hands. Of course she'd already seen its contents from inside Fort's head using her Mind magic, but that didn't seem to dim her enthusiasm at all. "Fort!" she shouted, and gave him a huge hug, avoiding the bag.

"Sierra!" Fort shouted in return, only to get all the air

knocked out of his lungs as she squeezed him tightly. Even without any air, he couldn't believe how great it was to see her. He'd been so used to talking to a Mind magic version of Sierra that he had forgotten how much better it was to see her in person. There was no one he felt closer to, not even Cyrus, considering how much of Sierra's life he'd felt like he'd lived through her memories, back when he'd first arrived at the Oppenheimer School.

"It's been so long!" he told her when he could breathe again.

"I was in your head, like, twenty minutes ago," she said, grinning widely. "All I did since then was reach out to the other two, and show you where they'd be so you could open portals."

"I meant since we were together in person," he said, blushing a bit.

Sierra laughed, then hugged him again. "I know, Fitzgerald. I'm just messing with you! I can't believe how good it is to see you for reals too, instead of just in our minds—"

"Is this the big emergency?" said a voice, and Sierra immediately pulled back, turning to find Rachel Carter passing through her portal. "More importantly, where is—"

She was interrupted as Jia Liang arrived, throwing nervous glances back through her own teleportation circle. But as soon as Jia saw Rachel, both girls brightened and hugged with even more excitement than Sierra and Fort had. Fort rolled his eyes.

"You two just saw each other, like, a week ago," he said.

"Shut it, Fitzgerald," Rachel said to him over her shoulder.

"A lot has happened since then," Jia said as she pulled away from Rachel. "*You* two got expelled, and now they won't even let me go to class." She shook her head. "They're guarding me constantly, because Agent Cole thinks I'm going to steal a book of magic or something."

"Tell her we did that already," Rachel said, her tone joking but her face showing she wasn't thrilled about how Jia was being treated.

"I can't stay for more than a few minutes," Jia told them, giving Rachel an especially apologetic look. "I didn't want to take the chance of a guard walking in if we opened a portal to my room, so I told them I had to use the restroom. They won't wait long before checking on me." She glanced back through the portal behind her, where the ugly green tile of a bathroom in the second Oppenheimer School gave Fort unpleasant flashbacks.

"So what couldn't wait until tomorrow, Fort?" Rachel asked, her eyes on Jia.

"Um, here's the thing," he said, looking down at the ground, suddenly less excited about showing them now that he'd heard about what Jia was going through. "Remember when D'hea, the Old One of Healing, was going to destroy the world because he thought all the dragons were gone? We didn't know at the time that Damian actually *is* a dragon, so I convinced him to just make a new one out of magic. . . ."

Rachel began to groan loudly, while Jia just stared at him with her eyebrows raised. Meanwhile, Sierra had covered her mouth with her hand but wasn't able to hide her laughter. "Are you serious, Fort?" Rachel said. "You and I *just* got expelled. Jia's basically a prisoner—"

"I mean, Dr. Ambrose is sneaking me the Healing book every so often," Jia said.

"And you brought us here to share that you've got a *baby dragon* in there?" Rachel finished, pointing at the bag. "Is that what you're saying?"

A tiny *meep* escaped from the bag, followed by clawing noises.

"Well, kind of?" Fort said, and Sierra burst out laughing.

"Wait until you see this thing!" she said, laughing harder. "It thinks Fort is its daddy!"

Rachel snorted at this, while Jia reached up to cover her mouth, just like Sierra had a moment ago. "Come on, Sierra, this isn't funny," Jia said, but her voice broke a bit as she tried not to laugh.

"She's right, Mindflayer," Rachel said to Sierra, her own mouth twitching violently. "It's incredibly serious. I mean, does Fort even know how to change a diaper?"

This set all three of them off, laughing so hard that they missed the very annoyed looks Fort was giving them. "Hey, *all right*," he said, setting the bag down. "It's not funny, okay?"

"Fort, tell them what you named it!" Sierra said, having trouble breathing now.

"What?" Jia shouted. "You have a name already?"

"Please tell me it's Fort Jr.!" Rachel said.

Fort rolled his eyes. "First of all, it's a *she*. I think."

This set off even more gales of laughter.

"But her name isn't important!" Fort shouted over them. "What am I supposed to do with—"

"He named her *Ember*!" Sierra said. "Is that not the most adorable dragon name you've ever heard?"

Rachel and Jia both stopped laughing long enough to shout "Awwww!" at him, but that was the least of Fort's concerns. He should have warned Sierra, but there hadn't been time.

"*Don't* say her name, Sierra," Fort whispered, not liking how the duffel bag had stopped moving. "Ever since she learned it, she's been—"

A *whoosh* sound from within confirmed his worst fears as a small flame began to spread through the duffel bag.

"Nice!" Rachel said, quickly snuffing it out with a magical gust of wind. "You didn't say she was already breathing fire!"

A low growl emerged from the burned section of the bag, and slowly a scaly black head about the size of an apple pushed out. Ember's black scales glinted in the light of the green portals, and her red eyes stared suspiciously at Jia, Rachel, and Sierra. Behind her, wings the size of her body unfurled, and she briefly stretched them before wrapping them back around herself protectively.

Rachel gasped. "I take it all back—she's the cutest thing ever, and I *want* her." She leaned down, extending a hand. "She's like the size of a house cat. Come here, Ember!"

"No!" Fort shouted as Sierra quickly stepped out of the way, knowing what was coming. Ember pulled in a deep breath, ready to send out another plume of fire, but Fort picked up the bag before she could unleash her flames on Rachel and turned the tiny dragon to face him. "No, dragon, we do *not* set people on fire!"

The dragon began to purr, rubbing her cheeks full of fire against Fort's hand. He patted her head awkwardly. "Good girl, Ember. Good girl!"

Immediately she released a plume of fire several dozen feet long off over his shoulder, the heat of which almost caused him to drop the bag.

"Whoa!" Rachel said, scooting back from where she'd been squatting. "Looks like someone is cranky!"

Ember's eyes darkened, and she turned back to Rachel and Jia, smoke rising from her nostrils. "She would have burned down my aunt's apartment if I hadn't teleported her flame away," Fort said, spinning the duffel bag so she couldn't see his friends. "I think she might be hungry." He picked her up to look her in the eye. "No more fire when people say your name, okay? *Okay?*"

She stared back at him for a moment, then licked him sloppily on the face.

"What do dragons eat?" Jia asked. "If it's people, I'm not okay with that."

"Damian always liked hamburgers," Sierra said, then coughed to hide another laugh as Fort shot her a dirty look.

"That was in his human form," Fort said. "D'hea, the Old One of Healing, said dragons ate gold and silver." Ember slowly climbed out of the bag and up onto Fort's body, digging her claws painfully into his chest to climb up to his shoulder. From there, she curled her long neck around his protectively, her eyes still watching the others with suspicion. "Is that something you can magic up, Rachel?"

"Gold and silver?" Rachel said. "You think I wouldn't have done that for some spare cash if I could?"

"It must be possible," Jia told her. "Your magic is all about elemental control, after all. We probably just haven't found the right combination of words."

Rachel looked at her thoughtfully. "Maybe, but I don't know that I have any spell words for changing something into something else."

Jia wrinkled her nose. "This is why the books are so frustrating. I know a few different words for that, but if I tell them to you, you won't be able to remember them. We need to figure out a way around that."

"*Hello*, baby dragon over here!" Fort said, waving his hand. Ember raised her claws and mimicked him, giving the others an even dirtier look. "I can't exactly wait around for you to figure out how to turn rocks into gold. I need to feed her something soon, and then, I don't know, get her somewhere safe to hide, like a cave or—"

"Hey!" Rachel shouted indignantly, as Jia looked just as shocked. "Are you joking? You can't just abandon a baby animal like that!"

"She's a *dragon*!" Fort said, as Ember growled at Rachel. "I'm pretty sure she can take care of herself!"

"She's a baby and seems to think you're her mom!" Rachel said. "You *have* to take care of her, Fort. She doesn't have anyone else!"

"Seriously, Fort," Jia said. "The fact that she's a dragon makes it even more important that you watch over her. Think about what kind of panic there'd be if someone found her. Or even worse, if Colonel Charles got ahold of her."

Fort opened his mouth to respond but had no idea what to say. He couldn't keep a *dragon*, not in an apartment . . . not even if he was still at the Oppenheimer School. If he somehow was able to keep Ember hidden, she still needed to eat, not to mention probably go for walks or something. And what about when he started school again? He couldn't take her there, not without setting off mass hysteria.

"See?" Sierra said to him. "This is what I've been saying. She's *yours*, Fort. Think of her as a pet."

"Actually, that's a great idea," Jia said, and held up her hand. It began to glow with blue Healing magic, and Ember hissed at her warily, but as the magic filled the little dragon, she quickly calmed down, then fell asleep on Fort's shoulder.

"Hey, what'd you do?" Fort said, trying to make sure his dragon was okay.

"I put her to sleep—calm down," Jia said, unleashing a second spell. As the blue light passed over the slumbering dragon, Ember's black scales began to morph into fur. Her ears pulled in, becoming more of a small triangle on top of her now rounder head, and whiskers pushed out of her snout.

And just like that, a small black kitten snored quietly on Fort's shoulder. Apparently Jia's spell took age into account, because Ember was even smaller as a cat than she'd been as a dragon.

"There," Jia said with some satisfaction. "That should solve all your problems."

"Um, what?" Fort said incredulously, not even able to count the number of ways that was wrong.

"Now you can keep her at your aunt's place with no problems!" Jia said, then glanced at Rachel. "See? That's just *one* of my changing spells. We really need to figure out how to swap spell words, so you can use it to change lead into gold or whatever."

"Totally," Rachel said. "And I'm glad we were able to solve your problem for you, Fort. You're welcome."

"Um, what?" Fort said again. "This doesn't solve *anything*—"

"Since we're already here for Fort's fake emergency, let's quickly cover the actual important stuff," Rachel continued, ignoring him. She held out her hand to count on her fingers. "One, we need to find Excalibur, from whatever time Ellora sent it to; two, we need to track down Merlin, so he can train Jia and me like he promised, which is a problem since Damian destroyed Merlin's cottage, and we might not be able to find him now; and three, we'll need to somehow locate the Timeless One, the Old One of Time magic, who could literally be anywhere or any*when* in time. And we need to do all of that within a year, or the faerie queen will basically imprison us in her world for the rest of our lives." She paused, then looked up at Ember, asleep. "Oh, and four, I'm going to need to cuddle that cat ASAP!"

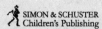

READ & LEARN

with *simon* kids

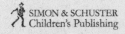